HYPER LYNX

THE LYNX SERIES

FIONA QUINN

HYPER

Lynx

Fiona Quinn

THE WORLD OF INIQUUS

Ubicumque, Quoties. Quidquid

Iniquus - /i'ni/kwus/ our strength is unequalled, our tactics unfair – we stretch the law to its breaking point. We do whatever is necessary to bring the enemy down.

THE LYNX SERIES

Weakest Lynx

Missing Lynx

Chain Lynx

Cuff Lynx

Gulf Lynx

Hyper Lynx

STRIKE FORCE

In Too DEEP

JACK Be Quick

InstiGATOR

Uncommon Enemies

Wasp

Relic

Deadlock

Thorn

FBI Joint Task Force

Open Secret

Cold Red

Even Odds

Kate Hamilton Mysteries

Mine

Yours

Ours

Cerberus Tactical K9 Team Alpha

Survival Instinct

Protective Instinct

Defender's Instinct

Delta Force Echo

Danger Signs

Danger Zone

Danger Close

This list was created in 2021. For an up-to-date list, please visit FionaQuinnBooks.com

If you prefer to read the Iniquus World in chronological order you will find a full list at the end of this book.

THE PLAYERS

The HYDRA
The Mastermind – Indigo (Deceased)
The Moneybags – Sylanos
The Private Army – Omega
The Political Cover – The Assembly

The Diner
Jim – the owner
Destiny – server
Barb – Server
Nicole – Server
Huahine – Short-order cook

Strike Force
Gator and Christen
Striker and Lynx
Jack and Suz
Deep and Grace
Blaze and Faith
Reaper and Kate
Axel
Randy

CIA
Oliver
John Black
Johnna White
Casper
Cho
DiSalla

THE PLAYERS(Continued)

FBI
Special Agent in Charge Damian Prescott
Special Agent Steve Finley
Dr. Gupta Ph.D.
Modesty (Destiny) asset

Cerberus Tactical K9
Ridge and K9 Zeus
Ryder and K9 Voodoo

Delta Force Echo
Ty and Kira

Davidson Family and Friends
William and London Davidson – father and stepmother
Christen Davidson - daughter
Karl Davidson – eldest son

Rochambeau Family
Mama Rochambeau
Gator
Genevieve
Auralia

LONDON BRIDGE IS

London Bridges falling down,
Falling down,
Falling down.
London Bridges falling down,
My fair Lady.

Build it up with iron and steel,
Iron and steel, iron and steel,
Build it up with iron and steel,
My fair lady.

Iron and steel will bend and bow,
Bend and bow, bend and bow,
Iron and steel will bend and bow,
My fair lady.

Build it up with silver and gold,
Silver and gold, silver and gold,
Build it up with silver and gold,
My fair lady.

1
———

It was such a relief when my phone's buzz suddenly yanked me awake.

Mentally thrashing through an endless dream, I was too exhausted to stay asleep.

I had gone to bed last night braced for torment—whether it showed up as warm, loving pictures or angst-filled ones. Either would make my heart bleed.

Today was Mom's birthday.

In my life, which was overflowing with heroes, she stood out as the miracle maker. I missed her dearly.

All day yesterday, childhood memories had been popping up.

My brain had been feeding them to me like bon bons.

Closing my eyes, I savored each one.

The flavor on my tongue of Mom's extra-special raspberry chocolate rum cake. The warmth of her voice as she whispered, "You're my favorite," into my ear. The earnestness in her eyes as she gave me good counsel or just stared out the window, thinking.

I remembered Mom as bright slashes of color on her pallet as she brought her imagination into a tangible form on a canvas.

Whenever I saw a bouquet of flowers, she was there in the

richness of the hues and the delicacy of the petals, easily bruised and crushed.

She was still part of my every day.

Painfully sometimes. Joyfully sometimes.

The emptiness she left was only made more acute this last week as I probed around my memories like a tongue finding and fiddling with the space from a lost childhood tooth.

Only this ache didn't come with the expected Tooth Fairy reward. Or knowing that another tooth would come in and replace the baby one that had fallen out.

Nothing could replace Mom.

There were just certain days that were more biting than others. Her birthday was always the hardest for me.

My life growing up had been enchanted. My parents had given me the Willy Wonka gold ticket of childhoods. Living a working-class lifestyle, my father *seemingly* owned a garage and acted as a mechanic. I believed that to be true until last year. That's when I discovered that the garage was a cover story for his actual job as a CIA officer.

Though my family didn't have a lot of material trappings, I never felt want. My parents filled my life with the colorful, the exciting, even the fantastical at times. And they brought into my unschooled education a parade of amazing people to mentor and teach me, despite Mom's being sick for almost all of my life.

Mom's imminent death had been part of my every day. And because I kept expecting her to die and then she didn't, I convinced myself she'd always beat the odds. That she'd be able to stay in her bed where she'd always been, making a nest of pillows for me to join her. I'd cuddle up to listen to her read to me. Or I'd draw quietly while she slept…

Dad had positioned the parental king-sized bed in such a way that we could watch through the window as airplanes flew low in the sky on the way to one of the D.C. airports. We'd tell each other imagined stories of the great adventures that the passengers had just lived.

Mom's gentle smile and creative way of viewing life…

I still needed her.

I never really got a chance to mourn her passing. Not properly. Right after her death, my life had spun out of control. I became the focus of a serial killer who started a parade of criminals through my life.

They were now in my past.

And I was slowly recovering both physically and emotionally from the years of terror.

In my toolbox of valuable skills, I had my mother's example of sheer *dogged* perseverance that had helped me through those terrible times.

Mom had heroically clung to life for as long as she could. As my last remaining relative, her big goal was to stay alive until I was a legal adult; she hoped to see my twenty-first birthday.

Valiantly, she made it until I was nineteen and a half.

Then one day, to my great sorrow and equally to my great relief, she just stopped.

Her transition to life beyond was peaceful, where her illness hadn't been.

That day, I had carried a tray with her preferred breakfast—a pot of orange pekoe tea, toast with honey, and a banana—into her room.

The stillness as I pushed through the door stood like a sentry. It stopped me from entering.

Hovering in the hall, I looked through the crack and realized that the room was empty though Mom was in the bed.

She had traveled from this world to the next, joining Dad on the other side.

Mom must have known it was close; she went to bed that night with my pink baby blanket and had it clutched to her chest.

When I was very little and couldn't sleep, Mom would wrap me in that soft pink blanket and carry me out to the tiny balcony off the living room in the Washington D.C. apartment where I lived my entire life until it burned to the ground.

I loved that apartment. It was the center of my own special universe.

Outside, with the white noise of the highway buzz, Mom would cuddle me into her as she soothed me.

I would block the smell of the city by burrowing my nose into Mom's dress. The savory scent of garlic and onions, spices, and lemony dish detergent, would fill my nostrils.

It was bliss.

All the strains and upsets of my little life fell away with the steady cadence of the old-fashioned wooden rocker's creaks and thumps.

Mom hummed nonsensical notes instead of any recognizable melody. Her cheek rested against my head, so she could turn and plant kisses in my hair when she took a breath in to hum again.

When she did sing an infrequent song, it was usually something monotonous and straightforward like *Row, Row, Row Your Boat*.

The truth was that Mom's talents were visual, and she had minimal capacity to find a beat or a melody.

It embarrassed her because dad and I both had good voices. Dad had been in a band all through college. He'd had to make a choice at some point to give that up to follow his career with the CIA.

Imagine sitting on a dorm room bed and thinking: Will I be a spy or a rock star?

My dad was a rock star to me, even if he made the choice to let his music become an avocation.

Mom liked to listen to us singing together, but I think she felt left out.

Before I went to sleep last night, my fiancé, Striker Rheas, had shown me a YouTube of a teenaged *acapella* group singing rock.

There was one young teen who tickled my fancy. He held the tempo with his beatboxing, which he took *very* seriously.

As well he should.

He had carrot red hair, porcelain skin, and looked completely cherubic as his mouth made the sounds of cymbals crashing. I could just imagine him showing up at the audition, wanting to participate in the group, and being told his voice wasn't up to standard. Undeterred, he found a way to join in.

Mom would have *loved* that.

And so, as I lay in bed with Striker beside me, not wanting to toss and turn and interrupt his sleep, I was thinking again about Mom.

In my imagination, I pretended to wrap myself in the pink blanket, sending myself down memory lane onto the balcony. And there, I imagined baby me lying in Mom's arms as she monotoned, "Row, row, row your boat."

And that was what I had done all night in my dreams.

It hadn't been a pink, fluffy-blanket, sweet dreams kind of boat ride.

It was the nightmare kind.

The danger is imminent kind.

My mother had stood on the bank with her bare feet in the roiling waters, one hand clinging to a branch, the other cupped around her mouth screaming at me, "Row faster, Lexi! Faster! You have to get away! Go. Go. Go!"

And because I believed my mom, trusted my mom to always do the best she could to protect me and keep me safe even in a dangerous and turbulent world, I rowed.

Hours of frantic rowing.

And now, with a rubbery arm and physical exhaustion, I

reached for my phone buzzing on my nightstand before it woke Striker, grateful—even if it was a wrong number—that by waking up, I had made it to shore and could stop.

I stroked my thumb across the screen and whispered, "Hello?"

"In a moment, you will get a call from the FBI. Take the call. Accept the invitation. Out."

The phone went dead.

2

STRIKER CAME AWAKE BESIDE ME. "Who was that?" He scrubbed a hand over his eyes and scratched through his short-cropped, rusty-blond hair. "What time is it?"

"Spyder," I whispered, turning the phone to check the readout. "It's almost five. Go back to sleep."

Striker rolled onto his side and bent his arm to elevate his head. His features were hard to read in the dim indigo of near dawn coming through my bedroom window. "And?"

I tipped my head. "A call's supposed to come in from the FBI. Spyder told me to take the meeting."

"All right, Chica." He shifted the covers off him.

I wish he hadn't.

Striker went to bed naked last night. His morning ready-for-a-tumble body was darned enticing—broad shoulders, tight abs, those thigh muscles, and—*Whew*!

If only I knew when this FBI call would be coming through, I might have taken advantage of waking up before the alarm rang.

"But I'm going to remind you," Striker tapped my hip, refocusing me, "we already have a meeting on the books today at eleven hundred hours. Spyder wouldn't have called like that if it wasn't high priority. This meeting at the CIA is, too."

I pulled myself up to sitting, punched a pillow, and laid it against the headboard, leaning back—the "ready for a conversation" position. "Do you know what's going on at the CIA? A gist? A whiff?"

"This is what I know." He pushed himself up to sit against the headboard beside me.

I would have felt a lot more guilty about his losing sleep if Striker wasn't the kind of guy who could get by on four hours of shut-eye and then head out to compete in a triathlon.

Must be nice. That definitely wasn't me.

Coffee would help.

"The original meeting was scheduled," Striker said, "with a room full of people connected with a case. Once Iniquus Command confirmed with the CIA working group that I was bringing you with me, that roomful narrowed down to three."

I shrugged. "So, maybe it's not that important, and it would be okay if you take notes and catch me up later?"

Amusement twitched at the corners of his lips. *So darned cute.* "I'm going to speculate based on tone."

"Okay."

"This is an ongoing mission that needs to be solved. They can't figure it out. They called Iniquus in, hoping for a fresh perspective." I didn't need to see his face. I could tell by his tone that Striker found this turn of events entertaining.

I drew my brows together. "And that amuses you. Why?"

"Because I don't think they know what they have headed through their doors. Or maybe they do, and that's why they made the changes from a roomful down to the three main players."

"More?"

"I know exactly how this is going to go down. You're going to listen to their information, then you're going to say something so obvious that they're all going to look like buffoons for not spotting it themselves. The fewer witnesses to the thrumming, the better. If the lore about your solve-rate spread to this group, they're trying to limit the reputational damage."

"Psh." I got out of bed, picking up my cell phone as I moved.

"You think I'm kidding?" He clicked on the side lamp.

I turned just in time to catch the full-blown dimple action of his grin.

He wasn't playing fair. I needed to be focused and professional for this incoming FBI call, not caught panting and sighing into the phone as I played with Striker.

Striker laced his fingers behind his head. Uh-huh. He knew *exactly* what he was doing with that display of his.

As my heart thumped a "go get him and have some fun" beat, I turned to my panties drawer and dug around.

"Iniquus Command has bets laid amongst themselves on the outcome of today's CIA meeting." Striker's face had returned to stoic, but his voice betrayed him. He was enjoying this a tad too much.

I turned and stared at him. Bets? Again? I hated that. "No pressure, though."

"I'm not worried about it. Neither is Command."

Striker and I both worked for Iniquus Security. We do the things that the alphabets would like to do on their own, but red tape and politics shackled them.

At Iniquus, we didn't have to deal with those kinds of constraints. Our sole purpose was to get the bad guys into the hands of prosecutors and protect the innocent.

Striker commanded Strike Force, one of the five specialized Iniquus operations groups. I was attached to Strike Force, though I wasn't under Striker's command.

A good thing.

I didn't think I'd want to be in an intimate relationship with someone who had power over me.

I've been working at Iniquus ever since Strike Force stepped into my life to protect me from a serial killer four years ago.

Wow…four years? Yeah, though I was nineteen when that all went down, it still seemed like yesterday—a string of devastating events over a few short months—Mom's death. My mentor, Spyder McGraw, went off-grid, leaving me rudderless. My apartment building burned to the ground. I met my (soon to be ex-) husband Angel, and a whirlwind romance led Angel and me to the courthouse for quick wedding vows. Immediately after Angel and I said, "I do," Angel stepped onto the bus taking him to the airport and off to Afghanistan where his Ranger unit was deploying. And that was when a serial killer left his first letter under my door.

Striker strode into my hospital room, scooped me up, and stole away with me to an Iniquus safe house after I survived the killer's attack. There, Strike Force's job was to protect me and keep me alive, so I could testify.

I figured a few crimes puzzled out while I was sequestered in the safe house, and Iniquus Command recognized the skills taught to me by one of their own, Spyder McGraw. And that's how I came to be part of the Iniquus family.

Spyder…

Wow, I haven't seen Spyder since Christmas.

Hadn't heard a word.

That he called, commanded, and hung up…

Typical Spyder.

It was a puzzle. To figure it out, I needed more pieces.

I was champing at the bit to hear what the FBI wanted to say to me.

I moved to my closet and rifled through the hangers.

CIA and potentially FBI today, what did I want to wear?

I pulled out a pair of gray dress pants and a pale-blue, short-sleeved summer sweater. With my phone, panties, and bra gathered, I took everything into the bathroom to get ready.

And wait for the phone call.

Yup, Spyder had poked his Anansi-trickster head out from his hidey-hole.

A lifelong family friend of my parents, after Dad's death, Spyder took up the role of a second father. I loved Spyder for everything he has taught me through the years. My ethos. My code. My stability.

If Spyder said jump into the lava lake, I'd jump knowing that he would have weighed everything and trusted that I could successfully swim to the other side.

Somewhere, there was lava.

And Spyder had said jump.

3

———

Emerging from the bathroom, I lifted my nose to the scent of coffee wafting up the stairs.

Bless you, Striker.

I'd admit it, last night's row-dream was ill-timed. I didn't feel game ready. The shower hadn't done the trick. But the coffee…

I hustled down the stairs to the kitchen, where Striker leaned his hips into the counter. He was wearing his butter-soft, over-washed jeans that were missing their top button—and nothing else. He crossed his ankles comfortably as he cradled a mug.

I looked up at the kitchen clock and then back at the staircase.

If only the call would come in from the FBI, I'd know if there was time to jog up the stairs and work off some stress with a little sheet-aerobics.

"Chica," Striker said as I turned back to cast a longing look down the length of his body. "If you keep licking your lips while you eye me like candy, I'm turning your phone to airplane mode and throwing you over my shoulder to take you back to bed."

"Promise?"

He stalled with a tip of his head, then reached for the mug he'd already doctored for me with milk and Splenda.

"Lexi, you need to pace yourself. This isn't going to be the easiest of weeks."

I accepted the mug, sliding onto one of the kitchen chairs, repositioning to face Striker.

"It's your mom's birthday. Were you dreaming about her last night?"

I lifted my chin, asking with my body language why he guessed that.

"Row, row, row your boat?"

"Ah." I took a sip from the mug. "I'm sorry if I kept you awake. Yeah, I've had a flood of memories about my parents over these last few days. It's the most curious thing…"

"Tell me."

I waggled my hand toward my back. "It's like they're both right there, looking over my shoulder."

Striker's brows laced. He was probably afraid of what new woo-woo channel was playing on my psychic network. While Striker usually dealt with my psychic senses just fine, he still didn't love that I could see, and sense, and do things in the ether where he had little dexterity beyond the senses typically developed by SEALs in the field.

During his military career, Striker built those capabilities—the sense of eyes on him. Reading a room. A hovering foot that just knew there was a tripwire hidden. But that was the extent of it.

And for me, that was baby talk.

"Your parents are just checking in?" His voice sounded one part hopeful, two parts braced. "I don't remember you mentioning ghosts as part of your experiences."

I waggled my hand again, like an antenna trying to home in on a signal. "Ghosts? That doesn't sound right. It's not the term I'd use. Presence? Yeah, I don't know that I've experienced my parents hanging out with me in quite this way since either of them died." I scratched at my chin.

"No words? Just a sensation?"

"Exactly. Like they're worried. Like…" I looked up at the ceiling. "Yeah, I don't know—just kind of hanging out over my right shoulder.

Striker rubbed the back of his neck. "All right, Chica. But if you pick up a *knowing*, I get to hear about it straight away."

I gave him a mock salute and picked up my coffee, taking a deep, satisfying inhale before I put the mug to my lips.

A *knowing* was the word I used when a psychic phrase came to me. It used to be that they happened all the time as a child. Simple silly things like waking up to the nursery rhyme Humpty Dumpty, and I would know that Dad would be making eggs for breakfast.

Since Mom died, the childish *knowings* had stopped. Just like before, information was presented as children's rhymes, baby songs, or even kid stories. But they were never innocent.

Now, they usually presaged life or death horror.

It was understandable why Striker was worried that last night's "Row, row, row your boat" had worked its way into my dreams.

I stilled. *Shit. Was it a knowing?*

With that thought, my phone buzzed on the table. The vibrations bobbled it against the hard surface, sending it spinning.

I snatched it up.

"Hello?"

"Lynx? It's Finley." Steve Finley used my Iniquus call sign. He was an FBI special agent whom I had crossed paths with on many an assignment. His lane was domestic terrorism. That he was the one calling was information.

"Good morning."

"I got a text saying this wasn't too early to call." Finley's voice sounded tired. "Five is a shitty time to reach out, but this was my window. I hope you understand."

"No worries. I was waiting for you while I got a cup of coffee in me."

"I've been chugging coffee for the last twenty-four hours. If I got shot, I'd bleed caffeine."

"No evil eye, no evil eye, no evil eye." I chanted with a grin.

"Ha! That's right. No need to curse myself into not making it through today."

My smile fell off. "Are you in danger?"

"Me? No. I'm at the office and plan to stay here at least through this evening. So you got the warning call to expect me?"

"FBI in general. I'm glad it's you in the specific. I like working with people with whom I've already built a rapport. It saves time."

"And our time is very compressed. Have you eaten breakfast yet?"

"Just coffee."

"We'd like for you to come to FBI Headquarters to be read into the program and talk to our specialist this afternoon. Does that work for you?"

"I'm headed to Langley at eleven. Let me give them a two-hour window and an hour to get from Point A to Point B. Would fourteen hundred hours work?"

"I believe so. I'd like you to do me a favor, though. I'm going to text you the address of a diner. If it works in today's schedule, we'd like for you to go there for breakfast and put your eyes on a young server named Modesty Turlington."

"Modesty? As in shy?"

"Yes, well, I don't know about synonyms, but her parents named her Modesty on her birth certificate."

I curled my fingers and looked at the hang nail I'd been worrying. I lifted it to my mouth and nibbled it off, leaving a raw red spot. "I knew a couple once that called their son 'Brave.'"

"And was he?" Finley asked.

"Hard to tell. I never saw him in a situation where he needed to be particularly courageous. He's four years old, though. I guess time will tell."

"A name with big shoes to fill." I could hear the smile in Finley's voice. "Out of curiosity, did he have any siblings?"

"His sister Pam."

"Those names seem on either end of a naming spectrum."

"Their last name was Lamb. So it's Pam Lamb and Brave Lamb. I'm sure they had their reasons."

"Surely…"

There was a long pause that I filled by taking a sip of coffee.

"About Modesty," Finley continued. "I'd like you to get a feel for her before you get any other information about the situation. So we're hoping you can go by her work and get eyes on."

"Okay, if I do that, she's going to see my face, so I should dress for my role."

"Here's the deal, Modesty was raised in ongoing difficulties, and like many children who were in survival mode—"

"She developed intuitive skills," I filled in.

"Exactly. She has an advanced BS meter. We need someone in this role who is authentic. Someone with a background story that sounds like it parallels hers. And we need someone her age."

"How old?"

"She's eighteen. Dressed properly, you could pass as a teenager."

Striker had crossed his arms over his chest as he listened to my end of the conversation. I could tell from his eyes that he was absorbing, processing, and assessing the situation the FBI was thrusting me into.

"What about my background parallels hers?" I spun my mug around as I concentrated on not only Finley's word choices but his tone. There was determination laced into his words.

"*Seeming* parallels. The jigsaw pieces are the same, but the final pictures are different. Some aspects that you share—raised by a community of people. The elders in that community taught you instead of your going to school. You were taught specific skills that are esoteric—meditation practices amongst them. You have a wide perspective but can't really relate to the norms of what school kids experienced."

"I can rebuild an engine but have no idea about which dinosaurs died in the Mesolithic, or even if there were dinosaurs in the Mesolithic?"

"Yeah, like that. Your knowledge and experience are quite different than most. Same with Modesty, but to be sure, she doesn't have your skills. She was taught things more in line with agriculture and making hammocks."

"She's escaped a commune?"

Striker moved around uncomfortably.

"More later," Finley said.

"Okay." I pulled a noisy breath in through my nostrils. "So if I escaped a commune, I'd have little… My job this morning is to get my eyes on this target and get a read. I can do that."

"Perfect. Thank you." There was a long pause. "Spyder told you to expect my call. You know two things about me, I'm domestic terror, but I work for the Joint Task Force, which has an international scope. In this assignment, you'll be trying to lace these ideas together."

"Yup." I glanced over at Striker; our gazes caught. Held.

"While this is a big deal to the FBI—millions of dollars in fraud—this case has bigger ramifications. We've been working with Spyder since he brought us in on his findings. The implications stretch to a case that the two of you have been working on. So he asked us to bring you on board. We're happy to have you."

Wow. That right there was a HUGE piece of information.

"Happy to be had." The air had caught in my chest.

Spyder and I had been working to bring down the group

Spyder had named "Hydra," a criminal network that had been run by a mad man, now deceased. He had created a monster by using established entities to engage in a crime network, enriching everyone in their group through a parade of illegal activity. Omega, Iniquus's rival, did the security aspects. Sylanos had been a software pirate back when such a thing was prevalent. He'd acted as the money bags. And here in the United States, the group called "The Assembly," which was made up of our highest-ranking politicians, judges, police, and other power jobs, closed the circles to protect the bad guys should they be caught.

It was sort of like back in the Civil War, the Mason's gave their members a Freemason card to carry with them. Should the soldier ever be captured, they were to present the card to the enemy. The enemy would then hand the captured soldier over to a Mason from their side of the conflict. It was one of the original "get out of jail free" cards. No matter your side, your Masonic brethren would keep you safe.

Same with the Assembly.

Assemblymen, and they were *all* men, felt that their membership made them god-like. They weren't subject to the laws of men. Rape. Theft. Murder even… Nah, none of that mattered. Not when the police chief, the DA, and the judge all wore their little Assembly pins. Signals, just like the Masonic papers had been, that they were subject to different rules.

They were allowed to act with impunity.

Spyder had worked against them for over a decade. We dropped an atomic bomb of data exposing much of their criminal activity about a year and a half ago. At that time, the Assembly was so enmeshed in American politics and the three branches of government, it was quite a societal upheaval.

I thought we'd mostly succeeded. But according to mythology, you cut off the head of the Hydra, and it keeps growing back.

Holy moly, I'm back to fighting the Hydra.

Striker caught my gaze.

I realized my brows were up to my hairline, and my eyes were held wide and unblinking.

"See you at two o'clock then, main entrance. I'll wait for you and bring you through security," Finley said. "Call me if the time needs to change."

"Will do. Bye." I rolled my lips in.

"That doesn't look good." Ridges crisscrossed Striker's forehead.

Pressing my thumbs into my temple to stop the sudden throbbing, I took in a deep breath. "It's fine. That was Finley. He wants me to go get breakfast at a diner." I stopped as I heard a ping and checked my text messages. It was an address. "They need someone who is a good parallel for a subject of interest. Same general age. An unusual background—"

"That someone might read as cultish? You said cult, right?"

"My words, not Finley's. If you think about it, yes, my childhood could be described in such a way that it could seem very cult-like. I can choose my words carefully."

"And they'll give you support? Cults aren't always safe playgrounds."

"I was speculating. That wasn't the information Finley gave me. Right now," I lifted my mug and drained the coffee, then passed it to Striker's outstretched hand, "I need to figure out what a teen runaway would look like. Then go have breakfast and size things up. The FBI will read me into the program this afternoon."

"Spyder's involved with a cult runaway?" Striker asked.

"That can only mean one thing." I pressed a kiss onto Striker's cheek.

"He's taking another run at the Hydra." Striker reached for my arm and held me still. "Christen's getting into town Monday morning."

"I can't wait." I smiled. Christen was flying in from a forward operating base in the Middle East, where she was a pilot with the Night Stalkers. She'd saved up her leave time so she could marry my teammate—one of my best friends, Gator Aid Rochambeau— then head off on an extended honeymoon.

Striker and I got to stand with them as part of the wedding party—an honor.

"I'm bringing it up because you'll have the wedding on your mind," Striker was saying. "And we're heading to the CIA."

I tipped my head back so he could clearly see my eyes. "I won't cause a scene."

"No?" He released my hand.

"What do you think I'm going to do? I could maybe walk across their sacred CIA seal, stand in front of the hero's wall, and yell out to all that will hear, 'I was told I was a widow. I grieved my dead husband. I picked myself up, moving on with my life, only to discover that it was a CIA ploy. Angel was alive all that time. I was *promised* a private divorce, sealed by the courts, in exchange for my silence about their black ops mission.'" My voice was ramping up. "'You reneged, CIA. You tortured me with my grief, CIA. And then, didn't even follow through with this teeny tiny ask on my part.' You think I'll do that, Striker?"

"Might." He set his mug on the counter. "I wouldn't blame you if you did." He crossed his arms over his chest. Protector- mode. "But you'd probably be arrested for voicing classified information." He tipped his head and sent me a warm smile. "Christen and Gator really want you to wear a dress to their wedding and not prison orange."

"Yeah, well, I'll do my best. And you?" I took a step back to give my neck some relief. I was five foot six, and Striker stood head and shoulders above me. "You have every right to burst into the CIA feeling as angry as I do. After all, the CIA's decisions affect you, too. We can't be married until I can do it legally. Our relationship is constrained by their lack of action. It means nothing to them. It's still unfathomable to me that Angel agreed to their black ops plan. Think of all the pain he caused. All the grief —mine, Angel's family. His Abuela Rosa." I laid my hand on my chest. "She nearly died of a broken heart. I..."

My lungs forced the trapped air out in a fast stream.

Heat washed over me as my emotions collided.

Waves against the rocks.

I was done playing with the CIA.

But the CIA was a formidable adversary.

Something needed to move this along. I just needed a plan that would release me from their shackles.

I guessed it mattered how loud and how ugly I wanted to get.

4

I PLOTTED IT OUT. I could take the Metro to a bus and then walk a block. That way, there was zero chance someone would see me getting in and out of my car.

When I had dressed this morning, I had put on some basic makeup, but I decided to wash it off and scrape my hair into a ponytail. A pair of ripped jeans, a t-shirt with a stain, and a pair of old tennis shoes, and I'd call it done.

I twisted this way and that in the mirror.

This look was neutral. It said very little about me.

Yeah, this was a go.

I wondered what kind of "pocket debris" I should gather. The minutiae that went into my pocket or my purse so that anyone looking would find artifacts of the life I wanted them to believe I led.

A bit problematic since I didn't have a handle on my role yet.

No purse. I'd carry my phone, some crumpled low denomination bills, a Chapstick…

Yeah, the less I had with me, the more malleable my character would be for me to construct in the future.

Metro and city bus cards.

Ready.

Striker was standing at the bottom of my staircase, keys in hand.

I quirked an eyebrow. Did he think he was coming with me?

"You're taking public transportation since you don't have time to develop a cover car, right? I thought I'd give you a ride to the Metro, so you don't have to figure out what to do with your keys."

"You're so smart." I stood on the bottom stair and gave him a gratitude kiss. "And darned cute." I sighed as I stepped off the step.

"I hear you, Chica. I'd much rather stay home and play but—"

"Duty calls."

***

"Oh, wow." I put my hand on the window as the bus rumbled down the street. I knew *exactly* where I was.

Bouncing over the potholes, the lights of oncoming traffic chewed through the early morning fog. Sirens and the flashing red lights of an ambulance passed by on the other side of the road and thrust me back in time to when I had looked up this very street, watching rescue lights coming toward me.

I pressed my forehead against the cool glass, the hiss of air conditioning sprayed upward from the tiny, perforated holes. Sweat slicked my skin with the recognition and was dried into a salty tightness freezing my features as my system took the hit.

In my memory, I was back, reliving the horror.

That dreadful rain-slicked night, Dad and I had been driving along, belting out a song on the radio. We had been having a wonderful time when suddenly my life cracked open.

It was a feeling of utter helplessness. There was the boom of impact, the shrill wrenching of metal, the tinkling of glass shards as they hit the pavement.

Our car was upside down in the ditch.

With ringing ears and blood dripping into my eyes, I turned to find Dad dangling from his seatbelt.

My door was mangled, but with the window broken out, I was able to wrestle myself free. I dashed around to Dad's side of the car and reached in, trying to rouse him.

The next part was a blur. Pulling my Swiss Army knife from my pocket, I'd cut him free.

Should I have cut him free?

Even now that I'd been trained and had worked with the local rescue squad, I was conflicted about my decisions.

I hadn't found a pulse. But that might have been the tremble in my hand, like a hummingbird's wing, flapping against his carotid.

I couldn't tell if he was breathing. But I was in shock, myself. Maybe my mind was stuttering. Maybe I'd just missed his shallow inhales.

It doesn't matter. It's over. What I did was what I did.

Right or wrong.

With his safety belt cut free, gravity tugged Dad from his seat.

All I could do was try to protect his head and then drag him out of the wreck to the hard surface of the road where I could perform CPR.

Was he still alive in the driver's seat?

Would he have survived had I waited for the rescue crew?

I'll never know.

The what-ifs were always there in my memories of him. They coated the images of my amazing dad with my shame and guilt at not having helped him.

I didn't know how I got Dad as far as the road.

I didn't remember ripping open his shirt or positioning my hands.

I did remember the compressions.

I tried. Tried for a long time. Tried until I knew that even if he came back, by some miracle, that his brain had been deprived of oxygen far too long.

That realization came on the tail end of exhaustion.

It was a whisper and not the gnashing of teeth and screaming to the heavens. I simply crawled up to rest his head in my lap, and I chanted, "Please be okay, please be okay." Though, I knew that "okay" had nothing to do with being alive or smiling at me again. It was more like a wish that his soul's journey be gentle.

That he be at peace.

I had stroked my fingers over Dad's hair and thought about the night when Mom had died the first time. They had shocked her back down to Earth again. Before she was fully conscious, she had lifted her arm to point and said, "Oh, I want to be there."

As painful as it was in that moment for me, I was sorry the doctors had saved her.

The conviction in Mom's voice was so powerful. Whatever she'd seen was good. That place that Mom didn't want to leave— that's the place I imagined my dad had reached.

Now that my bus had rumbled closer to the diner. I was out of the vicinity where Dad had laughed his last laugh, sung his last note, breathed his last breath.

I closed my eyes and tried for a slow, steady inhale.

My stop was next.

If I was going to try to parallel Modesty's situation, my eyes should look haunted.

I looked over my shoulder and whispered, "You two obviously want my attention."

Ghosts...

I didn't disbelieve in ghosts like I disbelieved in vampires. I had never experienced them before. The otherworldly? Sure. The psychic realm? Yup, I spent a lot of time training and working in the ether.

Ghosts…

Somehow that wasn't something I'd really thought about before. If what I was sensing of my parents was ghost-like—ha! My parents died, not specifically protecting me from evil, but I had always felt that they had died in service to me. Though, now that I lay down those thoughts for scrutiny, it wasn't quite right.

Certainly, when I felt my parents close, I never saw them as apparitions. They had no visible form. And yet, there they were.

The bus came to a stop, and I stood, gripping the pole, waiting my turn to exit.

I wasn't in the mood for this. There, I'd just admit it. I was in the mood to go by the florists and get my mom some of her favorite sunflowers, take them to the graveyard, and hang out with my folks.

Talk things out.

Let the wind carry my words and sprinkle them in the distance like the seeds of a dandelion afloat on the breeze.

It would be nice to rest against my parents' headstone with a sketch pad and draw just like I did as a child while Mom napped.

What I didn't want to do was climb off this bus and go look Modesty in the eye. Read her like a book. Bring my findings to today's meeting.

Meetings.

Two of them after this.

It wasn't a good day for that. My concentration was blown, and my body still hadn't recovered from the hours of somnambulant rowing.

I nodded at the bus driver as I sidled past.

She shot me a look of sheer boredom.

Or maybe she was exhausted and despondent, too.

Spyder wants me here, I reminded myself as I stood on the sidewalk, looking around as the bus continued its circuit.

The weather was reflecting my gray drippy mood.

I gave myself a good shake, forcing myself away from Memory Lane. I needed to be focused and strategic as I laid the groundwork for this new mission.

This was the point where mistakes had the greatest impact on outcomes.

Whoever this woman Modesty was, she had a role to play in something big and bad. I just needed to figure out why she was under the lens of an FBI terror specialist.

5

———

OKAY. Deep breath.

According to my phone app, the diner was just down this street and around the corner to the right.

I decided to cut across the parking lot and come up behind the restaurant. It would give me a chance to peek and see if a car was parked out back with an out-of-state license plate.

It was still pretty early, six-forty. Usually, I'd have another twenty minutes before my alarm sounded, or one of my dogs, Beetle and Bella, woke me with their tongue laps.

This week they were staying with their trainers, the Millers; they were learning how to do cadaver scents on waterways. It was good that they'd be having fun learning new things and enjoying the outdoors this week. Their training was pre-planned, freeing me up for whatever Christen and Gator needed from me to make their wedding beautiful and memorable.

Lousy timing for Spyder to put this new mission on my radar.

Ah well, it was hard to schedule the bad guys.

The parking lot over here was empty, but around the diner, it was much more congested.

The website had said that the diner was open all night. I

assumed that this was the on-the-way-to-work breakfast rush in full swing.

I hoped so.

I wanted to be able to slide in and hang out, getting lost amongst the comings and goings of workaday folks.

As I got closer, I heard a commotion on the other side of the fencing that enclosed the dumpsters.

A young woman's words were hard to decipher as they warbled with fear.

Men's voices—one angry and taunting, the other finding whatever was going on to be funny as all get out.

Could this be Modesty in trouble? Should I intervene?

The first rule on a mission was typically "Don't stick your nose where it doesn't belong." Spyder had shown me enough videos and talked me through enough scenarios during his mentorship that I realized stepping in and thinking I understood the dynamics of a situation just wasn't a thing.

It's one of the reasons why I didn't carry concealed. Imagine seeing a man shoot someone; I pull my gun on him and shoot, later to find out that he was an undercover cop, and he was taking down a terrorist. Or equally awful, I pull my gun and hesitate, trying to grasp what was going on. The undercover cop sees me with a gun pointing at him and pulls the trigger a second time.

I was not a superhero. It wasn't my role to play one. If something terrible was happening, I should call the police. Possibly make a distraction.

Still, I was trained that unless I knew the backstory, stay away.

Easier said than done when I heard a woman in distress.

I melted into the background to get a read on the situation. This technique was what my martial arts teacher, Master Wang, called shadow walking. It was the technique taught to Ninjas so they could move through a space without being detected.

In this technique, the shadow walker must observe the colors around them, not just that a tree trunk was brown, but it was light and shadow, crease and crevice, flecks of gray and white, green and tan. If I used a solid color when I shadow walked, I could always be seen. When I thought of the process like painting a canvas, I was successful.

This was a honed skill that took years and years of practice. Master Wang said I was a stellar student, the best he'd seen. Learning as a child, shadow walking was one of my favorite things to do. I'll admit that at that time, my whole goal was to win at the hide-and-seek games the kids from my apartment complex played in the park just up the road from our apartment building. Sometimes it even got me out of a punishment at home when disappearing meant I wasn't at the scene of the crime of the missing cookies.

I always thought of it as a mental ghillie suit like the coverings snipers draped over themselves so they could lie unseen to the enemy.

To do this, I had to imagine the hues and shades of my surroundings dappling over my body.

My success had a great deal to do with my mother teaching me art skills. My eye perceived variants in colors that were missed by the untrained eye.

My mother's art training blending with Master Wang's martial art training.

Both were tools in my toolbox.

Useful, applicable tools, especially in situations like this one.

As I started training under Spyder's mentorship, time refined my shadow walking goals.

Since then, too many times to count, shadow walking was the difference between my life or my death.

Now, using the technique, I rounded the dumpster to find

three men triangulated around a waitress. A bag of restaurant trash in each hand, her back was to the dumpsters.

She was trapped.

Projecting the color of dumpster blue and rust patches out in front of me. Stilling my breath to observe, I watched the young woman trembling.

She was a tiny woman. Maybe five foot two. A hundred—a hundred and ten pounds.

The men, in comparison, were hulking. My guess was that these guys did construction or landscaping. Their muscles had the look of men who didn't need to go to the gym because their jobs built their bodies up. While they dressed in clean jeans and T-shirts, their dusty boots with mud-caked along the edges made me wary. They'd have steel toe reinforcements. Lethal weapons if they knew how to kick.

I was wearing tennis shoes.

Realizing that I was assessing my own clothing choices for my ability to fight in them, I slipped behind the trash to drop my shadow walking concentration. There, I quickly texted Iniquus Operations Control a message that there was an emergency unfurling, send a police car with backup.

Iniquus monitored all of its operators when they were on task. The control room would have my location up on their map. As soon as the message dropped, they'd shift into go mode.

After I saw the "delivered" indicator on my phone, I turned off the volume. An ill-timed ping could endanger me further.

"Look, guys," The woman was pleading. "I've been on my feet for the last eight hours earning the money. I need it to eat. I have kids."

Robbery?

I took in a breath, calmed my system, and dropped back into my shadow walking mode, so I could observe.

If this was Modesty, her being hurt might create issues

moving the mission forward. I had no idea if Modesty had children or not. Of course, this woman could be lying about the kids to garner sympathy.

If she handed them her money, and they went away, that was one thing. But now that I had my eyes on the men, I realized that was not their plan.

One of the men kept glancing over to a mustard-yellow car, the sides lacey with rust. No hubcaps. I read off the license plate to memorize it—in case that became important.

The man with the snicker, his lower lip distended with a plug of tobacco, reached out and gave the waitress a shove, sending her back two steps.

She slammed into the diner's cement wall, her head making a stomach-churning crack.

"*Please*." Her knees buckled. Sliding to the ground, she gripped the garbage bags, using them to form a barricade in front of her.

She looked young. Vulnerable. About the right age to be Modesty…

I wished Finley had given me something beyond a name.

I wished she'd let go of the garbage bags already to have her hands free. Instead, she was all but hugging them against her as if the restaurant waste was the buffer she needed to stay safe.

She eyed the kitchen door and licked her lips as if she could taste freedom on the other side. Her gaze bounced to each man and back to the door, quick glances as if she were trying to gauge if she took off running, could she make it inside?

But also telegraphing her intent to the men.

The guy with the white shirt and the lizard logo moved between her and her escape route.

There was really nowhere else to run. All of the other businesses in the strip mall stretched along the far side of the parking lot.

"Go ahead and hand over the money," the guy with the turquoise blue shirt said, low and reasonable. "We need to eat, too. I'm hungry. You hungry, Benji?" His gaze shot to the smallest of the three.

"Starved." He sent a lascivious lick of the lips the woman's way. "I think good things are coming. A morning quicky and full belly after. You're going to be nice to us, aren't you?"

The waitress worked the disgust from her face. Manipulating her lips as if trying to remember how to form words. "If you come inside, I'll buy you breakfast."

I strained to hear her. She was barely audible as she put together the men's intent.

Blue T-shirt sent his gaze first to one of his band and then the other.

It seemed to me that he was assuring himself they were all heading toward the same goal. Then he sent a broader sweep to make sure no one was around to interfere in what would happen next.

His eyes slid right over me, where I held in the shadow of the dumpster.

It was getting closer to decision time. What was I going to do?

How far away were the cops?

While this shadow walking was a massive tool in my spy craft toolbox, it took enormous concentration. It was hard to compartmentalize, holding both the shadow and thinking strategically about what needed to happen.

All three of them glanced over at the yellow abomination of a car.

"Come on now." The guy with the blue T-shirt took two long strides in the waitress's direction, reaching down to her. "Let's go for a ride."

She slapped his hand away and cowered behind her garbage bags like a toddler behind her blankie.

"Throw her over your shoulder," Blue T-shirt ordered the guy he'd called Benji.

"The car's too far for me to carry her," Benji whined.

"Go git it," Blue said as if Benji was the dolt of his three-man crew. "Drive over here, and we'll just shove her in."

Benji pulled a set of car keys from his pocket.

If I let him get over to their car before I acted, it would be one less adversary, should I have to get in the mix.

"No," the woman wailed out. The one word held, rising in volume as it slid up the scale.

Good job! That should bring out some curious eyes if anyone was near that back door.

Someone who could help.

A chef with a butcher knife or cast-iron skillet…

I *didn't* want it to be me. That would make my next step in this FBI task harder. I wouldn't blend in later if I stepped into this mess now.

I'm not a superhero, I reminded myself, again.

These were three beefy guys with steel-toed boots. They obviously enjoyed hurting women and weren't afraid to commit a crime.

And too, it was highly plausible that if I stepped in, the men would still be successful at what they'd determined to do, then her fate could also become mine.

6

A GALLOPING HEART pumped adrenaline through my system. Sweat slicked my skin. I was having trouble maintaining my breath—a crucial component to retaining my shadow walking protection.

I definitely didn't want to be spotted before I chose to be seen.

One thing I knew—cops coming or no cops coming—if the men shoved this woman in their car, things would turn very badly for her. The chances of getting her out of that situation unharmed were slim to none.

Not that I'd allow them to take this woman without somehow trying to protect her.

This so totally sucked.

Benji took off at a jog toward their vehicle.

Lizard grinned like a mad man.

Blue reached for the woman's wrist, dragging her toward him.

She pressed her hips down to the ground. Hoisted a few inches up, her feet made odd duck-like paddles toward him to keep from tipping over.

If she faceplanted, she was done.

There were very few moves that could get you up and safe if

you were face down with weight at the small of your back. Even with my experience and training, that was the position I called "mercy" because the attacker's benevolence was really the only thing that allowed someone to survive.

Still, she gripped the garbage bags.

Did she even know she was doing that?

Terror made the brain do odd, short-circuity things.

Let go of the darned garbage! I sent her thought commands.

As she opened her mouth in what looked like it might form a scream, Blue yanked her arm, pulling her to her feet, and in a single, almost dancerly move, he spun her into him, slapping a hand across her mouth.

Her eyes stretched wide and unblinking. Her forehead was etched with a lattice of frown lines. She snorted like a bull as she tried to drag enough oxygen up through her nostrils and exhale.

Her limbic system was obviously lit on fire.

Mine was getting there, too.

There was no way I was letting these men push that woman into their car. I no longer cared about consequences. The evil in front of me took precedence over the evil I was supposed to be stalking.

Blue wrapped his free arm around the woman's waist and lifted her off her feet. His lips were pressing kisses onto the woman's neck.

Benji had reached the car.

Lizard had circled in front of me, away from the waitress's flailing legs.

Let. The. Garbage. Go. Already! I pushed out the thought command. It had zero effect.

Okay, with Benji at the car, this looked like the best scenario I would get.

Dropping the shadow walking technique, I took a step forward, using my momentum to raise my leg in a front kick that I aimed between Lizard's legs, lifting him off the ground as I aimed for the sky.

He shrieked out in high-pitched horror of pain and surprise, grabbing at his crotch.

Bent over, gasping, he gave me the perfect target for a push kick. I tugged my knee into my chest. Leaning backward, I thrust out to catch him in the ass.

His arms flew wide and flailing against the momentum of my attack.

He skidded face-first into the black top.

Blue spun toward me. His face red, eyes bulging with rage. He tossed the waitress to the ground with such vehemence that she rolled with her bags and lay there, stunned.

Blue clapped his hands together, a body language signal of impending violence.

There were two things I needed to be hyper-aware of—avoiding blows to my head and Lizard grabbing at my legs. Their steel-toed boots could be lethal in a fight.

Lizard was still clutching at his crotch, eyes streaming, gasping for air.

"Looks like we're going to have two treats instead of just the one." Blue's snarling words were designed to intimidate me into cooperation.

Fear of physical pain made most female crime victims compliant.

This was obviously not his first rodeo. He knew how to intimidate and control.

Blue's eyes slid to Lizard. "Get off the damned ground," he spat.

Benji had made it into the car; I could hear the engine turn over.

The screech of tires assaulted the air with its nerve-torturing cacophony. As Benji's too heavy foot pressed the gas, the balding tires finally found their grip on the black top.

The danger quotient just went up exponentially.

The bad guys' car rocketing toward us, I took advantage of Blue's inattention.

He still hadn't figured out that I was a trained adversary. And I knew now that he was the kingpin, the others his lackeys. Slice the head off the king, and the others would flail.

I spun like a dancer to cover the space between us.

It was a martial arts move that I loved because it wasn't at all the norm one saw in a street brawl. It would confuse his brain.

I needed every advantage I could get.

Distant sirens told me that I'd have help soon. Would it be soon enough?

In a fight, a lot of harm could fall in a very short time frame.

My calculations didn't slow me. They were part of my training. A fight wasn't physical moves by themselves. It was a chess match. It was about keeping a cool head in a heated exchange.

The opponent with ice in their veins conquered the hot head.

Still, I had no illusions. My success wasn't a given.

This was still a three against one fight. And size and number matter.

You're not immortal, I reminded myself. Mostly, that was Spyder in my ear, teaching me to be humble and strategic, or my ego might just put me into a scenario that I couldn't control.

On my last spin, I balled my fist, pulling my hand to my shoulder and exposing the boney cudgel of my elbow, the hardest part of the body.

Elbow strikes were my favorite strikes. I could do a lot of damage to my opponent with little danger to myself.

I clipped across his chin.

The force twisted his head to the full extent his neck would allow, like an owl with bulging surprised eyes.

His reaction was more information. He should have spun with the strike to sap the blow of its power.

Now perfectly positioned, my fist against my shoulder, I flung my arm outward, my knuckles catching his temple in a back fist that pitched his head in the other direction, throwing him off balance.

"Fuck you, bitch." I heard Lizard off to my right. Still crawling on the ground, he was part of my awareness, but he wasn't my focus.

Blue chambered a punch, stepping into it to give his arm the power of major muscle groups. He swung at me. Street brawler with experience. That twist to the shoulder gave him a longer reach and used his back muscles and glutes.

I was a much smaller, much lighter adversary.

And it occurred to me, this was no longer about trapping two women and putting them in his car to take us off to do what they willed. Blue now had to save face in front of his posse.

That might make him reckless, throwing haymakers instead of jabs and hooks.

I was able to duck under the next poorly executed punch.

That kind of swing happened when you didn't have a plan.

As I pressed up from the squat, I blocked his arm, making sure he couldn't grab at me. My ponytail, which made me look younger for this assignment, was a fighting liability—nothing I could do about it now.

Using my own momentum as I rose to my full height, I tipped to the side, my weight on my stability leg, my right leg pulled to my chest. Instantly, I extended my round house, aiming the top of my foot to line up just under his ribs. If I were lucky, I'd kick the wind out of him, leaving his diaphragm convulsing so he couldn't inhale.

The trick was to get my foot out of the way before he could grab my leg and drop me to the ground.

Oof. He coughed and wretched as I spun again outside of his reach.

From my peripheral vision, I saw the waitress scrambling to her feet.

Still, she hugged the garbage bags to her like shields.

Lizard was up on all fours, making strained moans.

I took the opportunity to kick him in the gut. He arched up like a cat then vomited.

When I stepped down and swung back to find Blue, there was his fist crashing into my cheekbone. But unlike Blue, I didn't just let a punch land, or it would have knocked me out cold.

Spinning. Spinning.

Where were the police?

Blue grabbed my shirt and dragged me into a bear hug, lifting my feet from the ground.

His hands were meaty and powerful, the kind of hands that built strength through use.

I was mighty protective of my head. I'd had two major head traumas in succession, and unless I wanted to be spoon-fed from a wheelchair, I needed to protect my brain at all costs.

I couldn't grapple with this guy. He stood almost as tall as Striker did.

I grabbed his pinky fingers and bent them backward as I dropped my chin to my chest, then flung my head back, breaking his nose.

That level of pain surprises the nervous system and freaks it out. For a split second, his power grid was knocked offline.

He dropped me.

I scooped my foot behind him, placing the sole of my tennis shoe on his calf as I rose up to stand on his leg, driving his knee into the pavement, his weight and mine coming down, hopefully crushing his knee cap.

Benji was out of the car with a baseball bat in his hand.

Nope, that was my line. I wasn't going to die here today.

I grabbed the waitress by her uniform and tried to lift her and move her toward the back door and the relative safety of more people.

She curled in tighter around her trash bag.

Shit.

"Help," I yelled at the top of my lungs. "Help!" And knowing that the word help rarely got people involved, I added, "Fire! The diner's on fire!"

The bat was lifted over Benji's shoulder. He was ready to knock one out of the ballpark.

I ducked under the blow, pushing the waitress's head down further.

Benji shifted tactics. He swung the bat over his head and was going to cudgel me with it.

It was the move I had anticipated.

What I had processed, and Benji had not, was that his buddy, Lizard, was behind me, his hands splayed on the black top as he tried to rise to the fight.

I spun, dove, and rolled over Lizard. It hurt like hell. But it was nothing compared to the excruciating pain that Benji inflicted on his buddy as that bat crashed against Lizard's spine.

The wood made a sickening thwack.

Lizard dropped unconscious. Possibly dead.

That had been a vicious blow aimed at *me*.

Benji didn't seem to register that he'd probably paralyzed his friend. Benji was hard focused on me.

The waitress laid in the path to the door on my left.

The dumpster was to my right.

Two men on the ground and an enraged Benji in front of me.

Their car, with the engine still coughing and choking, cut off my only line of escape.

I scrambled in the only direction that would keep the waitress safe, and me too. I planted my foot on the bumper. Praying that the rust could hold my weight, I scrambled up the hood of the car to the roof.

"Get down off there," Benji yelled.

"Help!" I screamed.

"Get down off my *goddamned* car."

"Help!"

Suddenly more engine roars, more tire squeals. This time it was the good guys. Iniquus had sent the calvary, and the D.C. P.D. were screeching their brakes as they came to a halt.

The waitress had finally gotten herself together. Dropping the garbage bags behind her, she pulled open the back door and slung herself inside.

Huh. Well, you're welcome, I guess.

I had my India Alexis Sobado ID on me.

Did I just blow my op?

7

I SLID from the car's roof, keeping the vehicle between the officers and me.

Benji scrambled to get back in the driver's seat, but the officers popped their doors, pulled their weapons, and shouted, "Hands where I can see them."

I didn't want to be involved in everything that would happen next. I didn't want to give them my ID, or a statement, or my contact information when I'd be summoned to court to testify.

None of it.

I glanced around me and focused on the mud-splattered cement block wall behind me, painted in cheap "whatever's in that there bucket" tan paint.

Shadow walking with prep time and an even countenance was one thing. But my adrenaline was a geyser.

My heart was pumping so hard I could almost hear the squeeze and release.

When I was younger and working with Master Wang on this skill, he made me sprint until I could hardly breathe, then I was supposed to disappear.

We would have sparring matches that put me on the mat,

gasping in pain and exhaustion, and he'd command me to shadow walk. And I did.

This wasn't exactly like riding a bicycle.

This was a fine-tuned skill that had required me to put biofeedback sensors on my fingers and learn to drop my pulse and respiration rates after extreme exertion just like the Olympic biathlon folks did when they had to cross country ski to their mark, unstrap their rifle and shoot a bull's eye, before taking off for their next target.

I was sorely out of practice.

Still, I tried.

Standing against the wall, I projected the colors out in front of me like a mask. I slowed my inhale, moving my trembling hands behind my back. Any movement, *any movement at all*, would pull the human eye in my direction—a holdover from our caveman days when wild animals were our greatest threats.

In the whole "fight or flight" limbic response, it was the reason why we also developed "freeze."

We self-paralyze when our survival-brain thinks stillness might protect us best.

Please, don't let me freeze up here and now. I begged my brain.

Luckily for me, Blue was enraged, pinning attention to him. The cops didn't have time to do but the most cursory scans of the environment.

He didn't get to kidnap the girl, didn't get to steal her tips, had a broken nose, broken kneecap—I was betting—and from the way he was clutching his chest, I'd say I broke a couple of his ribs as well.

Just desserts.

The officers traced a circuit into the scene with tiny shifts of their heads. Using their peripheral vision, they took in their partners' actions and reactions, making sure they weren't advancing toward the three bleeding, angry men on their own.

From what they could see, there were no women involved.

If I had arrived on the scene, I would surmise that these guys had gone after each other. Three good ol' boys, friends, who had a falling out, "That's all it was, officer. Nah, I don't want to press charges," I could imagine them saying.

This was a quandary.

What should I do?

If they were just going to get off with a slap on the wrist, they might try this same thing later with another woman. If I stepped forward and told them what had happened, I could blow an FBI op.

Spyder was central to this. He wanted me involved, which meant it had national if not international implications. Yeah, in the hierarchy of crimes, the FBI mission was my highest pursuit. What I'd do is tell Finley about this so that he could maybe chat with the D.A.

If the woman didn't come out and say anything… What did I know of her circumstances? Maybe she had a reason to be under the radar, too.

Maybe that was Modesty.

The cops moved in as the two conscious brutes found their way to their knees as instructed.

As my body settled, my heart re-seated, my lungs filled naturally with a long, slow inhale, shadow walking became easier, more reflexive.

The officers told the men to lace their fingers and put their hands on their heads.

The men seemed submissive, and I didn't trust that.

They had been much too belligerent and bellicose for them to simply allow the officers to cuff them and put them in a car. They hadn't even offered up an explanation for their blood and injuries. They said nothing.

This told me that this scenario had played out for the friends before.

Lizard was out for the count. I could see the shadows changing on his shirt as his chest rose and fell. Not dead.

They had a strategy. I could see the two telegraphing messages to each other with their eyes.

I had no way to warn the officers and remain in the shadows.

My hands behind my back, I reverted to my childhood power move of crossing my fingers. I sent out a mental warning.

Of all my psychic skills, pushing a message to someone else wasn't one of them.

This was a crime scene. The police were the professionals. Even if they could see me, anything I did or said would not be received as assistance. I'd be perceived as a criminal, cuffed myself, taken down to the jail, and booked.

Iniquus would have a lawyer there before the fingerprint ink was dried.

I wasn't worried about that.

I was worried that I was expected at the FBI and the CIA today.

Obviously, I failed at my psychic mind-meld with the officer. He looked a little too relaxed as he stepped up to Blue, another stepped to Lizard to check his vitals, and the woman officer went toward Benji.

As if in trained choreography, the officers reached toward their belts to pull out their cuffs.

Blue sneezed. A big fat sneeze tipped his head backward then rocked him forward. Folding at the waist, blood shot from his broken nose.

The officer jumped away from the spray.

It was a signal.

And a technique.

Blue released his hands from where they'd been posted on top of his head. Grabbing up his shirt, he wiped at his nose. When he did that, Blue dropped his hip to the blacktop, freeing his legs. Already bent from being in a kneeling position, all Blue had to do was extend his leg and clip the officer in the kneecap with his steel-toed work boot.

Eight pounds of pressure was all it takes to break a knee.

For sure, that was exerted exponentially.

The officer was down.

Blue grabbed the Taser from the cop's left hip and fired it into the injured officer.

I had *no* idea what to do.

Interference would make me a target—the officers were clueless that I was on their side.

Leaving them to a fight with one man down was antithetical to who I was.

I was frozen by the memory of Tasers and guttural screams.

Gator had been Tased the night I was kidnapped. He was Tased because he was trying to protect me. His tortured body on the ground convulsing with agony had been entirely my fault.

As this officer made the same sounds as Gator had that horrible night, the memories bit into my brain and made it stutter. Right action that night was to do what Gator had told me to do, what I had been trained to do in such a circumstance—run.

But I hadn't done the right thing. Instead, I ended up being kidnapped.

The memory sizzled my brain. Dragged me away from this life-or-death scene to the one that Gator and I had survived. A PTSD flashback that left me vulnerable.

I forced myself with sheer will to focus on the here and now.

With no weapon, no badge, and no good plan, all I could do was pray for inspiration. In my mind, I was frantically clawing through the files of strategies that I'd been taught—by my friend Dave with the DCPD, my mentors Master Wang and Spyder. I was coming up empty-handed. This wasn't a scene they'd prepared me for.

Action might get me shot by the cops.

So far, the officers hadn't been focused my way. Nothing put me onto the police officers' body cams—yet.

But inaction had its risks, too. Just standing here against the wall could well snag me in a way that blew my op.

Shadow walking used brain trickery to succeed.

I couldn't hide from a camera lens. The more still I could hold myself here against the wall in the blue-gray shade of the dumpster lid, the more possible it was that I'd be missed by an officer on the scene now, or later by a supervisor reviewing the tapes.

The melee with the police grew fiercer. I was ready to drag my phone from my back pocket and call dispatch to get the officers more help.

Then suddenly, the sizzle of a Taser.

8

———

THE AMBULANCE ARRIVED with backup as the echo of Benji's screams faded.

He was face down and cuffed. The Taser probes still pierced his skin. The officer's finger rested on her trigger, ready to light him up if he made a single aggressive move.

Unconscious from the bat to his spinal column, Lizard had already been cuffed when Blue pulled his escape plan.

Blue—

Blue had a gun pointing at his back.

With things seemingly under control and every officer's body cam focused away from me, I eased along the wall. Rounding the corner, I made my way next door to the gas station, where I could check my appearance in their bathroom mirror and regroup.

I second-guessed myself.

Cameras would be everywhere at the gas station.

Again, I wasn't quite sure how to play this.

How bad did I look?

Did I have blood in my hair from the head butt that broke the guy's nose?

No, the gas station was a bad decision. Everyone would be

gathered to figure out what the commotion was about. Better to slip into the diner. Hopefully, everyone inside would be caring for the waitress, focused on her. I could slip in, head to the bathroom, and wash the sweat off my face.

Except for the bruise that I could feel swelling, I might just look like someone who was coming in on a foggy morning, with temperatures that made my hair and clothes wilt.

Walking through the front door, the tinkle of bell chimes jangled my nerves. They alerted the staff that someone had come in. They could pull unwanted eyes my way.

I was surprised to find everything looked…normal.

The clanking of silverware against the dishes. The blast of morning news on the television. The conversations. It all continued as if there hadn't been a battle out back.

I tucked my head down, eased up the aisle toward the restrooms, pressed open the door.

Ah, here she was.

The waitress stood in front of the mirror, glaring at her image.

She didn't have a scratch.

Her whole body trembled with shock as adrenaline left her system.

When I moved behind her, she flicked her eyes in my direction, but she didn't seem to recognize me.

Terror does strange things to the brain.

"You okay?" I asked. I caught the name on her name tag, Barb.

Her gaze slid back to her reflection in the mirror without answering me.

She still didn't seem to be aware that I was at the crime scene or had helped her.

Yanking the elastic from my hair, I bent at my waist, fluffing my fingers through the loose strands, feeling for any moisture that would be Blue's nose blood.

I didn't feel any.

When I stood, I pulled the ponytail back into place.

Turning on the cold tap, I stuck my hand under the soap dispenser, careful to avert my eyes from hers. Since Barb didn't recognize me straight off, I didn't want to do anything that made her focus on me, place me, and call attention to me.

The soap stung as it hit my knuckles, raw and puffy.

Barb moved to a stall, and I was able to check out my face. Yeah, that punch had left a mark. Some abrasion, some swelling, my skin was discoloring into a bruise. It wouldn't be too visible for another hour or so—enough time for me to try to get eyes on Modesty and get out of here.

Probably, I could get this covered up with makeup before the CIA.

I pulled out my phone and checked the time.

How was it only 7:10 in the morning?

Awful.

All of it.

It didn't bode well for the mission. As soon as that thought popped into my head, I pushed it back out again. There was no need to plant those kinds of seeds.

This was a fluke, that's all.

Monday, I'd take this back to Strike Force, and I'd walk them through every move and thought that I could put together. We'd do a tabletop re-creation of the event, thinking it through in retrospect.

A retired Navy SEAL, Striker as commander of Strike Force, brought this to our team as a strategy to make us more effective. We'd reconsider *all* of it. They'd critique *all* of it. Not with blame or shame. Together, we'd find the holes in my thoughts, actions, and reactions. In this way, I could fine-tune how I responded in the field during future events.

That was one of my weaknesses, choosing feelings over training.

Sometimes I just felt obliged to act.

Two years ago, I felt impelled to let the kidnappers truss me up and shove me into their van because there were innocent lives at risk.

And today, I felt compelled to protect that young woman—before I knew if she was the FBI asset, or person of interest, or whatever other way they might characterize her.

If I were wrong about my choices, Strike Force would call me on it.

My team only wanted everyone to succeed and go home safe at the end of the day. I wasn't concerned about their critique of me.

I *was* worried that Blue had caught me on the cheek with his slug. I rolled out of it, dispersing the energy, but I could feel my sweat stinging the abrasion.

Striker would have a fit.

The doctor warned me about taking any more blows to the head.

And I would be standing in Christen and Gator's wedding party in a few days. Banged up me wouldn't look great in their photos.

All right. Enough distraction. Time to get to work.

I dried my hands, checked my pocket for my phone and cash, and moved into the diner.

An elderly man, with his pants hauled up almost to his armpits and a graying afro, got up from his stool at the counter. He pulled out his wallet, left a ten-dollar bill on top of his check, and shuffled out.

Two police officers, adjusting their duty belts, sidled past him at the door.

Shoot!

Okay, if I had been in the restaurant eating, there's no way I was outside getting clocked by Blue. I slid into the old man's seat and lifted the untouched toast to nibble.

The waitress, coffee pot in hand, stalled in front of me, looked down at the bill, the man leaving, then me.

Our gazes held. Destiny was the name pinned to her uniform shirt. She gave me a nod that read of deep understanding. Scooping up the bill and the cash, she slid them into her pocket. She picked up the man's coffee mug, stuck it in the sink, and placed a fresh mug in front of me, filling it full.

Okay, what was that look of understanding? If she had been on the run without funds and hungry, maybe she too had slid in front of a half-finished meal and gobbled it down. Or maybe she thought that I was in trouble with the police now prowling the restaurant.

Either way, she was protecting me.

I would play the role of starving runaway. I slathered the toast with butter and jelly and gobbled it down, closing my eyes as I relished the taste, then wiping my eyes.

Destiny glanced toward the restrooms as Barb power-walked toward the cash register and the grizzled old man with a dirty apron who stood there, taking people's money.

"Jim, I quit." She put her apron on the counter.

Jim didn't seem perturbed.

A cop pointed at Barb. "Hey," he said.

Barb looked around for an escape. I turned back to the leftovers on the plate. I could watch the cops and Barb in the mirror behind the condiment shelf. I reached over next to me to gather a set of napkin-wrapped utensils.

With the napkin on my lap, I used the knife to carefully remove the parts of the food that the man had touched. He left plenty for a hungry runaway, potatoes, eggs, he'd eaten all the bacon, only a small piece of fat remained. I was going for it. This was an excellent cover story.

I peeked up to see Destiny's reaction. Modesty… Destiny. She could have changed her name for protection. Sure enough, she'd blanched. Her hands trembled, sloshing coffee from the pot. She set the pot on the counter. Grabbing up a rag, she crouched to the floor, cleaning up the spill.

I wasn't convinced that wasn't done to hide from police eyes.

"I don't want any trouble," Barb said. "I just want to go home."

"Can we go somewhere and talk privately?" the male officer asked.

"No." Barb's face was red and angry. "I'm not going anywhere with *any* man. No way. No."

"Did you know the men who attacked you?"

I wondered how they knew that she was the focus of the attack. She had no physical signs of the altercation.

I pulled the elastic from my ponytail and let my hair fall across my cheeks as I bent over the plate, scooping up a forkful of potatoes.

"Did you know any of those men?" he asked.

"No. I was taking out the trash."

Jim crossed his arms over the expanse of his chest, resting their weight on the bulge of his stomach. "Someone attacked you? That's why you're quitting?"

"Second time this week. On Tuesday, the man just took my tip money. This time they wanted to shove me into their car and take me for a ride."

"Same men?" the officer asked.

"Aren't all men the same?" She looked over at Destiny. "Make the guys take out the trash. Don't go out back alone. Good luck to you." Then Barb pushed past the officers and headed out the door.

I bent over my plate, pretending not to care what the heck was going on between Barb and the police.

"Anything I can get you, officers? Coffee? Doughnuts?" Jim asked.

Ding. Ding. Ding. I knew how the police figured out a waitress had been attacked—that was the message I'd sent Iniquus. They would have conveyed that to dispatch. Man, I was slow today. I needed to focus.

Spyder depended on me to do a good job here.

As the police walked back out the door, I stood up to walk over to Jim, picking up Barb's apron. "Looks like you have a new opening for a server. I need a job."

"You have experience?"

"Sure."

He ran a thick index finger up and down the length of his nose while he assessed me. He pointed at his cheek in the same place where I had sustained the hit. "I don't need no trouble like Barb had."

"My cheek? That's not trouble. That was just an accident going in your ladies' room. That lady who just quit yanked open the stall door into my face. So any trouble I'm having already walked out that door." I pointed at the front, where a couple of men walked under the tinkling bells.

"Barb did that?" Jim asked, looking for the lie.

"No. Barb didn't do that. My face was in the wrong place at the wrong time. Barb didn't mean to hurt me."

He pulled out a clipboard from under the counter. "You can work Barb's schedule. I'll give you a trial week. At the end of the week, I'll see. I don't pay you nothin'. You get what you make. I don't like doin' no reporting to the IRS. No paperwork for you to fill out that way."

"When's my first shift?"

9

———

AT MY HOUSE, on Silver Lake, I climbed from the Lyft. "I've given you a tip and a good review."

"Hey, thanks, I appreciate it," the gal said as I closed the passenger door.

My teammate Reaper and his wife Kate were climbing the stairs to the duplex. I owned the building and rented out the left side to them.

Kate was cuddling her infant Little Guy to her chest. "Hey Lexi," she called out softly.

I raised my hand.

Reaper backed down the step, the diaper bag slung over his shoulder. His gaze hard on my face. "What happened?"

I reached up and touched my cheekbone. Yeah, the swelling had gotten worse. "I stopped a kidnapping." I gave him a one-shouldered shrug.

He looked at his watch. "A little early to be playing Wonder Woman, don't you think?"

"Yeah, but whatcha gonna do? The bad guys don't keep office hours."

"The blow to your cheek…" He twitched his head this way

and that as he ran an assessing look over me. A retired SEAL, there wasn't going to be much that was missed by his scrutiny. "Did you take any other hits?"

"Just the one. Beefy fist, though. Had I not rolled with the punch, I would have face-planted."

He frowned. "You called Dr. Carlon?" Dr. Carlon was a traumatic brain injury specialist who treated both of us for our ongoing issues with head traumas—Reaper sustained his from his time with SEAL Team Six. Me, well, I got mine from dodging criminals.

Dr. Carlon was cutting edge with her approach and one of the kindest, most accessible people that I knew.

"I called her first thing after the situation cleared. If it's an emergency, go to the ER. Other than that, she can work me in on Monday afternoon."

"Too long."

"I'm not going to the ER for a swollen cheek."

"I'm not going to lecture you, Lynx. But I am going to insist you take my appointment with her today." He pulled his phone from the cargo pocket on his Iniquus camo pants. "I'll call and tell the receptionist that's the plan. I can wait until Monday for my checkup. You can't."

I touched my throbbing cheek. "Are you sure?"

"I insist."

"I insist, too," Kate said. "You know what we've been through with Reaper's brain injuries. You do *not* want his experience. It's a terrible way to live, for everyone involved." She sent a glance toward her husband and swallowed. "You just don't want that. Take the appointment."

I nodded. "What time?" I still had the CIA and FBI…

"Four-thirty," Reaper said. "And I can see you're mentally checking your to-do list. But this takes precedence."

"Four-thirty. I can do that. Well, you're right. No matter what was on my agenda, I would move it for this." I touched my heart. "Thank you so much."

"And now that I've buttered you up with my doctor's appointment," Reaper said, "we have an ask."

"Sure." I started climbing the stairs to give Little Guy a kiss.

"We were hoping you'd watch the baby tomorrow night," Kate said. "Reaper and I are getting some things together for Gator and Christen's wedding."

"Oh, that's an easy yes. Tomorrow is the neighborhood parents' night out."

When I was first hiding from the serial killer, I bought my house. It felt safe to live across the street from my dad's good friends, the Murphys. Dave Murphy was a detective with the D.C. P.D.

It felt safer knowing someone I loved was nearby.

This was a working-class neighborhood. The parents were in jobs that didn't allow for frills and extravagances. While they might come up with the money to pay for a movie or dinner out, add in the cost of a babysitter, and that was prohibitively expensive.

Once a month, I have a neighborhood sleepover. All the kids come and camp out on my living room rug or under a blanket fort made with my dining room table. This gave the parents a reliable night that they could depend on to relax. The following morning, we had a potluck brunch and hung out together. It was really lovely. I looked forward to my time with my neighbors, whom I regarded as family.

I petted a hand over Little Guy's silken strands of hair. In his sleep, he was making a silly smile, drunk on his baby formula.

Though he was five months now, Little Guy had never been to one of the sleepovers. Kate wasn't quite ready for that yet. Even being right next door, she was still a mama bear and didn't like to leave her baby with anyone other than Reaper, so Kate's leaving the baby with me was a big deal.

"We won't leave him all night," Kate qualified. "We thought we'd work on the wedding list and then get some dinner out. Home by nine."

"It's fine. No worries." My cheek throbbed when I sent her a smile.

"Thank you," Kate said as she made her way through her front door.

"I'm calling Dr. Carlon now." Reaper looked down at his phone screen, scrolling with his thumb as he moved through the screen door and out of sight.

"Thanks," I called after him.

I checked my phone for the time. It was insane all the things that had happened and how hours on my clock didn't seem to keep up with the frenetic happenings of today.

I had an hour before Striker would pick me up for the CIA.

Could I get myself spiffed up enough in that time that he didn't freak out?

Hmmm. Doubtful. But I'd try, starting with a shower.

When I was Spyder's mentee, one of the things that Spyder had impressed upon me was that I should maintain a low profile. No one should be able to trace my professional life back to my personal sphere.

Stakeouts, placing surveillance, interacting with the crime players, I should always be incognito.

This morning, I had sort of complied with Spyder's directive. It had been my intention to play it very low profile. I was just going to slip into a back booth, pretend to play on my phone, and get a lay of the land. Gathering a few impressions of Modesty,

Destiny? This would mean I could bring my observations to the FBI with me.

Still, I wasn't sure I'd connected with the right person.

I guessed I'd find out this afternoon at the FBI.

With my hair in hot curlers, I studied my face. Yeah, I thought that the makeup lessons Spyder had given me would mostly hide this.

Spyder was a skyscraper of a man, thin like a flagpole. His gorgeous skin so richly dark, Spyder was blue-black. I'd once heard someone describe the color as blackberry—I agreed, with the metaphor, not just in his coloration but the fact that he was sweet and nourishing but protected by thorns. As striking in appearance as Spyder was, he couldn't easily change his appearance to go undetected. So Spyder had learned to manipulate his energy. Calm and cool, he rarely attracted attention to him unless he wanted to. And he rarely wanted to.

Since my looks were more malleable, Spyder taught me the CIA techniques for highlights and shading to transform my facial features into something I decidedly was not. Smoke and mirrors. Colored contacts could change my blue eyes. Temporary dye transformed my blonde hair.

Today, I wanted to set a tone. Not under the radar…hmm. Girl next door. Innocuous. Yeah, that's what I would do.

I picked up my makeup brush and got to work, seeming to repair this morning's damage.

I released my hair from the hot curlers and combed my fingers through the strands to make gentle curls and waves, then I pulled a headband in place. That took about five years off my face. I smiled at the effect in the mirror. I looked like a teen.

Under the radar and unexpected were the traits I liked to cultivate. Bonus, the curls fell softly over my cheek.

Now for the right outfit…

I moved to my closet.

Striker and I had three places between us. My house here in D.C., Striker's house on the Bay, and we also had an apartment on Iniquus campus where all of the operators had living quarters should worse come to worse, and we needed to be all hands-on deck twenty-four/seven.

That seemed extreme. When would that ever be required?

Well, it had when Spyder and I were taking down the Hydra and two of the three heads—Omega as security and the Assembly as the political and legal power—came crashing down.

This week, though, because I'd be having the kids over, and because I wanted to have time in the evenings to read through my mom's journals, I was home.

And it felt good.

I pulled a pink dress from the rod, looked it over, and put it back.

Next, I chose a yellow fit and flare with a mid-century feel to it—the days of innocence. Yeah, I'd go with this one.

I laid it carefully on my bed. My fingers touched the white sheet.

The fabric wrapped into my fist, a memory flashed of another time when my hand was holding a white sheet in just that way.

I was back on the road next to the crushed tangle that had been our car. Dad's head rested in my lap. On that day, when the siren's wail pulled me away from my prayers for Dad, I had looked up to see a man standing with one hand on a tree across the street, vomiting. The next time I looked up, police officers were making him blow into a device. They were handcuffing him; they were walking him away.

A woman, dressed in a rescue worker's jumpsuit, had snapped a neck brace in place to protect my spine. She gently leaned me onto a backboard.

I reached out for my dad's hand, but he was already tucked under a white sheet.

With a shake of my head, I forced myself to look at the yellow fabric on my dress. To bring my attention back to the here and now.

Why were these memories flooding back to me?

It felt like the accident had happened just yesterday and not back when I was seventeen.

Those emotions felt fresh and raw.

I put my hands on my knees as I panted through an anxiety attack.

I was going to make it through today.

I would make it through tomorrow.

Then the wedding.

And everything should go back to normal after that, right?

10

Wʜᴀᴛ I ɴᴇᴇᴅᴇᴅ ɴᴏᴡ ᴡᴀs something happy.

I wanted to disperse this gloom and doom energy before making my way to the CIA with Striker.

Since Little Guy was coming over early tomorrow, I should think of how I would entertain the kids and get set up while my hands were free.

I opened the door that led to the storage area under my staircase, where I kept my kiddo supplies. First, I tugged out my collection of cartoon character sleeping bags and the pile of pillows. Next came the laundry basket where I kept a fresh stack of pillowcases, the pile of fort building sheets, and the bag of clips to hold things in place.

I pushed that to the side to make room next to me for my box of old-school children's movies.

The last time we had our overnight, we decorated cupcakes, and I didn't want to do repeats. Every time the kiddos came over, I wanted things to be fun and new. I dragged out the box I had of art supplies, picking through the loose button bin, the bag of toilet paper cardboard cylinders, and the jar of googly eyes.

Uninspiring.

My hand landed on a box of finger paints I'd picked up at a close-out sale. I looked them over. The thing I liked about this set was that these were professional finger paints—who knew that was a thing? The pigments were rich, and they stayed moist and silken so they could be blended and manipulated on whatever surface the artist was working. And they were water-soluble, which was a huge bonus when it came to kids and art.

It was satisfying to use one's fingertips to experience texture.

I loved eating my kitchen grandmother Jadda's traditional Middle Eastern and African recipes where I could pull off a piece of injera or pita to use as a utensil. Scooping the food into my mouth using my fingertips, feeling the heat and moisture, and the bread's grain made the flavors come alive in my mouth.

Same with fingerpainting. Getting right in there with the tactical experience of paint on the sensitive pads, swirling over the paper, I thought of it as full-contact art.

I thought it was a blast, so joining in with the kids would be totally fun for me, too. Later, when our communal painting dried, I could hang the length of it on my wall. That way, in the morning, when their parents came for brunch, they could ooh and ah over the clever artistry.

Next out was the roll of newsprint I'd bought for a song when I first moved here. No matter how much the kids and I used from the roll, it never seemed to grow smaller in circumference.

I dragged it over to my dining room table, where I put down four layers to protect the wood underneath. Taping the corners to keep everything neatly in place, I put the paints in the middle.

Art could be our starter and could be ongoing, then snacks, movies, stories, and bed. And I could easily do that with Little Guy in my arms with Striker's help.

Oh! Art shirts to keep the kids' clothes clean.

Striker came in and found me dragging the bag of old extra-large T-shirts out. "Hey there," I called over my shoulder.

He saw my cheek immediately. Nothing ever missed his scrutiny. That was why he was stellar at his job. "What happened?" He came to a halt beside me, stabbing his hands onto his hips.

"Three guys wanted to kidnap a woman." I stood. Grabbing the bag's handles, I walked the shirts into the dining room and set them on the chair.

"And you stepped in instead of calling the police." He strode after me, closing the distance until he stood at my side, eyes scanning my length just like Reaper had done.

"I called the police. The police came and arrested the men. I shadow walked out of there. The police didn't see me."

He gently pinched my chin between his fingers and thumb, tilting my head back, turning it this way and that. "Not right away, you didn't. You tangled with them, or you wouldn't have that shiner on your cheek."

"It got a little rough, but that's the worst of it."

"You can't take anymore strikes to the head, Chica." He crossed his arms over his expansive chest and rocked back on his heels, ticked. "You're not made of steel. Did you go by the hospital?"

"No, but I talked to Reaper."

Striker canted his head.

"Look, I took a Lyft home, and on the way, I called Dr. Carlon. She was booked through next week, except for emergencies."

"And you didn't count this as an emergency?"

"I made an appointment to see her. And if you can let me finish before you get too upset with me, Reaper has an appointment this afternoon with Dr. Carlon. I'm taking his appointment, and he's taking mine since the first I could get was Monday." I smiled. "See how responsible I was?"

"The responsible thing to do was to leave the crime to the police."

"Three men were going to drag a waitress into their car. You know what would happen to her."

"I get why you would do it." He looked down at his boots for a very long moment. "I'm so proud you would do it. I hate every second that you put yourself in danger's way."

"Same here. That's exactly how I feel about you jumping out of helicopters in the Gulf of Aden, swimming up to the pirate boats, and rescuing hostages. Do you honestly think that it doesn't impact me?"

He stepped forward and gathered me gently into his arms, dropping a kiss into my hair and again onto my lips as I tipped my head back.

"I got a job at the diner," I said. "So that'll be a bonus for getting to know the woman the FBI is focused on."

"But it's a rough neighborhood?"

"Not that bad. I spent a lot of time there as a teen."

"Why in the world would you do that?"

"Dad died in a car accident. The guy who caused the crash was charged with DUI and something else—murder, manslaughter…but all the charges were dropped because he had diplomatic credentials. Spyder told me I couldn't take direct retribution, but Spyder didn't stop me when I tried to stop my dad's murderer."

"I'm not following."

"The diplomat liked to get drunk at a bar in that area."

"Seems strange for a diplomat to go into a dangerous area for a drink."

"He came from a country that prohibits alcohol. Shame maybe? That's what I thought at the time. Anyway, I was watching him and disabling his car so he couldn't drive drunk and hurt another family."

"That's not sustainable."

"No. It wasn't. The guy is dead now, so no need to be thinking about it. Memories are bubbling up, is all. It's because I was in the neighborhood."

I felt my parents' presence as I said that; there was an eagerness, a *Yes! Yes! Pay attention!* to the sensation.

Striker nodded. With a delicate touch, he petted over my bruise with the pad of his thumb. "How bad was the punch?"

"His knuckle grazed me as I spun."

Striker didn't answer. I know he tried hard not to smother me. It was a balancing act of being loving and concerned and knowing that I was a magnet for crap.

Hmm, I should stop using that phrase as it applies to me.

Spyder would tell me that what we put out in the world comes back to us. I didn't feel like my external life over the past five years was a reflection of my internal thoughts.

In this instance, I knew from Spyder's spiritual convictions and basic psychology that if I think it, I'll bring it into being.

Believing that I'm a magnet for crap means that I will consistently find crap to roll around in.

Like today.

It wasn't my moral or ethical duty to intervene beyond making a call to the police.

I could have gone inside and alerted the restaurant that the woman was in danger.

But I didn't.

And I helped.

There was risk. I'll have to admit, things could have gone very badly. One of those blows could have landed. Blue had me off my feet. Shoved into the back of the car and held by the three men might have turned out to be all kinds of horrific.

Yeah, I didn't want to think about it.

"You can't do that anymore, Lexi. You just can't. And you're going to be mad at me for threatening you, but so be it. If this happens again, I'm going to talk to Command."

"And tell them what? I was doing my job."

"That your job needs to be constrained to the Puzzle Room and to outside meetings with our contractors in their offices."

I didn't know what to say to his threat. I understood it, I guessed. He meant it from a place of concern. My knee-jerk reaction to this threat was pretty juvenile—*I'll show you who you get to boss around.* The reality was that he loved me and wanted me safe. What happened to me had ramifications for both of us.

Granted, his job was a heck of a lot more dangerous than mine. But there was only one time I've ever known him to get injured. Shot. It took me days to speak to him. It was a weird way to cope. But that's what I did.

Would I ever say to Striker, if you get hurt, I'll tattle to Command?

Not the same.

He didn't have ongoing health issues like I did. Two traumatic brain injuries put me at high risk for awful things now—depression, anxiety—and really awful things later—Parkinson's, dementia.

Command had instructed me not to play with violence of action. No daring deeds of do or die.

But honestly, when I replayed the scene this morning, anything I did had its downsides. If I'd run inside, the time it took me to raise the alarm, they could have scooped Barb up and been gone.

Life was life.

I couldn't go around swathed in bubble wrap.

Striker reached over and squeezed my shoulders. "I was blowing off tension when I said that. I'd never go to Command behind your back. You're a hero, saving that woman today. I'm proud of you."

"You're conflicted about me."

"Absolutely. But only about some things. I don't want you in harm's way because I love you."

"Okay."

"Mad at me?"

"If I am, you're pretty far down the list. I'm still dealing with the adrenaline spike from this morning, mourning my mom, and then I got upset after passing by the spot where Dad died. Now, we're headed to the CIA, and they're on my shit list. But I have to smile and help them with their problems."

"Is that why you dressed like Nancy Drew?"

I smoothed my hands over my skirt. "You think I look like Nancy Drew?"

He tugged at a curl. "Mystery of the Fire Dragon."

I stilled. I was a huge Nancy Drew fan when I was little. There were childhood pictures of me wearing bright yellow Playtex gloves as I went through my day. I was ever concerned that I would come upon crime scene clues and destroy evidence when I left my own fingerprints behind.

I had inhaled Carolyn Keene's work, and I knew *precisely* the cover he meant.

Young Nancy was in a yellow dress with a scoop neckline, a matching belt around her waist, and a full skirt. Around her neck, she had a simple necklace. I reached up and touched my own strand of cloisonné beads. He was right. It was a Nancy Drew dress; only Nancy had much shorter hair than I did.

"You recognize this dress from a Nancy Drew novel. And you even remember the title?"

Striker sent me a grin. "Yeah, well. I had this babysitter."

I chuckled at the thought of Striker being so young that he needed someone to watch him.

"She was reading that book when I met her. It was the first time in my life when I had a sexual impulse."

"Toward Nancy or the babysitter?"

He reached up and rubbed the back of his neck. "I'm not sure that I can tell you. But what I did was hide the book and a flashlight under my pillow when I went to bed that night."

"To read?"

"To look at Nancy's boobies on the cover and to want a Nancy all my own."

"Ha."

"And so my babysitter would need to come back and get her book. It was a win-win in my six-year-old world." He cuddled me into his arms. "See? I got my wish."

"Well, Nancy Drew or not. We have a meeting with a crime to solve." I sent him a wink. "I just need to put my magnifying glass in my purse. It's the role I plan on playing. Speaking of roles, you ready to *roll* on out of here and go to the CIA?"

"Yeah, I'm just going to use the head, then we'll *head* on."

I smiled at the play on words because he wanted me to.

Striker turned toward my guest bathroom. "Are you ready?"

No, actually, I wasn't.

No part of me wanted to be helpful to the CIA when they were failing to live up to their promises to me.

Now, I needed to see if there was anything about this meeting that might give me leverage. I needed the CIA color code group to follow through with their promise and help me get a divorce from Angel.

How could I get their attention?

Sitting next to Striker, I adjusted his passenger seat back a bit, leaning my head on the rest.

"I don't like the idea of you driving until Dr. Carlon checks your head," Striker said. "It would be terrible if you passed out and hurt not only you but innocent people who are driving with you."

Wow! When he said that, it was like a bolt of lightning between my eyes.

There was a long-ago memory that was clawing its way up my nervous system, trying to find the light of day.

"What was that look about?" Striker pulled his safety belt in place.

I waggled my hand over my shoulder. I was indicating that the "essence of parents" I felt hovering over there had spiked.

Yes! Yes! Pay attention was the impression I was picking up.

I wished I had the right vocabulary for this sensation, experience…

Pay attention to *what*?

I didn't offer Striker anything else by way of explanation. "It's fine. I agree. No driving until my head is deemed safe."

He nodded. "Once we're done at the CIA, we can grab something quick to eat at a drive-through, a late lunch. Then I'll drop you at FBI headquarters. From there I'd like you to take a car service to Dr. Carlon's office. I'll meet you there at four-thirty.

I pressed my lips together.

"Is that sour look for me?" he asked.

"No, I'm mad as hell at the CIA for not facilitating my divorce from Angel. I've been seething about it all day. You'd think that they'd do this for the child of a former CIA officer if not for the justice and correctness of it. Maybe some atonement of the pain they inflicted on me and Angel's family."

"They're stopping you from moving forward with your life." He glanced back to make sure the street was clear, then pulled out and started us down the road.

"Yep. And you, too."

"I don't care about a wedding, to be honest, Chica. Those vows are in my heart. Heck, I'll tattoo them across my chest if you'd like."

"Seems extreme." I brushed at my skirts.

"I imagine that seeing our friends marrying this year—Deep and Grace, Gage and Zoe's wedding in June—and now standing up with Christen and Gator makes this more upsetting. As for me, I don't need to make my vows in front of anyone but you. They're already my bond. And I don't need a piece of paper saying we belong to each other. We belong. If you wanted, we could just create a contract and sign it. We could even go through the mechanics of the wedding if our friends and family want that. It could just be a ceremony without the legal ramifications of you being married to two husbands."

"I don't lie. That would be a whopper if everyone thought we were legally married, and we weren't."

He turned the car right and let his eye graze over my face before focusing out the front window again. "The only place that it might make the slightest of differences is when we have kids. And we decided to wait five years and then see if it's good timing for us. Most importantly, of course, is your mental wellbeing. I'm worried that these circumstances make you feel caged in."

"Exactly. A prisoner of circumstances."

"Understood. And I agree. It's not fair that the CIA hasn't followed through. The problem is, even with all of our contacts and Iniquus's network, we can't leverage those connections because we can't tell anyone this is happening."

I adjusted the seatbelt strap over my chest. "Do you think it has anything to do with retribution?"

"How do you mean?"

"Spyder and I were working to take down the Hydra. Lots of Assemblymen wound up in prison. High-level Assemblymen who might still wield power from behind bars. Or have friends who want to pile on because they're mad."

"They shouldn't be able to connect your name or even Iniquus to that data dump to the press that started the ball rolling. If retribution were at play, I'm not sure how we'd be able to tell or what we could do about it." He reached over and took my hand, brought it to his lips, and kissed my swollen knuckles.

"The biggest problem today is this chip I've got on my shoulder. I need to leave it behind when we walk into Langley. I'm not going in as Mrs. Sobado, the wife of a black ops officer. I'm going in as a representative of Iniquus. I need to keep those roles clear."

"You're going to do fine. Hey, after we leave Dr. Carlon's, why don't we get a bouquet and go visit your mom. Sunflowers were her favorite, right?"

"Yeah." My face crumpled.

He remembered my mom's favorite flowers. Striker was an amazing guy. My guy. My heart and soul. Not being married to him felt like things were just dangling, unfinished. The constraints made by the CIA's inaction were like a paper-thin popcorn hull that wedged into my gum line, and I couldn't pry it out. So there it was, rubbing and irritating me. Constantly.

Striker drove quietly while the emotions flooded through my body then receded. "I'd like that. Thank you for remembering." I finally managed, referring to his suggestion about taking flowers out to the cemetery.

"Of course."

I rubbed my eye. "I still don't know why you can't go to the CIA on your own."

"Like I was telling you this morning before your coffee kicked in, my take is that your reputation proceeds you. I'm guessing here, but I'd bet that the CIA officers' expectation is that when you come in and look over their materials, you'll pronounce some grossly obvious answer. I'm sure they'd rather that beat down be confined to their top three officers."

"Let's say that's exactly how things go. How would your being there help them?"

"I'll probably be just as stunned by what you come up with as they are, so I'll be sitting there with my mouth hanging open in awe along with them. And since I'm your colleague, it spreads the embarrassment around." He pushed down the turn signal to indicate a left turn and rolled to a stop at the red light. "Yeah, I get the feeling that they're afraid of you, and they want me there to protect them."

I snorted, the laughter bubbling up and spilling over.

Striker sent me a grin. "You laugh, but I'm serious."

"No pressure. So my role is puzzler? But honestly, is this setting you up for another boots-on-the-ground mission? You just got back from being down range. I'd like you to be home for a bit if it's possible."

"Yeah, there's a chance that if this turns into a case, they want

Iniquus to work, that they'd want to read me into the program for next action steps."

Striker's phone rang, and he answered. As Striker ran through logistical data on a case that I wasn't working on, I turned and looked out the window to give him what privacy I could.

It had started to rain.

As big fat droplets spattered the windshield, Striker flicked on the wipers.

I looked down at the cubby in my door to reassure myself my umbrella was there.

Posting my elbow on the armrest, I watched the passing scenery.

We drove by a church cemetery, mildly neglected, in need of a weedwhacker.

The headstones were darkened by the rain.

I pulled up a picture of my parents. *I'm not going to go see you guys tonight at the cemetery,* I thought. *I want to visit when it's dry and sunny. When I'm in a better mood and handling things.*

My attention caught on a mother walking with her toddler posted on her hip. She had a broad umbrella with fanciful colors covering them. The toddler held her legs straight out, I guessed, so her yellow rain boots with big googly eyes and duck-billed toes didn't slip off her feet. Her little baby's arms were tight around her mom's neck, and she looked like she might just close her eyes for a nap.

And just like that, I was back wading around in my memories:

My dad's funeral had been on a rainy day.

I had hidden under the overwide umbrella in a black dress and my gray rain boots with the splashes of bright pink roses. My hands rested on the wheelchair handles as I looked down at the pale skin of my mom's scalp. I found myself counting the thin strands of hair that still held in place, that defied her medications' decree that they release from their follicles and fall away.

How odd that those few strands of brown felt like perseverance. Like hope.

She reached up, and I wrapped her ice-cold fingers in mine.

Spyder stood to my side with the umbrella handle in his tight grip. I could feel his energy radiating outward, encircling Mom and me.

That was unusual.

Like most of the special operators I knew, Spyder typically wore his energy next to his skin. He was usually vacuum-sealed in it. Spyder said those who learned to manipulate their auras survived; they were less visible to the enemy.

I wondered if that was how death found my dad. His aura was expansive and bright.

The Unitarian minister hovered over Dad's coffin and raised her hands in benediction just as the sharp crack of lightning snapped at the clouds like a whip lashing out to move things along. The imperative was met by thunderous hooves galloping across the sky, making my dad's friends pull in tightly and cower against each other.

The reverberations in the air made me shiver.

We hadn't expected rain that day. I looked down at the wheels on Mom's chair and watched them sink deeper into the clay. I wondered how we'd get her out of here after Dad was lowered into the ground.

None of this was something I had imagined.

I knew that the possibility of going to my mom's funeral was very real. It was only a matter of time before her illness claimed her.

Well, that was true for everyone, wasn't it? A matter of time until we died. But that time had seemed out in the distance when I thought about me, or Spyder, or Dad.

Dad was so strong and vibrant. He sparked with energy and vitality.

My mom... Well, the doctor said he didn't know how long Mom had for sure. He said that it helped that Mom had a spirit hungry for life. Though if you looked at her that day, you'd say that spirit had been chewed up and swallowed down by her pain.

That they were lowering *Dad* into the ground, as my mom sank into the mud by his side... It just wasn't what I had prepared myself for.

"May his soul rest, and may all of his friends, family, and loved ones find peace," the minister concluded.

Spyder put his hand on my shoulder, and I turned to look at him. "Lexi, I need you to hold the umbrella over us. I'm going to carry your mother to the car."

Obediently, I reached for the handle and watched my dad's best friend scoop Mom into his arms.

Spyder was incredibly strong. He lifted my mom with reverence.

She looked so fragile. Drained of life force. Bereft.

Bereft was a good word. It glued together the sound "bare" and the sound you make when you're sucker-punched in the stomach. That's how I felt. I was seventeen, and I'd lost my hero, my dad; it certainly felt like a blow to my diaphragm.

Like I couldn't breathe.

Like I was going to die.

Dutifully following along beside Spyder, I had to reach my arm straight up to cover his head with the umbrella.

We settled into the car and headed back to the church for lunch. There were far too many people who came to pay their respects than would fit into our tiny apartment.

I sat in the middle between Spyder and Mom as Stan, Dad's cop buddy, drove.

No one spoke. It had been a very quiet day.

Pay attention was the impression I was picking up from that parental energy behind my shoulder. It was like my parents were right there in the car with us. All I had to do was turn my head, and there they'd be.

This sensation… I both liked and *didn't* like this. I wanted my parents to be near, to guide me. I thought that was a thing. Sort of like praying. But this wasn't supportive as much as it was anxiety-producing.

When I thought that, I got another distinct impression that they wanted me to feel angst.

Was that a thing?

I have a friend, Sophia. She was haunted by a…mmm, my mind wanted to call it a ghost, but it wasn't. It was something right out of Hollywood—The Mummy. Sophia was an archaeologist who accidentally removed a ring from a sacred place. And until she found a way to put it back, her life had been a series of horrific events.

Maybe I'd picked up some kind of *being*—some *force*—masquerading as my parents?

No, that…that didn't seem right.

This sensation was stressful. And to be honest, I was full up on stress today.

If this kept up, I'd talk to someone who might have experience—like a medium or something. Maybe my mentor Miriam Laugherty, who helped me develop my ESP skills, would know. Though, I didn't remember her ever saying that she could commune with dead people.

There weren't a lot of folks I'd talk openly about such sensations.

If this was my mom and dad, I should listen if they were trying to warn me.

And if this was the brain trauma… Well, I'd have to report that to Dr. Carlon.

Thinking my brain was manifesting hallucinations was a whole lot scarier than thinking my parents were haunting me.

Remember. You must remember, something in my head was saying.

Remember *what*?

I wriggled uncomfortably in my seat.

Yeah, I'd never experienced something like this before.

Striker reached for my hand. "You're singing it again."

I turned to him. "What's that?"

He was off the phone now. "If my kindergarten memory serves me right, that's London Bridge is."

"Huh. Probably just thinking about London Davidson." She was, after all, planning that big pre-wedding shindig that no one —outside of Christen's dad's friends—wanted to attend. It would put me face to face with the Assembly. And I loathed them all.

"Not a knowing?"

Hmmm, a *knowing*?

I had two warning systems that I generally relied on.

When I got the heebie-jeebies, I knew it was time to get the heck out of Dodge because I was imminently at risk. The few times I ignored those feelings that screamed "run!" were the times that I came to regret.

I didn't have heebie-jeebies right now. That part of me felt calm.

The second way was much more cryptic. When *knowings* showed up, a crisis was headed my way. Usually, those warnings flashed like bright throbbing red words. Danger! Danger!

Striker had brought London Bridge is to my attention. It didn't feel like a *knowing*. There was no oscillating background with throbbing neon-colored words painted across my psyche.

I supposed it was nothing.

I *hoped* it was nothing.

But now, with this weird sensation of my parent's etheric concern and just a general "get ready, it's going to be bad" trepidation, this next week felt perilous.

12

ONCE WE PRESENTED our IDs at Langley's guard station, parked, and walked the expansive lot, we'd made it to the front doors of the CIA.

Luckily, the rain had stopped.

Oliver, a suit with a noncommittal expression, met Striker and me out front, guided us through the doors, and badged us past security.

Our footfalls on the highly polished terrazzo clacked sound waves into the gleaming white halls, where they bounced and echoed.

It was a lonely sound.

I've been here on several occasions. There was a mausoleum-like quality to those cold stone walls. This somberness must be hard to walk into each day and maintain warmth and contentment as a person. To me, the sterility was dispiriting.

Iniquus could be that way.

When our guests came into the front atrium, they were met with designed rigidity. The monotone was supposed to have a machine-like quality to it, everything humming along.

The colors were chrome and black. The workers' clothing styles depended on their job titles, but always in requisite grays.

Except for me. Command preferred that I stand out amongst the Iniquus throng, wearing bright colors. It was a psychological stratagem that worked like a charm. Amongst the military-like hardness, I was a spot of soft and gentle. The bad guy could tell me all the secrets because I was different, benign, an ally against the hard men in gray.

Though Striker was dressed in a suit and tie for this meeting, he'd be back in his camouflage tactical pants and his gray compression shirt this afternoon when he returned to the Iniquus campus.

Striker makes anything he wears look good, and his dress pants sure did good things for my libido, but his shoulders were too broad, his biceps too pronounced for him to look comfortable in the confining cut and fabric of a suit coat.

I wanted to reach for Striker's hand, but such a move was frowned upon in a business setting.

When I twitched as if to reach for him, he seemed to remember that he and our guide were both well over six feet tall, and my legs were much shorter. Running to keep up with their aggressive gait made me look ridiculous as I chased after them.

Striker paused and changed his pace to match mine.

We passed by oil paintings of men from long ago, staring down at us as we made our way toward the elevator banks.

There was no buzz here. No conversation. It was as if everything that might pass between humans was so secretive, so dangerous that it couldn't be allowed to seep into the air.

Up ahead, I watched a man with a lithe frame walking next to a woman with straight jet-black hair that fell just past her shoulders.

She wore a white pantsuit. Even with her red high heels, she barely came up to the man's chest. They held their shoulders rigid and walked with stiff backs. I could imagine that there was something dangerous afoot, and they were both trying to hold their secrets tight until they were in some SCIF—sensitive compartmented information facility—where the mystery could be revealed.

The woman looked back over her shoulder and caught my eye. Her body gave a small convulsion like a doctor's hammer had tapped her knee to watch her reflexes. Her eyes flicked up to the man, and she muttered something softly enough that the walls couldn't bat the sounds and amplify them, booming out an echo for me to hear.

The man rolled his shoulders then nodded.

He seemed, through his posture, to tell her to move along. But there was something unusual about the exchange. I could swear the woman knew me and had warned the man not to turn around.

How odd was that?

As the two passed a guard, a command was issued.

The guard gave a quarter turn and faced us. He held up his hand to indicate we should stop.

Oliver lifted his badge showing his high rank.

"Wait, please," the guard said as he raised his arms on either side of him, effectively forming a gate.

As the man reached out to press the elevator button, his head swiveled just enough my way that I recognized him.

"Black!" I called out. What in the actual heck?

"Madam," the guard said.

"Black!" I didn't care one iota that my voice pinged around the hall, pulling attention to me. "John Black. I need a word." I projected my voice out. There was no way he didn't hear me.

Everyone heard me.

Black reached for the elevator button again as if his pressing it hard enough would provide him with a quick escape.

Black was with the color code. He was one of the officers who did whatever they did all under the team's name: John for the men and Johnna for the women and some attached color.

Grey, the man who developed my husband Angel, moving him from his job as an Army Ranger into CIA black ops, was part of that team. Grey was the one who thought it would be just fine for me to be gutted by Angel's death.

Somehow, their team thought it was a good idea to tell Angel's friends and family, his *wife,* that Angel had been blown into smithereens on some dusty road in Afghanistan. We'd be sad and move on.

Well, I *didn't* move on. I found Angel, saved him, and was promised a damned divorce.

"Black!" I crouched under the guard's arm.

The guard snatched at me as I ran toward Black.

I slapped his hand away, racing the last few steps to catch up with Black as the doors slid open, and he climbed on the elevator.

The guard yelled, "Stop. Gun."

I reached my hand out to block the doors from closing. Hell no, Black wasn't getting away from me.

In that same breath, Striker lifted me off my feet, pushing me up against the wall.

My bruised cheek pressed painfully into the cold surface.

Striker covered my body with his.

It was singularly the most astonishing and violent thing that Striker had ever done to me.

I stilled, dangling like a rag doll, in shock that he'd manhandled me that way.

The rumble of the elevator told me that my chance to put pressure on the color code group to release me from Angel was lost.

Striker pressed his full body against mine. "It's fine. Everything's fine. That's a colleague of hers, and she just wanted a word."

Our guide was saying. "I'll take responsibility." From where my face was pressed into the wall, I could see Oliver hustling to the elevator bank and pressing the button. "Let me just get another elevator car."

"I issued an order," the security guard growled.

With his arm around my waist, Striker lowered my feet to the ground, continuing to wrap me in a blanket of Striker protection.

I seethed.

I had no idea what Black said to the guard, but it was enough that the guard pulled his weapon on me. It was enough that Striker felt the need to shield me with his own body and put himself in danger's way.

How dare Black?

I had been on numerous cases with him. My puzzling skills had kept ops in play, saved Angel from his torture chamber. I deserved a moment and a whispered conversation.

A guard and a gun?

Are you freaking kidding me?

My whole body trembled with rage.

Striker kept a tight hold on me. Though where I would go or what he thought I would do is beyond me.

The guard didn't seem convinced that I wasn't a threat.

His pistol was held against his chest, barrel facing toward the ground, finger along the trigger guard, the ready position should he need to punch out, align me with his sights and take me down.

For cripes' sake.

"Come." Oliver was obviously distressed by the turn of events. He was scooping the air, trying to herd us forward as the new elevator car bounced into place, and the doors yawned wide. "Come."

With Striker's arm around my shoulders, we took the few steps forward and climbed onto the car.

"That…" he started, then stalled with an exhale, punching the button. "Yeah, that was unexpected. Mrs. Sobado, I apologize there was obviously some miscommunication."

I glowered.

"This meeting… I feel that things have gotten off on a bad footing. This is…" Oliver rested his index finger on his chin and repeatedly swiped at his cheek with his thumb, a sign that he was thinking quickly and trying to be strategic with his words. "There is a dangerous situation unfolding. It's very time sensitive. I'm told that you are… We think that you can… I hope that didn't upset your equilibrium. This meeting has consequences."

I didn't reply. It had been a long day already, and here it was just eleven. I still had the FBI and a trip to the doctor. My cheek where it hit the wall was throbbing. I shrugged my shoulders to get Striker off me as we reached our floor.

I wasn't mad at him.

He did the right thing. I wouldn't have stopped. Through his actions, Striker might have saved me from being shot.

Who knew?

Still, I tapped my foot aggressively while the doors opened, my arms folded tightly under my breasts.

"Your cheek," Oliver said. "I, uhm…shall I get you an icepack?"

13

———

"I'M GOING to lay this out for you with as much information as I can." Casper was the way he introduced himself, nothing more—not even a title. That was true for all three men in the room, a name and a blank face that said, "don't ask for any other identifiers."

Casper was short and balding. His figure was that of a man past his prime who ate a lunch of vending machine snacks at his desk. His skin drooped on either side of his chin, and I thought a little sunlight with its boost of vitamin D would probably serve him well. "Much of this case will remain redacted information. This makes your job difficult, I'm aware."

"What job is that?" I asked. I sat kitty-corner with Striker at a conference table too long for the five people in the room. There was a bank of windows off to my right with a view of the expansive, park-like setting outside. The walls, covered in neutral paint, were peppered with various awards and citations, a few pictures from decades past.

I wondered if Oliver was coming back. He'd left us at the door with an odd little bow.

There was no coffee station set up, just a pitcher of water in the center of the table with some glasses upside down on a cork tray. They were too far away for me to reach without standing and bending over the table.

The three suits sitting with us were named Cho, DiSarro, and the head guy, Casper.

Casper's eye had caught on my cheek and then slid away. He didn't ask.

Probably wise.

To say we were starting this meeting off on the wrong foot would be putting it mildly.

If Striker didn't have the car keys in his pocket, I might just have headed on out the door and explained to Command that I wasn't feeling well after this morning's fight.

I might just do that anyway. I didn't need Striker's car. There were car services readily available in D.C. I used them all the time because they were usually cheaper than parking prices.

Casper cleared his throat. "Our leadership has concluded over time that we here at the CIA might have an institutionalized view of things, especially as they become higher-risk cases and are assessed by our senior staff." He faced Striker, looking him in the eye and seemingly cutting me out of their dialogue.

Striker noticed it too, and I could tell he was highly amused by the crinkles at the corner of his eyes. Though, his face would be read as stoic by those who didn't know him well.

"As you might be aware, the CIA started a program called Red Cell many years ago, developing ideas about where a big threat might emerge that we hadn't considered."

"Creative minds—" Cho started.

"Exactly," Casper cut him off. "Not to say that there isn't creativity at work here at the CIA just that—"

"The culture becomes homogenized as people are given promotions," I said and was ignored.

My dad was one of the creative minds that the CIA had hired.

When I thought he was working on cars in the closed bay of his garage, he was often processing through various data points with field officers, helping them come up with creative solutions.

When I was thirteen, Dad and Spyder were talking through a case over their ubiquitous games of chess, I mentioned something I thought was quite evident, and Spyder raced out of the garage. When he came back, he spoke with my parents, offering to mentor me. And that was how I started training in earnest for what I had thought would be my future career in the intelligence field. Iniquus was happily where I landed. I wouldn't do well here at the CIA.

I wanted to butt heads with *everyone*. Okay, maybe not Oliver. So far, Oliver was okay.

"That's the concern. And it's why we invited Iniquus in." Casper gave Striker a nod. "Again, there is little I can say about the case. This might prove helpful as you won't be crawling through the weeds. Or it might prove too daunting." He sent me a sad smile as if anticipating my failure. "If you walk out of here today," he now turned to look specifically at me, "and you haven't offered us any new ideas, we remain in the same position as we were when you walked through the door. So don't worry if you're not able to come up with anything that our officers are able to use."

Yeah, we weren't going to become besties. That was clear. "But there's a box to be checked on some form? Run this by an outside creative?" I asked with a tip of my head.

He pressed the flats of his hands on the table, his fingers splayed wide. "There's a directive that I'm following through with. It's not meant to be an afront. It's just—" He waved his hand toward me. "You're what? Early twenties? You haven't even got a college degree? You've been on the job with Iniquus for—"

"She's been contracted with Iniquus for three years," Striker said. He didn't add anything that would bolster me. But his eyes danced with merriment. He leaned back like he was going to enjoy the show.

I hoped I could live up to Striker's expectations.

"With no formal training in anything that I can discern." He raised his brows then let them drop, inviting us to draw our own conclusions to that thought. "Iniquus, though, has a golden reputation. Our partnership with them over time has been beneficial to the CIA. This isn't a mission that we're handing off this time. Striker is a task force commander." He nodded his respect toward Striker. "And we've never been disappointed. Since he came up through the Navy to the SEALs and later to Iniquus, I have to assume he's escorting you. Monitoring you as a supervisor? Mentor?"

"No, sir, Lynx isn't under my command." Striker pulled Casper's eyes off me. "She heads her own department at Iniquus."

"Oh?" He focused harder on me with masked incredulity and confusion. "What department is that?"

"My title is Iniquus puzzler."

"Puzzler…" He stopped and laughed. "Sounds like you're comic book arch-nemesis." Casper focused back on Striker when he didn't get a rise out of me. "I see. I guess Iniquus command got the memo about the institutionalization of viewpoints and diversity." He chuckled. "What could be more different than the hardened and experienced special operators turned private security professionals than hiring," he turned toward me, again, "someone like…you."

I focused on the muscles around my eyes, contracting them hard, so my eyeballs didn't roll. I was here representing Iniquus, and I'd already created issues downstairs. Whether Casper was trying to be offensive to see my reactions as a test or if he was being perfectly sincere with his disdain made no difference.

Striker had suggested they had removed the other folks slated to come to this meeting so that I didn't embarrass the leaders on this mission. Having sat through that, I had another take. These three, well, maybe not the three—this guy, Casper, probably thought this meeting was a waste of time, and he wanted everyone to focus on their work piles.

"Okay," I said in my girl-next-door, fluffy-bunny voice, "well, now that we have that cleared up. How about I listen to what you're willing to share. I'll give you enough feedback to feel that you can ethically check that box for having tried an 'outside the CIA loop' brain, and we can all move on with our day."

Striker rolled his lips in, a momentary break in his stoicism that I thought was him trying to hold back a snort of laughter.

I so wanted to live up to Striker's belief in me.

"I mentioned the Red Cell," Casper said, opening his laptop and focusing down as he tapped the keys. "The Red Cell is a working group of highly successful authors. Thrillers, science fiction, post-apocalyptic writers have the breadth and depth of knowledge to construct their plots. They have the kinds of creative minds that made them curious enough to seek answers, develop relationships with folks with a wide cadre of expertise, and more importantly, they see the not-so-obvious holes that a criminal could burrow into and exploit."

"Ways that a terrorist could work a loophole into a noose to hang us all," Cho said.

Casper tapped the enter button to start a PowerPoint into action, the lights in the conference room automatically dimmed. "The Red Cell suggested we contact a Seattle artist to participate in this effort."

"A specific artist with a specific medium?" I asked.

"Right. That's right." He shifted around and sent a side-eye to Cho.

Just then, a tap sounded at the door. Oliver stuck his head in, looked around until he locked eyes on me, and then held up an ice pack.

That was nice of him.

"I'm fine, thank you."

Oliver nodded and backed out again, slicking the door closed behind him.

Clearing his throat, Casper tapped the computer, and the graphic on the screen changed to show an art gallery.

In the gallery, people milled about looking at what seem to be modern versions of death masks.

Before photography was around, when a loved one died, if the family were wealthy enough, they'd often commission an artist to come and make a cast of their loved one's face out of wax or plaster. Just in that form, they could be kept as a memento of the dead person or could be handed to a different artist when the likeness was commissioned as sculpture or perhaps an oil painting.

This display in the gallery looked like a combination of death mask and oil.

Interesting.

Each installment included a box beneath the mask.

"This installation opened last year. The artist collected human debris from around Seattle. It might be a hair from the public bathroom, fingernails, cigarette butts from the sidewalk, chewing gum stuck to the bottom of a park bench."

Strange hobby.

DiSarro pushed away from the table, pressing into the arms of his chair until the seat back squeaked, then coming upright again. "I took these pictures when I went up to Seattle to see the exhibit and chat with the artist. To be honest, from an intelligence point of view, I was pretty uncomfortable with this. I wasn't sure if her collection was ethical. And in this circumstance," he pointed to the screen, "I'd say it deserves a good conversation amongst ethicists because while some of the collection was made of objects that were knowingly discarded as litter—the gum and cigarettes—the hair, I guess, is my main issue."

"Because she was collecting DNA?" I asked, figuring out that ethics plus body debris could only mean DNA.

"Exactly," DiSarro replied.

Was this a trick?

Hair wouldn't matter. The only DNA in the hair is if the follicle is still attached. That doesn't happen in a normal hair shed. The hairs that fall out of our heads and the hairs that come out on our brushes and combs are hair at the end of the cycle. The follicles are gone. Hair, to be useful, would need to be pulled out to retain its follicle.

"I don't see hair being a DNA ethical issue if it's randomly found." That got me a nod of approbation from Cho.

"I guess saliva on a cup might be a better example of someone inadvertently leaving their DNA behind," DiSarro said.

"So this art installation has something to do with the artist using DNA?"

"Glenda Leibowitz is a Ph.D. candidate in electronic arts," DiSarro said.

Striker leaned forward. "I've never heard of that." Striker paints in oils, but he loves innovative ideas. He was going to enjoy this case if it had to do with applied art.

"Leibowitz collects a piece of DNA from the city's assorted human debris. In her lab, she sequences specific genomic regions and enters that information into a software system that she developed. The program then creates a file of a model of the face of the person whose DNA she sampled."

That's messed up, I thought. But said, "Creepy."

Casper tapped the computer, and a close-up of one of the masks was on the screen.

"How does she get from computer analysis to art object?" Striker asked.

"These are 3D printed portraits that are life-sized." DiSarro pointed at the screen. "Those boxes underneath contain the street sample that started the process."

"An artist did that? Not a geneticist?" I squinted at the screen, wondering how close she was able to get to reality with her project.

My friend, Dr. Zoe Kealoha, worked with blood markers. She had developed a number of ways to identify someone without going through the time and expense of using DNA testing.

I was trying to recall what she had said about what scientists could now tell with DNA. We had talked about this because of an article I'd read about how anthropologists wanted to see if they could find some functional DNA in a long-ago human. I had asked Zoe her thoughts on whether or not science could tell what they would have looked like.

Scientific algorithms could identify age, sex, even body mass index with fair accuracy.

It became a little more complicated with trying to get a face to match the sample. The whole nature versus nurture thing has an impact not only on our psychological development but also on our physical looks. Maybe the person's DNA said the gal should have an athletic BMI, but she learned stress eating as a coping mechanism that wouldn't line up. Maybe the DNA said she should have straight black hair, like the lady walking with Black earlier, but she wanted to dye it red and add a curly perm.

Zoe said that while DNA was better than a random guess at figuring out what folks look like. One of the main problems with developing a useful image—beyond what humans do to change their appearances—was that our facial features are a composite of gene interaction.

While Zoe's research with blood markers was meant to determine if someone was wrongly accused, it could not say definitively that the person was innocent or not. For that, law enforcement needed DNA. It had its place. But using it to narrow a search by reconstructing the face of a possible criminal through the DNA sequence?

I was skeptical that this artist had the ability to produce statistically correct replications.

"It's rather genius what she came up with," DiSarro said, warming to the subject. "In the lab, she cuts the sample into the smallest size she can, puts it into a test tube with the proper chemicals to break it down, sticks it into a centrifuge, rinse repeat until she obtains the purified DNA. A Polymerase chain reaction helps her to focus on that targeted genome. Then she has to send it out to a lab for sequencing."

"It's a reputable lab?" I asked.

"In our case," Cho said, "since this is about criminality and not art, we handed her about a thousand base pair sequences from our crime lab. There was a chain of custody and a high-level of forensic professionalism."

I focused on him. "Until you handed it to her."

"Even then. We set up a lab that would maintain the evidentiary integrity."

I nodded. Set up a lab for her? With that expense and the expense of bringing Iniquus on, this was a big "get" then.

"Okay, you used Leibowitz's artist skills to find a bad guy. But now, you're not sure if you have the bad guy or some rando who happened to leave some DNA behind?"

"Exactly." Cho shifted his weight in his seat and sent a fleeting glance toward Casper as if admitting such to me was a no-no.

"What did she collect?" Striker asked.

"CIA officers did the collection. Cigarette butts. Luckily, our target smokes."

"How do you know that?" I asked.

"What?"

"That your target smokes. I mean, if you knew what your

target looked like, you wouldn't have needed this process, right?" I canted my head. "A crime happened, and there was a fresh butt on the scene. Someone thought, 'Could be our guy, let's test it out.' But in practicality, you don't know that."

"With one sample, I would agree," Casper said. "However, we have four instances where a butt was found at the crime scene, and the DNA matches on all specimens. We feel confident that we have the right DNA. So we offered it to the artist, she made a face mask. We found the guy on surveillance cameras at the time of the crimes."

Knowing this about DNA, if I had ever become a serial criminal and had a vicious streak with an enemy who was a smoker, I'd collect their old butts in a little plastic baggie in my freezer. I'd leave one or two behind at each crime scene. That way, the investigators would say precisely what this CIA officer was saying.

I wasn't giving a lot of credence to the cigarettes. But this was a fascinating and ethically questionable new tool that might be deployed. I was looking forward to talking this over with Zoe. Maybe she and I could take a trip to Seattle and go see this installation.

Good? Bad? Yeah, rules should be put in place, and I'd like to hear Zoe's take on it since she was a stickler for ethics.

"But you're not convinced that it's the right guy based on other... No." I tapped my chin. "You think you have the right guy, but you don't have evidence other than his proximity, and you've found holes in your speculation. Enough holes that you don't think that this will make it through the grand jury when you hand it over to a prosecutor. What crime? What continent?"

"Espionage. Europe," Casper said.

"Foreign player?" Striker asked.

Casper stuck his tongue between his teeth and lip, making his mouth bulge outward. It was a modified signal that he was feeling aggressive, if not violent, about the subject. "American."

This was actually more interesting than I thought it would be, in a creepy and disturbing way. "Please continue. I'm assuming that you went to the extremes to engage with this artist because this person of interest didn't have a DNA sample in the government data banks. And I'm betting that no one in his family did one of those home DNA testing kits because they wanted to know where their ancestors came from, so there was no familial DNA to track down."

"Correct," Cho said.

I blinked as I processed the information. "So what traits could the artist use to develop her conclusions?"

"Gender, eye color, weight ranges, anything important that could change facial morphology." DiSarro reached up to rub the space between his eyes and swept a thumb up his cheek bone. "She said there are about sixty-ish traits that she's analyzed. Putting those trait parameters into the software program, she prints off a 3D structure that could model the person's face."

"You tested her theory?" I asked.

Casper leaned forward and typed into the computer. Up came a picture of DiSarro next to one of the creepy pigmented death masks. It was a close, if not an exact likeness.

Simultaneously amazing and disturbing.

"From there, she creates a sculpture and paints them hyper-realistically," DiSarro concluded.

"Okay," I said. "Now, what do you want from us?"

14

CASPER SWIPED his hand down his tie. "We started with a customer question—how did the top-secret information get into the hands of the bad actors. We sent that question to our relevant collection specialists who determined which collection platforms —" He turned to me, offering an avuncular smile. He was going to slowly lead me through an intelligence cycle, baby step by baby step.

"Cigarette butts?" I asked with a bat of my lashes, trying to move this along.

"This includes human intelligence—people who will give us useful data." He turned his attention to Striker, who sat stoically listening. "In this case, it was determined that we needed assets." He caught my eye. "An asset is a term that the CIA uses, but we use other synonyms like sources or agents. We aren't CIA agents." He pointed at each of the three.

I wasn't sure what response he wanted here—surprise? Astonishment? A slap to my forehead that gosh, I'd been using the wrong terminology?

"Targeters, operations officers, staff operations officers are all involved. These *highly* educated, highly trained, highly *profes-*

sional intelligence officers give the leads to our field agents for covert action."

"Who was your customer that posed the question?" I asked, trying to get him to stop with his CIA 101 lecture. Yeah, I was aware that he didn't perceive me as a "highly" or a "professional," but really, whatever. His reading of who I was didn't matter in my analysis, and soon I'd be out the door and headed over to talk to Finley at the FBI.

"The Pentagon."

"Thank you," I said sweetly. "And can you tell me which station was developing the assets?"

"No."

"Are one of you the collection management officer?" I looked from one man to the next. That was a no. "Who vetted the material that you're sharing today?" I thought maybe if I threw out my own CIA vocabulary that we could move on from kindergarten.

"I did," Cho said, looking decidedly uncomfortable.

"I appreciate your effort to bring me up to speed on the CIA processes. Since we have limited time in this meeting, I'd like to know what information you were able to glean from your Red Cell artist? What you wanted to accomplish by hiring Iniquus." I paused. "Other than checking your superior's boxes, that is."

Striker reached under the table and squeezed my thigh. I could interpret that as a warning that I was about to overstep. But I preferred to interpret it as Striker getting totally turned on by my take-charge attitude.

Casper chewed his upper lip. "I'm going to show you some video. Please watch carefully. I've printed off the image that was created by the artist. I was told that you are an expert at body language." He paused. "I think that's a pseudo-science without real applicability in this instance. But… I was told to run this by you, and that's why we're here."

For twenty-five minutes, we watched the surveillance videos.

Some were grainy security camera feeds, some much more high-tech and easily viewed and interpreted.

And honestly, I didn't know why I was here. Wasn't this obvious?

The footage came to an end. Casper tapped his computer again. The lights came up. "Body language interpretation isn't going to get us what we need."

"I agree with you," I said. "Well, body language is helpful here, but it's not going to give you the information you're asking for. Those are two different things."

"Yeah? What's that?" Casper leaned back in his chair, lacing his fingers and posting his hands on his head. It was an alpha body language move. He was spreading his arms like a frilled lizard to take up space and show dominance.

"You want me to prove that you're focused in on the right guy. And I can tell you -ish."

"-ish? How professional."

"That face you made, disdain. That's fine. I'm not particularly interested in winning you over. From your expressions, I can tell you that someone above you insisted that you call me in. You didn't want to do that, but you couldn't say no, so what you did instead was you contracted Strike Force to come. This is your baby, and you don't need some young whippersnapper coming into your office and blowing some information your way. Especially since you don't really believe in the science of body language."

Hmm, I hit the nail on the head. "And frankly, I've had a long day, and I have a lot of work to do." I checked the time on my phone. "I need to be at the FBI very soon. So let me just cut to the chase. You both do and do not have the right guy. And by that, I mean, you're focusing on the wrong crime."

"What crime do you think we should focus on then?" DiSarro asked.

"Conspiracy." I stood and walked toward the windows. The sun had popped out behind a bank of black clouds. I'd just use my own power move to make them squint at me. "I think I see your problem. Gentlemen, your officers are playing the three doors game on the Monty Hall show. You'll remember that game. There are three doors, one has the grand prize of a new car, and then there are two goats. Only one door is a winner. What you've found are the goats, which have their value but certainly aren't the big prize."

"What now?" Cho posted his elbows on the table.

"First a story." I leaned my hips into the ledge and crossed my feet at the ankles, looking comfortable and relaxed by design. "I would like to tell you the tale of Agent 355, during the Revolutionary War."

There was a great shifting around the table. I had felt the undercurrent of their disdain since I walked in. No one asked me to fetch them a cup of coffee, but they viewed me as Striker's subservient. Brought here for no discernable reason and now flapping my gums.

Whatever.

I planned to tell them my little story and then explain why they were chasing the goats, then walk away before I damaged Iniquus's reputation by being petty—which was the most benign feeling I was experiencing.

Black walked away from me at the elevator bank.

Saw me and decided to ignore me and walk away.

It had been eight months. And the CIA owed me my freedom.

"According to historians," I explained, "there's no information about Agent 355 other than they know she was a woman. Those who have tried, since Revolutionary times, to figure out the mystery have failed. It was almost like she was a time traveler. Oh, they thought they had her name a few times. Serenity Bryant, they postulated. The soldiers arrested Serenity multiple times.

They had a noose hung at the gallows awaiting a head and a neck. Now, it was really unusual that Serenity Bryant would be accused by the British soldiers. Serenity was the eldest daughter in a family of British loyalists. Her father wielded both money and prestige. Invariably, at trial, someone of equal social standing and who knew the family would come forward and say that it was impossible that Serenity had stolen the secret papers or had spied. She always had an alibi. She had been busy tending them on their sick bed or was busy caring for the poor the day the espionage had happened."

I leaned over the table and poured myself a glass of water. I took a slow sip, knowing full well I was irritating people as they wished I'd just get to the point.

But I had been trained in many things by my CIA operator father and later by my mentor, Spyder McGraw.

One of those things was magic.

With magic, if you just went right for the big bang of the reveal? Well, it wasn't very theatrical, and I didn't get the gasp at the end.

This was performative.

I'd get to the jazz hands at the finale.

"Agent 355 was dangerous to the Loyalists. The Tories thought that perhaps the spy was a maid in a high-ranking Red Coat household where, as she served, she would have contact with British officers and overhear what was said over cards or drinks. A lot is unknown." I gave a slight shrug. "One thing that is known about Agent 355 is that she helped to uncover General Benedict Arnold's plans of betrayal. And her work led to the arrest of Andre, Arnold's contact, by the Colonials. West Point was saved. Andre hanged."

Pens twiddled in the officers' hands.

"While Agent 355 is now listed as a woman named Abigail, a former slave owned by Anna Strong, in reality, the spy was a woman named Serenity Bryant." I paused for effect. "She was my seventh-great grandmother. I will tell you also that Grandmother Bryant was thirty years old when this took place. How did she thwart the gallows, and how did she spy for America? When you know the whole story, it seems quite easy and obvious. Serenity had an identical twin named Mercy. She had been married at the age of sixteen to a fifty-year-old Loyalist, Jacob Witherspoon, who moved Mercy to Williamsburg, Virginia." I glanced from man to man. "I'm sure that's a place near and dear to all of your hearts, having spent a good amount of time in the area during your training at The Farm."

Slight nods. Making this personal to them brightened their interest a bit.

"Mercy was amongst people who were arguing about the need for independence. Indeed, she had been outside of the Capitol Building on July fourth when Thomas Jefferson read the Declaration of Independence from the west balcony."

I lowered my voice to sound conspiratorial. "Soon after, there was a fire at their house on the Duke of Gloucester Street."

Heads nodded, recognizing the location.

"Mercy had been convinced about the righteousness of the Colonials' cause. So, when the fire alarm went up and the servants were shrieking for help, Mercy threw on a dark cloak and grabbed a satchel that she'd been preparing from her trunk. Slipping out into the night and disappearing, everyone thought she'd died in the blaze. No one even considered that she existed. And where did Mercy go? She was secretly transported via colonial sympathizers to her family's mansion in Seattle. There, she and her sister took turns being out and about. It took immense cunning, forethought, and courage. But they succeeded. And now historians call Serenity and Mercy Officer 355 as if they were only one person."

I smiled. *Tada!*

I held off on the jazz hands.

They didn't seem to have made the connections.

The men sent side eyes to their fellow officers to see if they picked up on some seed in that story that had relevance.

Seriously?

Finally, Casper pulled up his PowerPoint again and pointed at the image on the screen. "This guy is an only child. So while you offered up a cute story, it has no relevance here."

"Are you sure?" I asked. There it was again, the essence of my parents. If I could explain the sensation, it was like they were both nodding their heads at me. "That's right. Remember…" It was as if my parents took this opportunity to pull a long-ago forgotten family story out of storage, shake off the dust, and hold it up to the light for inspection.

What could anything happening to me now have in common with my Revolution-era grandma?

Pay attention!

"No, we aren't sure." Casper leafed through his papers. "He was adopted."

"An open adoption?" Cho asked. "Would we be able to track records? The birth mother? The hospital where he was born?"

"Foreign. The family moved here from Switzerland when the subject was still an infant. So I'd say access to those records would include a heavy ask from our allied country and might even show our hand."

"How would they have found each other if they were adopted in a foreign country?" DiSarro asked.

Casper leaned forward. "Depends on the birth country's laws, and if it were an open adoption, I would guess. We didn't find familial DNA here in the U.S., but that doesn't mean that someone didn't initiate the tests in another country."

I took another sip of water then set the glass on the window ledge beside me. "I was reading just the other day that a woman who had been adopted as a child found a paternal cousin through DNA&Me. She met up with the guy and asked for any information about her birth father. It turned out that her dad was wanted by the FBI."

"No kidding?" DiSarro was perking up. "What did the dad do?"

"He had been FBI with high-ranking security clearance. He came home one day, agitated, and decided to kill his wife and four kids."

"I'd say that was taking the definition of 'agitated' to the outer boundaries," DiSarro said. "When you think of it, the mom putting that woman up for adoption probably saved her life."

"Chilling," Cho said. "And he's still on the wanted list, which would make me want to keep that story to myself. Circling back to this crime." He pointed at the screen. "Let's assume for a minute we have two men—identical twins. What did you call them? Goats?"

"As a metaphor, yes," I said.

"It's possible," Cho hooked a hand around the back of his neck, "they found each other. I suppose it's possible they both liked crime. Though, I'm not really buying this theory." He gave a shrug. "I guess we could try to rule it out."

"You could rule it in by just paying attention to their photographs," I suggested.

"Their. Plural?" Casper raised his brows.

"Identical twins," I repeated. "Could you please put up the photos of the man at the coffee shop and then of the man on the park bench side by side?" I could feel Striker putting off warning vibes. And yes, I could hear my own tone. Irritation. It had little to do with this meeting; it had everything to do with Black...and maybe the CIA in general.

After a moment, Cho had them up.

I walked to the front of the room, standing in front of the

screen, and pointed at the photos. "Same day. From the time stamp on the photos, we know that these are also an hour apart. At some point, this man left the officer's line of sight. These men are not the same."

"Come on now." Casper flicked his pen onto the tabletop and leaned back in his seat. "Look at him. Hair, clothes, scuff on shoes, drip of coffee, *identical*."

I rubbed my forehead, working to modulate my voice to sound professional. "Subject on the right has a mole growing in his left eyebrow." I lifted my finger to point.

Cho played with the mouse and zoomed in.

"It is not in the eyebrow of the subject on the left." I turned and lifted my other hand to point at the exact location on the other image's photo.

The officers all leaned forward.

"If you'll zoom back out on both images, please." I waited. "Subject on the left has a white scar on his left index finger. It looks like it was from a burn. He also has that tear in his cuticle." I caught Cho's eye. "Can you zoom in on their hands?"

After he had the images adjusted on the screen, the officers in the room all shook their heads. "Son of a gun. Identical twins."

"Hence when you picked up the cigarette butts, you got the same DNA sequence," I said. "Research shows that small variances in DNA show up in identical twins or triplets. However, that usually only happens when the zygote splits into two very early. Rare. That early split explains why some identical twins develop hereditary diseases that their sibling does not. How they found each other and how they started this makes little difference. But you are dealing with identical twins unless, of course, they were triplets. But I don't think that matters. All of the surveillance photos are of these two. They were always meticulous about not leaving any fingerprints, I noticed. They were not as careful about the DNA, one because it's tough to move about without shedding

DNA, but also, when they were involved in their crimes, they always made sure the other had a solid alibi. Yeah, I'm convinced that they smoked and left the cigarette butts to purposefully confuse you. And it's worked for what…years?"

"Years," DiSarro confirmed.

"That doesn't explain how they get their crimes accomplished," Casper said.

"Well, the rest isn't that difficult. First, the conspirators used these two guys as goats, and the rest is based on probability."

"We're listening." Casper's voice took on the tenor that I had experienced so many times at work. They wanted to know the answer, yet…they knew when they heard it, they'd be embarrassed.

Oh, well.

15

———

"WHEN I WAS GROWING UP, my mother was bedridden," I told the three CIA guys. "Some days when her head hurt her too much to entertain me, Mom would put on the game show with Monty Hall. I loved that show because of the clever costumes that people created. Are you all familiar with what show I'm talking about?"

I looked around as the men nodded.

"One of my favorite games was the three doors game. Basically, Monty Hall picked someone from the audience. When the curtain lifted, there were three doors. Behind one of the doors was a brand-new car. Behind the other two doors, there were goats. At the time, I wanted very much to go play that game because I wanted a goat. And I had no need for a car."

The men's lips curled in. They were biding their time to hear something of significance.

Still, if you get to the reveal too soon, there's no razzmatazz. I hoped they'd grow to appreciate my metaphor.

"Now the person had a one in three chance of picking the car, and it's important to note, Monty Hall knew exactly where the car was hidden—the show didn't want the player to win. Let's say the player picked door number one. Monty would say, 'Okay, you have door number one. Let's see what's behind door number two.' Again, Monty knew good and well that there was no car behind door number two. He knew it would be a goat. The door opens. Goat says, 'mah.' Player knows that they started with a one in three chance to win, and now that the goat is revealed, they think they have a fifty-fifty shot at winning the car. What does Monty do?" I looked around for one of the officers to throw in an answer.

"He asks if they'd like to change their mind," Cho said.

"Exactly, and they almost always stick to their original pick. Well, almost everyone does. It's for psychological reasons that they stay with their original choice."

"But they shouldn't?" DiSarro asked.

"Statistically, no. Let me start with the psychology that's got your field officers stuck, then I'll explain the math. And this isn't just a chance to talk statistics. It's the strategy that these people of interest must have known in advance. They wanted to go on about their espionage, but they needed their chances of being caught to be statistically minimal. What that means is they wanted you to focus on the goats and lose the car. The goats in this metaphor are not committing acts of espionage. The car is. The goats are conspiring to keep you from noticing the car."

The men shook their heads at me.

"Step by step then."

Striker ducked his head to hide his grin.

"One, the psychology. Cognitive scientists have studied this phenomenon, and my mentor taught this to me because it's such a profoundly held human reaction, and in my line of work as Iniquus puzzler, I can't fall into the trap. When someone has made a decision, they stick with it. Here it is, ready?"

Head nods. Hand rubs. Worried faces. I could tell that it was dawning on these three that they were about to be grouped with the people who made bad choices based on applied psychology.

And that would make them feel like fools, just as Striker had predicted.

Welp, here I go.

"Let me give this example a name. Joe Shmo. So Joe Schmo doesn't like to feel bad about himself. If Joe makes some decision and loses, he feels awful. But if Joe were to change his mind *and then* lose, he feels much worse. Let me repeat that. If Joe sticks with the things that cause him to fail, that's bad. If he had picked the right thing, to begin with, and switched to the wrong thing, worse." I gave them a nod. "Put this information into the Monty Hall scenario. Joe picks door number one. The goat was behind door number two. 'Would you like to change your guess, Joe?' 'Nope,' says Joe. 'I'll stick with number one.'"

The men nodded.

"So door number one turns out to be a goat. Joe feels bad. But Joe would feel so much worse if when Monty gave him the opportunity to switch, and he switched. Following the new choice, Monty's assistant opened door number three, the number Joe switched to, and Joe finds a goat. Had he stuck with door number one, he would be a winner. Hmm. Are you following me? Stick to the original, fail, and feel bad. Switch and then lose, and you'll be beating yourself up for a long time. That's the psychology."

"Let me see if I get this," Cho said. "We have two goats—identical twins—showing up. Their job is to catch the attention of our field officers. Once our field officers decided to focus on the goats—"

"Right, but they perceived the two goats as one entity," I clarified.

"But once they targeted the goats—twins—human psychology said don't change your mind and look for anyone else."

"Exactly." I smiled. "Because if, in the end, the officers switched their attention onto someone else, and it turned out that the goats were the right target, they'd feel super bad. And that's where the metaphor stops being useful. The car, the real spy, is taking advantage of the confusion. The confusion is created by the two men. These men pulled the eyes off the spy. Also, they confused the heck out of your officers by being in two places at once."

The officers exhaled.

Casper asked in a small voice. "Did you happen to figure out who plays the car?"

I walked over to the screen and pointed at the woman with a baby carriage. "This is her getup that day. She's very good at her disguises. But you can tell it's her because she has this tattoo under her watch and when her watch moves, you can see it." I pointed to the computer. "May I?"

"Sure." Casper pushed his chair back out of my way.

I pulled up picture after picture, showing the woman in a variety of disguises. But in each instance, the tattoo was partially hidden under a watch or bracelet.

"Do you know what the tattoo is?" Cho squinted.

"Yes."

"Care to share?" Casper's nostrils widened like a bull snorting.

"No. Sorry. I recognize it. And I know what it symbolizes. But that's classified with the FBI. I could ask them if it's all right to share." Hmm, maybe this was the leverage I needed to force the CIA to follow through with me. But was I the kind of person who would put my country's classified information in danger because I wanted my life to be tidy?

"We play on the same team," Cho said.

"True. And yet, I have rules governing my security clearance. Sorry." *Not sorry.*

"Hey, Mrs. Sobado, can you finish with the statistics? The

person who picked door number one should have switched when given a chance?" DiSarro asked.

"Right. Their chance of winning actually doubles if they switched their answer. But you're not going to believe me until you see the stats play out for you. Just do an Internet search, and you'll find sites that allow you to play. You can assess the odds for yourself." I smoothed my hands down my skirt, drying my damp palms. "To conclude, gentlemen, the field officers were meant to put the focus on the twins. The twins weren't committing espionage. They *conspired* to thwart the spy's detection. The crime was committed by the car if you will. The woman who is spying knew that the chances of the officer settling their attention on her and solving the crime was the same probability as the game show contestants winning the car. I believe there's a fourth person whom I haven't identified today, playing the role of Monty Hall, who has manipulated the officers into thinking the twins were the prize and not the goats."

All right, maybe that wasn't the best way to present that information. But I was tired and distracted. And they were further along than they had been.

Interesting about the woman, though.

I'd bring it up over at the FBI if I saw Damian Prescott, who was working that case.

Striker stood. "Gentlemen, I believe this has been a productive meeting. Today you identified an issue. You wanted to assign culpability to a single man. Mrs. Sobado was able to identify that man as a set of identical twins conspiring against our government. She was able to identify the spy as a female with a wrist tattoo who is excellent at changing her appearance. I believe this information will help you move forward with your case. Mrs. Sobado is now due at the FBI, and we need to leave. Should you have further need of a creative way of assessing your crime picture, you now know that our Iniquus puzzler," he held out a palm in my direction, "is an amazing talent. Thank you for your time."

And he headed for the door.

I scooted after him.

Right outside, standing sentry, was Oliver. "I thought since there was that incident earlier that I'd escort you out. I don't want you to have any trouble."

"Thanks," I said, falling in line with the men as we made our way to the elevator bank.

Down we went to the main entrance.

We followed the hall toward the front door.

Making his way through the metal detector, a man stopped with his hand resting on his briefcase. He looked me dead in the eye. "Mrs. Rueben?" he asked with incredulity.

I stopped in my tracks. It was like an icy fist squeezed down on my heart, and my whole system ceased functioning for a moment.

I recognized him.

Maybe I recognized him…

Maybe my mind was making a collage of my past as I remembered my dad's accident and funeral.

But I could swear…

Spyder had asked me to hold the umbrella over my mom's head as we left Dad's internment. As I did, Spyder scooped up mom and made it over to the car. Stan drove the vehicle. Who took mom's wheelchair? Who put it in the trunk? I could swear it was this guy.

"Mrs. Reuben? I'm sorry, I…"

"Mrs. Rueben was my mother. I'm Mrs. Sobado."

He lifted his briefcase and walked toward me, his eyes unblinking.

"Lexi," I said, reaching out my hand, hoping he'd mention his name.

"Seth Toone." When his hand touched mine, a buzz radiated up my arm into my neck and jaw. It was like I'd whacked my elbow on a door frame. Painful and odd. How did he do that?

"You look just like your mother. It's shocking, almost." He was obviously flustered.

I wondered if he got the same zap I did.

"The last time I saw you, you were just a teenager." He pressed his fingers onto his tie. "It was at your dad's funeral." He swallowed hard enough that I heard the phlegm galumph down the back of his throat. "I worked with your dad. He was an amazing man. It's a stretch for a stranger to say this, but he would have been so incredibly proud."

I smiled. *Proud of what exactly*?

"You are the spitting image of your mother. Crazy. How is she?"

"Dead." But as I was saying that, my stomach clenched. It was a knowing. *London Bridge is Falling down. Falling down…*

"I'm so sorry to hear. My condolences. Forgive me for intruding." He gave me an odd little bow and walked away.

"Chica?" Striker's voice sounded far away.

"Hmm?"

"You okay?"

"Yeah, sure."

"You don't look okay."

Oliver was watching the scene unfold with curiosity.

"Yeah, I just had a thought. Something I should research a bit." It was an obfuscation, not a lie.

I could feel them, my parents, hovering there over my shoulder.

Their angst felt like handwringing. They were anxious.

My PTSD psychiatrist cautioned that I might have developed an enhanced knee-jerk reaction. Where I have a hyper response to a small stimulus. It's relatively common for survivors of physical assault to flinch larger, cry out sooner, act as if the thing that's happening to them is bigger, badder than it might have been perceived before the abuse.

I was in danger of becoming a hyper Lynx.

I smiled briefly at that thought.

Well, all that made good sense.

If my attacker wanted to hear my scream, and I held back to not offer the reward, it would be that much more pain that I'd have to endure, and he'd get the scream anyway. Why not just scream at first touch?

My psychiatrist said that was one way that survivors coped.

Another was that I might see everything through the lens of a survivor, hoping not to get caught up in another horrible event. My body was primed for anxiety. Anxiety might have no rhyme or reason. But as a thinking, puzzling person, I would try to find the source of concern to squash it. The problem with that strategy was that often there was no concrete reason.

She suggested that when anxiety percolated up like it had when I shook Seth Toone's hand, that I not try to adjust my antennae to a station to understand it.

Anxiety could just be anxiety.

Anxiety could have been triggered by something I didn't necessarily see on the conscious level as a threat.

The problem, she said, might come when anxiety brightened my electrical system. Needing to know why I experienced the physical reaction might lead me to search out a reason like, "Did I leave the stove on? Is my house burning down?" Doing that could lead to more profound anxiety issues.

Okay. I got that.

I have a friend under medical intervention for OCD where if she didn't check, double-check, triple-check every light, every appliance, and every lock, she was too anxious to leave the house.

Her issues started after a house fire in which their beloved cat died of smoke inhalation.

But that wasn't this. I didn't think so anyway. I meant…it could possibly be that I was lit up from the bad dream, the potential kidnapping and fight, my terrible interactions here at the CIA today, and the upcoming party filled with Assemblymen.

It was a lot for even the most even-keeled of people.

Was this me creating a story to explain my anxiety? Or was this truly my ESP warning system?

16

———

STRIKER and I were hand in hand, making our way across the expanse of Langley's parking lot. "Give Finley a call, Chica. Put off the FBI until after you've seen Dr. Carlon and had a good night's sleep."

"Spyder wouldn't have contacted me before five this morning if this situation could wait. I have to assume they have a small window."

He fobbed the car unlocked. "I get it, but Lexi, you're not superhuman." He opened my door for me.

"No?" I piled into the passenger seat and looked up at him.

Striker leaned in and kissed my nose. "Sorry. But no." He shut my door and rounded to his side of the car, where he climbed under the steering wheel.

"Are you afraid I'll have a freak out at the FBI like I did when I saw Black, and you won't be there to stop the scene from turning bloody?"

"Angry, violent outbursts can be caused by head trauma." Striker pressed the button to start the engine.

"I was neither." I pulled on my safety belt. "Okay, I was angry that John Black walked away. But I wasn't violent. It's completely rational that I would want to talk to him."

"You need to tell Dr. Carlon."

I posted my elbow on the armrest and planted my head in my palm. "Fine," I whispered.

"What's fine?"

"Fine, I'll bring it up when I go see Dr. Carlon. You won't stop trying to assess me until I do. Let's just nip that in the bud."

"I'm not the bad guy here." He put the car in gear and started to navigate his way out of the lot.

"No, you're not. There's been a parade of bad guys today, and you are most emphatically not one of them. I don't want to go to the doctor because I'm always afraid the other shoe's gonna drop, and she's going to tell me something devastating about my health." I pinched my lip. "I'm changing the subject. Did I tell you I got a job working at the diner? I start as a server tomorrow morning. The four to noon shift."

"So much for beauty sleep."

"You think I need beauty sleep?" I flapped my hand to tell him I was kidding, let the question go. "At the diner, when they put my name on the schedule, I noticed I'd be there with a woman named Destiny. I didn't see Modesty on the list. Hopefully, at the FBI, I'll find out if I found the mark."

"And not the wrong diner."

"I'm not saying that I didn't consider that. I triple-checked the text from Finley. And if that was a mistake, I just won't show up tomorrow. I'll mark it up to the Universe asking me to intervene with the gal being attacked."

"You're not a weapon for the Universe to wield." Striker's tone was emphatic.

"But you are, oh tip of the spear?"

"Okay." He lifted his hand to salute the guard as we passed the security check. "I get what you're saying. Let me clean that up. It's my druthers that you weren't used as a weapon by the Universe. Is 'Burger Go!' okay for lunch?"

"Yeah, that's fine. About tonight, thank you for remembering Mom loved sunflowers." I touched my hand to my chest. "But I think I'm going to skip a trip to the cemetery. I just want to go home and curl up on the couch with you. Watch some mindless TV, maybe. And go to bed super early so I can get up at three to get to the diner in time for my first shift."

"All right."

"I…hmm. Thinking about Mom this whole week… I'm not sure what it is that I'm feeling. Conflicted, I guess, is the best word. I wish she were alive. I wish I could introduce you to her. But I'm glad she's out of that horrific pain, you know?"

"Yeah, I know." He reached over and took my hand.

"She had wrung every possible kindness and joy out of her life even with the misery and pain she went through. I think that the biggest gift I was able to offer her in return was that she saw me as a capable adult before she died. She told me as much."

"You know, when I met you as Lexi at the hospital and learned about all the things you knew and could do, it was astonishing, almost overwhelming that you had that expanse of skills at nineteen."

"Oh, please. When you were that age, you were a SEAL, putting in your time and acquiring expertise to join SEAL Team Six."

"Stop deflecting, listen."

I pressed my lips together.

"I always wondered if you weren't busy gathering accomplishments so that your mom could see that you were a success and capable. That she'd know it was okay for her to let go of that pain."

I squeezed my nose then sniffed. "Yeah, you may well have something there. That pressure to be an adult as soon as I possibly could. Capable. I worked hard at it, from waking up in the morning until I fell into my bed at night. I don't regret it. Everything in my life, even the garbage things, served me. And the tools in my toolbox have kept me alive where other people might have failed."

"Would certainly have failed." Striker's voice was adamant.

"Okay, I'll agree with that. So I get to stay alive because my mom was dying, and I needed to demonstrate my competence to her." I paused. "I was thinking up at the CIA about nature versus nurture in terms of how DNA could or couldn't tell us what someone looked like. I'm really not sure that I agree with the artist's premise for her found chewing gum. But for an art installation, it's fine. For intelligence gathering? Murky."

"Agreed."

"It's an interesting thought, though. I wonder what I would have become with this same DNA but different nurturing background—if I'd gone to school instead of homeschooling, for example. If Mom hadn't been sick, and I didn't feel the need after Dad died to be the adult of the family. What career would I have picked had I not known Spyder?"

"An interesting series of questions."

"I also wonder what would have happened to you if your sister Lynda wasn't your sister."

"How do you mean?"

"Because she has—what shall we call it? A checkered past? Poor judgment? A danger gene that led her toward destructive choices rather than using them for good the way you did joining the Navy to become a SEAL. What would have happened without Lynda in the picture? You'd still be on SEAL Team Six."

"Maybe. I think it works out. By joining Iniquus instead, I get to do the same kinds of mission work. I'm still serving our country. And I got to meet you."

"Bonus."

"But I get what you're saying. Lynda and I come from the same gene pool—nature. But we put those genes to different uses." Striker pulled into the line at the Burger Go! "The usual?"

"Thanks." I laid my head back and closed my eyes while Striker ordered our lunch. Good thing he would be driving. I'd have enough time to shove the fast food in my mouth en route, then climb out of the car and run up the steps to the FBI.

And while Striker was driving, I'd have time to regroup.

What did I know going into this meeting?

Spyder had called. And hung up.

That meant that Spyder was in the field and took an opportunity to reach out.

That phone call was information.

I have worked with Special Agent Steve Finley on cases where he was up to his chin in the sewage of his poor choices on a mission. I had supported Finley when he was in desperate straits. He has given me a nod or a silent pause to convey information that I desperately needed to understand a situation. And that had made all the difference.

I really do respect Finley and his work. If he had called me this morning and asked for a meeting, I would have said yes even without Spyder's directive.

One - This FBI case is of interest to Spyder.

Two - Spyder wants me involved in this case.

Three - This case has to do with a cult or cult-like entity.

Four - Spyder used to be partnered with my dad. My dad had been in the CIA. Spyder has not clarified if he had as well. I assumed not. But that didn't mean that Dad and Spyder weren't working toward the same ends.

Five - Spyder's main juice in life, and I was speculating here because Spyder was nothing if not close-lipped about his…everything. I didn't even know what country he was born in, how he came to have the Scottish-sounding last name of McGraw when he looked as far from Scottish with his blue-black skin, high angular cheekbones, and soft East Asian accent as one could. But from what I had worked on with him and the seed I could glean, Spyder had always been interested in taking down the Assembly. Had my dad worked on that same mission? Am I following in Dad's footsteps? It was interesting. I have met several soldiers who were born while their dads were fighting in the Middle East. Now, as adults, they were barreling down the dusty roads of Iraq and Afghanistan, standing behind their big guns precisely where their dads had. Nothing had changed. Just another generation of fighters stepped up to do their duty.

Six - The Assembly met all the criteria for secret societies. It was an invitation-only group. White. Male. Elite. Once you were invited into the Assembly and were given the pin, you had it made.

This *had* to be about the Assembly.

It had to.

"Seven?" Striker glanced my way.

"What?" I asked.

"You were counting. You got to six and stopped."

"Yeah, that's where I'm stuck for the moment. I was thinking about the FBI meeting."

"Something you can brief me about?"

"You know as much as I do. I was wondering how involved this FBI case is going to be."

"Gator and Christen's wedding is next week." Striker budged up to the window, handing over the money to cover our order.

"Yeah." I accepted the bag, which Striker handed to me to distribute.

"No 'weeee!' No jazz hands? That wasn't a very enthusiastic, 'yeah.'" He rolled up his window and drove on.

"Oh, about Gator and Christin, I'm a thousand percent enthu-siastic." I unwrapped his sandwich and rewrapped it so he could eat and drive, then handed it over. "It's having to go to the party Thursday that's got my system tied in knots." I pulled out the straws, unwrapped them, and inserted them into our drinks.

Striker reached for a fry. "Gator stopped by for a chat about that."

"Oh?"

"Of course, we were invited to that pre-nuptial celebration because we're in the wedding party."

"Hmm." I picked up my soda for a sip. "They gave me the wrong thing. I don't recognize this flavor. It's like cherries."

"Try mine." He pointed to his cup. "Christen and Gator thought when they decided on a tiny wedding with the nuclear family and a handful of friends that they'd be able to manage to keep her family from posturing. Keep the Assembly away from them."

"It's complicated. I get that." I set his drink down. "Yours is wrong, too."

"After last fall, when her dad had brain surgery…even if Christen disapproves of who Davidson is as a human being, he's also her dad."

I nodded.

My dad had been so admired. Had led such a wholesome life. I couldn't imagine what it would have been like to grow up in the swamp of an Assemblyman's family.

I didn't know how Christen managed to walk away from both nature and nurture as an intact human being and an amazingly accomplished pilot. A good and ethical person, she was a testament to a strong inner core of values. I had to assume she learned those values from her biological mom.

"Gator and Christen want us to know we have no obligation to go to the celebration that her stepmom is organizing Thursday."

"We're in their wedding party." I started in on my burger. "Don't you think that would seem strange if we weren't there?"

"Does it matter what people think?"

"True story, I couldn't give a flying flip about the guests. But I do care about Christen and Gator. They asked us to be in their wedding party to support them as they started their new life together. It would kind of suck if we said we can't sit in the same room with people in a group that we detest. Especially knowing Gator and Christen detest them too. Support means support in sickness and in health. For better or for worse."

"Exactly. That's what I told Gator. He seemed relieved."

"I'm thinking about London and William Davidson. Can you imagine the level of...what's the word I want? Not selfishness. Not entitlement."

"Narcissism?"

"That's closer. The level of narcissism to say: Hey, you're getting married, and you want it to be a small intimate circle of people who know and love you, but I don't care. I'm having a big old shindig full of guests you've never met before. It's going to be lavish. It's going to be long. And on top of that, I'm going to make it formal knowing you both *hate* formal events and the clothes required."

"At least it's Thursday. Friday will be the rehearsal and a laid-back meal at your house to just chill and enjoy. Saturday's the wedding. They'll be off on their honeymoon, and we—"

"Will breathe a sigh of relief." We were right outside of FBI Headquarters. I balled up my trash and shoved it in the waste bag hanging on the back of my seat.

"We can do this," Striker said.

"Agreed. I wish, though, you didn't call it my house. It's *our* house."

"Our house then."

I leaned over and put my forehead on Striker's shoulder. "We were supposed to be married already. I'm sorry."

"Chica, it's not your fault. It's a party. It's a piece of paper. What it's not is the truth."

I didn't look up, but I did press a kiss into his bicep, so he knew I was listening and accepting.

Striker and his eagle eye saw a car pulling out, and he whipped us into the slot. "Ready?"

"No." I undid my seatbelt.

"Game face."

I sent him a vacant smile, holding my eyes wide and vacuous.

"I see that you've decided to go for blood. You may want to dim that sentiment just a bit." He sent me a smile, slightly crooked, double dimples, and merriment.

I batted my eyelashes at him. "Too much?"

"A tad."

I popped open my door and climbed out.

Finally, I was going to get some of my questions answered.

17

FINLEY HAD SAID he'd meet me at FBI Headquarters entrance and show me to the meeting. Instead, Finley sent this worker-bee to guide me to the meeting room while Finley finished up with a phone call.

I was glad I had chosen flats this morning. The security guard was my height, but he moved like an Olympic racewalker. His walking pace was my warm-up jogging pace. I had to shift my gait to that pre-jog glide, with my fisted hands held parallel, my elbows brushing the tops of my hips.

He kept glancing over his shoulder to see if I was still there.

He seemed exasperated that I wasn't keeping apace.

And yet, he did nothing to slow to my comfort level. I preferred Oliver.

You know what? This is stupid.

And because I felt passive-aggressive about the last five minutes of this foolishness, I called out, "I just need a moment," and swung into the restroom we passed by.

There, I went ahead and took advantage of the facility while I caught my breath and cooled my system. I wasn't walking into a meeting with the task force sweaty and breathless. It was unprofessional.

I washed my hands, combed my fingers through my hair, pulled my colored lip gloss from my pocket, and applied. Having adjusted my dress, brushing my hands over the wide skirt, I took a deep breath and exited.

The guard glanced over to me with a frown and started bolting down the hall again.

By himself.

Nope. Not playing. I've had quite enough of these power games for today, thanks.

At the other end of the hall, the guard came to a stop and waited for me.

When people act a fool, bad drivers cutting me off on the road or what have you, I think to myself, *they have a terrible case of diarrhea. If they don't get home immediately, they're going to foul their car. It's understandable.* Thoughts like that allowed me to be kind, sympathetic even, to their discomfort and behavior.

In my mind, I couldn't come up with a single reason—apparent or made up for the sake of charity—for his behavior.

Still, I sent him a smile. "Thank you."

"Lynx." Prescott looked up as I walked through the door.

"Perfect!" I called out as I caught his eye. "Just the person I needed to see."

He threw back his head and laughed.

"Hey, Finley." I gave him a finger wave. "Prescott, can I have a moment?"

Damian Prescott was a good guy. We'd been through a lot together. But the last mission I helped him develop was the mission where I found out Angel was still alive. I saw in Prescott's eyes, as he moved my direction, the shadow of pity in the way he held his face.

"Hi," he said and waved me toward the corner of the room. "I was thinking about you this morning when I saw your name on my agenda. How are you?"

"Okay. Thanks. And you? How's Raine?"

Prescott held up his left hand where a gold band gleamed. "Raine is miserable."

"I'm sorry to hear that."

"It'll pass. Morning sickness. We expect Baby Prescott around Christmas."

I reached up and gave him a hug. "Wow, such great news. Congratulations."

"Thanks." His grin fell off. "Have you heard from the judge about your divorce?"

"Nada."

He pulled his head back, giving him double chins. "Seriously?"

"Sadly so."

"I'm sorry. Is there anything I can do to help?"

"Possibly. But first, let me tell you that I was at the CIA this morning."

Prescott crossed his arms over his chest and rocked back on his heels.

"Let me preface this," I said. "I was in a meeting. I did not mention you by name. But I saw something of interest, and I was given permission to tell 'the right person' about what I saw. Their hope is that you'll give them a call."

"Who needs the call?"

"Guy named Casper. He didn't tell me his title or department."

"Ah, yeah. Okay. I know him. What did you see?"

I peeked around Prescott's shoulder to make sure that no one else in the room was listening. I'd be fine with Steve Finley, but there were people here that I didn't recognize. "Espionage case."

"Uh-huh."

"I was watching tapes to help pinpoint the spy."

"Okay."

"I saw a woman with a very distinct tattoo on her left wrist. She wore a bunch of different disguises, and in each, a watch or bracelet or long sleeve obfuscated the tattoo, but I would catch glimpses."

"The *Rex Deus*? Another player?"

I reached out and gripped Prescott's forearm. "Caution. I didn't see the whole of the tattoo. The video was often low resolution. But yeah, I think we found another member of that cell. Casper didn't share any of the details of that case with me. This was a visual puzzle they handed me. So I don't know the circumstances. But. Yeah. I'd give him a call and see if he'd share. I'm pretty clear that he doesn't have a clue what he's dealing with. At no time did he mention anything about our DARPA scientists or about terrorism. I'm handing this information off to you. Iniquus won't be pursuing that connection. I'm happily no longer part of that case. No need to loop me in."

"I'll reach out to him in the morning. Now go back, is there something I can do to help with the Angel situation?"

"I saw John Black at Langley. He ran from me and ordered a guard to keep me away."

"But why?"

I ran my tongue along my teeth and shrugged.

"Okay." He looked down at his shoes as he thought. "Color code hasn't followed up after eight months. It could be that they need Angel to sign the legal forms, and he's off doing something mission-wise. Perhaps he's off-grid, and they can't pull him out to sign court papers."

"You know, that would be the obvious answer. But I hadn't thought of that." I blinked. "That might be the reason. But that reason sure does suck. He could be deep undercover for years. I was supposed to get married in June. I abandoned all the plans.

Told my family to cancel their flights. And I couldn't tell anyone why. They think things are strained between Striker and me."

"I'm sorry."

"I'd like to know if your theory is correct. Or if there's another reason. If they'd just tell me, I might not be seething over this."

"I can't imagine. Well, I can…but still, it sucks. I'm sorry. And I guess what you want to know is if I have any contacts to talk to Angel's handler John Grey."

"That would be awesome."

"Let me put my head together with Finley. You know his girlfriend Anna's in the field right now, but she may have someone's cell number."

Finley walked over. "Is everything okay?"

"Lynx is making connections for us. I'll talk to you about it later. Is Gupta set?"

"Yes." Finley held out an open palm to indicate a seat at the table. "Are you ready, Lynx?"

I sure hope so.

18

———

"Hello." Dr. Gupta stood about five foot three, parting his thick black hair just above his right ear, making a cascade that rounded over his sizable pate. Everything about his head was overlarge, his eyes with their thyroid bulge, his lips and nose all looked like they had been suddenly downsized from a much larger face.

His demeanor, though, was incredibly kind and intelligent.

I felt an immediate affinity for this man.

Dr. Gupta and Spyder had much the same essence—the strength of a quiet soul. A state that I aspired to.

And as I thought that, I adjusted the time I needed to wake up tomorrow morning so I'd have time to follow my meditation practice.

"Hi, I'm Lynx."

He gave me a slight bow—weirdly, this was the third bow I've received today. Since my parents started to hover, there had been a lot of bowing. Coincidence? Could others sense their presence on a subtle body level and be acknowledging their elevated state?

I'd never know.

I bowed back, *namaste*.

Not quite sure what was going on, I wanted to know first and foremost how Spyder fit into this picture.

But that's not what I was going to get. I'd have to wait.

"Lynx," Finley said. "Dr. Gupta is a tenured sociology professor at Georgetown, where he focuses his research on secret societies. We asked him to offer a primer as we follow a lead brought in by our mutual acquaintance." He referred to Spyder.

I nodded.

"We're just waiting for Kennedy, then we'll get started."

Rowan Kennedy was FBI connected to Eastern Europe. Organized crime families were his emphasis. In particular, where the crime families used propaganda as a weapon. That these three people were involved in this meeting was more information.

International in scope, for sure.

As I thought that, Kennedy pushed through the door. He scanned the room and gave each man a dip of his head. And yup, when he focused on me, he offered that odd little bow.

So strange.

"Dr. Gupta, we're all here if you'd like to begin," Finley said.

Dr. Gupta stood at the front of the room. "Very well. I was invited here today to give you background on secret societies in general and then to give you an overview of The Grove in particular; for whatever reason this has become interesting to you." When he said that last bit, he held up both hands like he was signaling stop and rubbed them through the air. It was as if he were warding off anyone's attempt to fill him in; he didn't want to know.

I did, though. *The Grove*?

"Since we're here at FBI Headquarters, let's start with secret governmental societies. We are, aren't we? Bureaucratic secret societies. Here we have two efforts underway. We seek out secrets. But we also guard our own. Often, there is selective recruitment. No matter how you enter into the ranks, there are oaths of loyalty and silence. Is it spiritual in nature?" He shrugged. "Spy work has a moral code. And that code is probably very different than what the normal Jane Doe walking down the street operates under. For example, the CIA might find it important to kill someone, and that's allowed under the right circumstances."

He scratched his nose.

"But spy agencies aren't normally put into the same bucket as the occult. Occult, it has an evil, dangerous feel to that word. It's become that through our entertainment systems. Horror movies, for example. But really, occult simply means concealed. And we can agree that much of what we do here at the FBI is concealed. The main rule in a secret society is that knowledge isn't for everyone. It's for the select—emphasis on select—few. And it's the job of those who have the secret knowledge to guard it from others."

Hmm. Are we going after someone within an alphabet? What would that have to do with a waitress named Modesty?

I wish they'd cut to the chase. Being patient and focused today was proving to be a challenge.

Gupta picked up a fob and tapped the button. The lights dimmed. A screen dropped. There was a painting of the Illuminati.

That got my attention. All of the secret occult-like behavior and Illuminati-connected images were part of the group with the tattoos on their left arms like the one I saw this morning. Could it be the FBI and the CIA were tracking the same dangers?

"In human history, there have always been secret societies, and there always will be, I would surmise," Dr. Gupta was saying. "One of the things we expect to find when studying the various groups both historically and contemporaneously is that they have a charismatic or visionary in the leadership role."

He clicked the fob and up came the image of the seal for the Freemasons.

"Most secret societies aren't publicly secret. We know they exist." He pointed to the screen. "People know about the Masons. What they don't know is what happens within the Masons. Rituals, passwords, member belief systems, even individual identities may be obfuscated from public view. Think. Even in our colleges and universities, our campuses are rife with secret societies. These include what happens in fraternities and sororities—whether they're social or professional/academic in nature. Now, why would one choose to be part of a secret society?" Dr. Gupta's question was rhetorical.

So far, nothing new here...

"Secret societies promise their membership special status. The more exclusive the secret society, the more likely they will seek recruits amongst the rich and powerful. You might have heard about the Bohemian Club, for example." He put up an image of symbology. "This all-male group. It's filled with CEOs, politicians, financiers, and influencers. Among their history, you'll find names like Henry Kissinger and Ronald Reagan. Both of the George Bushes are Bohemian Club members." Gupta scratched his head. "Ancient history, I know, but when Nixon was considering his run for president—while he was never a member of the Bohemian Club—he was invited to go meet with them over a weekend. Nixon knew it was a big step toward being elected. Clout." Gupta pointed at the ceiling. "Power. Another group that acts that way is the Assembly. And we all know from the ongoing legal entanglements for the Assembly that those who were recruited and initiated believed that rules and laws were for lesser men. The Assemblymen believe that through their rituals they are the voice of god, and therefore they can do as they wish."

Assembly? Okay, now we're getting somewhere.

"This all leads me to our topic for today, The Grove."

The Grove... I tried to think if that had come up in anything Spyder had ever mentioned to me. But it didn't seem familiar.

"Here is the history." Gupta pinched at his lower lip, pausing as if to align his thoughts. With a nod, he began. "Just slip into your thinking caps three aspects of secret societies: selective recruitment, fanatical loyalty, rigorous discipline. Okay, with that background, we'll begin. The Grove started off as a progressive idea. Very progressive. June 4, 1919, Congress met to vote on whether or not women should have the right to vote. One of these senators was Marshal Leadbottom. Senator Leadbottom voted against the women. That night he died. Corpulent, to say the least, and older, it was assumed that he died of natural causes. With forensics, what they were in 1919, we'll never know.

"The next day, his wife Dotty, Dorothy Leadbottom, sold their house, their belongings, cashed in her stocks, jumped on a train, and moved to Hollywood, California. Once there, she was absolutely done with the misogynist lifestyles of the east coast elite. She purchased what was then named Athena's Grove."

He posted a picture of an ornate wrought iron main gate with an owl motif.

"There, she had cabins built to set up a community of women. These women were sour on males—mistreated wives, rape survivors, prostitution survivors, lesbians who didn't want to marry. Mother Dot, as she came to be known, enjoyed the classics and liked the idea of the Oracles of Delphi. The women, like any secret society, were chosen and welcomed. Once they lived in The Grove, they had rituals and initiations. They did have men come in, day workers paid for by Mother Dot's wealth. They did the manual labor and also—uhm…" He sent me a red-faced look. "Excuse me. These men also provided the women with sexual interactions if the women wished them.

"They were living a very nice life when the stock market crashed many years later. Mother Dot owned the land and the cabins. There, they grew and produced their own food. Expenses were meager, and Mother Dot had a stash of gold. They were financially ready to weather the storm. Going back just a bit, some of the women had children that came with them when they were invited to the Grove. Some became pregnant while they were there. Once they were adults, the girls could decide if they wished to stay or go on with a more traditional life. Some stayed. Some went. They always knew that they'd be welcomed for visits as adults. However, once they became adults, the male children needed to make their own way elsewhere. No men had lived at The Grove.

"With the Great Depression, many men were desperate. The women decided to allow one of the barns to be turned into a male dormitory. And a new man arrived on the scene. Mother Dot was very pleased. A doctor from Seattle, his family lost everything in the crash. The Grove would certainly be glad to have a doctor. He was given a cabin to live in and work from. Ward Blackburn was his name."

Finley caught my eye. "Our person of interest is Modesty Blackburn."

Interesting. I nodded. "Was The Grove considered a cult?" I asked.

"No," Gupta explained. "Well, not in the beginning. The distinctions and designations are hard for us to tell now. Secrecy is nearly absolute in the current iteration. A cult uses psychological control. None of what was happening under the women back in the 1920s was psychological control—except women holding money and power away from men. However, the secret rituals were to be kept secret. From what we can tell from the histories written by the women, they were having a great time being free of men's rule—including exploring their own sexualities." He coughed into his fist. "Back to Blackburn. He liked the setup at The Grove and wanted it for himself. Instead of being a laborer, he wished to have the women serve him. How could he make this secret society of liberated women into a subservient society dominated by the men, and him in particular? Well, we've pieced this together as best we can. Back in the time that Dr. Blackburn arrived, the puberty rituals lasted for three days. The first day the women who were already initiated went to the center grove to plan and dance and eat and enjoy. The next day the young ladies who had gotten their menstrual cycles that year would be invited to join for their ritual. On the third day, they'd all party together. It is reasoned that Dr. Blackburn, using his chemistry background, poisoned the punch, thereby killing all of the women who had been through the rituals. We believe this was studied by Jim Jones in Jonestown, killing his followers with potassium cyanide in the punch."

"I've never heard of this place or this event," I said. "You'd think it would be part of American lore."

"The secrecy of the society and the upheaval at the time…" Gupta ticked his head back and forth. "At breakfast, the doctor described a vision he'd had in the night. He was told that god would smite those who had abused the rule of the lord. He, Blackburn, would be put in their place as the leader of The Grove. He said he planned to discuss this that day with the elders."

"Who were dead," Prescott said.

"Right. They loaded up a truck with their bodies and left. We believe they were put on a boat and taken out to sea. Blackburn went back to The Grove, where the ritual of pubescence became a wedding ceremony that he presided over. Each man was told his number in The Grove hierarchy. In numerical order, the men could pick their bride from amongst the young women. The girls were traumatized by all of the women—their mothers and grandmothers, aunts and friends—dying. They went along, believing that god had done this. Since there were two more girls than men, Dr. Blackburn chose the first three wives that day, setting up polygamy as a standard. The men replicated the life that the women had led. Except now, the girls were not compensated for their work—it was slave labor. They didn't have autonomy over their destinies or their bodies. Girls could not leave."

"The boys?" I asked.

"Almost all of the boys followed on as had always been. Some boys who brought wealth or a male skill, like blacksmithing, could stay at The Grove. But they'd have to serve until they were much older to be offered a wife. Usually, the less desirable among the adolescents. And that all continues until today. The leader, Orion Blackburn, is Dr. Blackburn's grandson. He is believed to have twenty wives and possibly eighty children."

Holy wow! "Modesty is one of Orion Blackburn's children?" I asked. Kudos to her for escaping such a setup.

"Exactly," Finley said.

"I'm sorry to interrupt, but do you have a picture of Modesty?"

Finley tapped at his computer then turned the screen in my direction.

"She's calling herself Destiny, now."

"Noted," Finley said.

I caught Prescott's eye. He leaned in and whispered in my ear. "Lynx, we worked that case in Syria last December. The horror of women slaves who were offered as prizes to ISIS fighters. Is this going to be too much for you? Are you okay with working this case?"

Finley flicked a look of concern toward Prescott. He must have heard the exchange.

"Spyder wants me involved," I said. Yeah, the enslavement of women was a real, contemporary global issue. It had been so hard to be in Syria and see what that looked like firsthand. It was the reason why Angel had gone black ops—he was willing to suffer and sacrifice, to be tortured and endangered to save these women.

Angel was a hero.

Anything I was experiencing from not having a divorce from him was so small and petty.

I needed to remember that.

If, as Prescott suggested, the papers were held up because Angel was off-grid…yeah, his work took precedence. Those women's lives were much more important.

I felt some of the combativeness recede. The heat was removed from my pressure cooker thoughts.

But what in the world could The Grove, Modesty Blackburn, and Spyder have in common?

And what did the FBI want from me?

19

I'D LEFT THE FBI, my head spinning with questions.

Sitting in a Lyft that smelled heavily of lilac room refresher, I'd processed all the way over to Dr. Carlon's office. The driver was aggressively maneuvering through late afternoon traffic after telling her I was heading to the doctor for an emergency medical appointment.

She kept looking over her shoulder, perhaps fearful I might pop like a balloon and leave my insides all over her spotless upholstery.

Dr. Carlon said I needed to be more careful. I told her I could easily trip on the stairs at my house and bonk my head. I was always in danger unless I was flat on my back in bed, and that was no way to live.

Once again, Dr. Carlon suggested I adopt wearing a motorcycle helmet as a fashion statement.

When I finally met Striker at his car, I opened the door and climbed in, saying, "Dr. Carlon cleared me for fieldwork. She thinks I'm fine."

Striker said nothing, waiting for me to get my door shut, and my belt pulled across me and fastened tightly.

"I hope you're more comfortable with my medical status now." Leaning toward the car's radio, I flipped around the radio stations looking for some music that would take the edge off.

It wasn't a long drive to my house unless it was this time of day, and we were inching along with the rush hour traffic.

"That's it?" Striker asked. "I bet Dr. Carlon said to keep an eye on things. She'd never say you're a hundred percent."

"Right, well, I'll never be a hundred percent, we know that. Good enough is going to have to be good enough."

Striker flicked a glance my way, then pulled out into traffic. "Look, I don't want to fight with you."

"And you're feeling aggressive?"

"I'm…not aggressive. Protective."

I reached for his hand. Pressing a kiss into his bicep, I rested my head on his shoulder with a sigh. "Thank you. It's nice that you care."

He tapped my head with his cheek, then turned to press a quick kiss into my hair. "You said Finley was there at the FBI meeting?"

"Yup, and Prescott. Finley's domestic terror. Prescott runs that joint task force. But there's an international flavor to their caseload. Rowan Kennedy was there."

Striker looked my way, then merged into the oncoming traffic. "Kennedy's focus is psychological warfare out of former USSR countries."

"Interesting, isn't it? I asked Finley about that. Dr. Gupta was the guy giving us a lecture—a fascinating guy. I liked him a lot. You know, he reminded me a bit of Spyder." I bobbled forward as Striker had to use evasive moves to avoid a crash with the overly zealous driver to our right. "Not in his physical capacity," I continued, "but his general demeanor. Centered, unflappable—well, unflappable until he had to mention women's menstrual cycles and sexuality."

"He was talking about that in your meeting?" Striker sent me a quick glance. "Why?" he asked with a laugh.

"Just background on this secret society that Modesty Blackburn comes from. She's the daughter—amongst dozens of offspring—of their charismatic. I've been given permission to speak to Strike Force about the case, so I'm not breaking any laws here. But Kennedy added to what Gupta was telling us about secret societies. It seems that in some cases, charismatics are losing control of the narrative—the Internet age. The average Joe gets a lot of power. They can spin off the charismatic and enhance it. I think about it a little like fanfiction, right?"

"Keep going with that idea."

I settled back in my seat. Traffic was aggressive, and I didn't want to impede Striker's driving. "Yeah, so you have an author who develops their characters and the world the story takes place in. Everything we know is what the author wants us to know. An author, if they're good, really does manipulate us, don't they? They decide what emotions we should experience, everything from the gasp of discovery to sobbing heartbreak to book hangovers when the story is done. Yet, we're not ready to let go of the characters who became our friends…our family, even."

Striker sent me a grin. "What did Kate call it? Her book boyfriend?"

"Ha. Yes. I'll admit, it's fun to have a hunky hero to fantasize about."

Striker shot me a look. "Uh-huh. Is that a jab? I need to step up my game?"

"Book boyfriends keep me satisfied while you're downrange. Are you seriously jealous right now? I'm tired. I want to stop thinking for today."

"We're almost home, Chica. A hot bath, some cuddle time on the sofa, early to bed."

"Agreed. Now, in this case, we have a secret society, we add in a criminal genius mind, and I'm assuming that this somehow has a terror component that they didn't reveal to me. I'm not part of that piece. I'm working on the piece that tries to find out how to hook Destiny into being a resource."

"Puzzles."

"Yes, indeedy."

"Did they say when you're to start?"

"I told you this. I start at the diner tomorrow."

"Undercover."

"Yes."

He was chewing on the inside of his cheek. Displeased. "For how long?"

"As long as it takes, I guess. Hopefully not long. A lot of that depends on how well I do figuring this out. Interesting point, though…" I waited for him to finish his turn into my neighborhood.

"Yeah? What's that?"

"Finley asked if I was going to be at the party for Gator and Christen on Thursday night."

"How would he know about that?" Striker aligned his car with Kate's, put on his blinker, and draped his arm across the back of the seat.

"Good question."

There was a moment of silence while Striker backed into place and cut the engine. "Why would he care?"

"Also, a good question."

"Did you ask?"

"It wasn't a good time. Too many ears."

"What did your spidey senses tell you?"

"Felt like tightrope walking. I think since they're keeping a watch on the Assembly and this party is on their radar. Since all roads lead to Rome, I'm guessing that this case I'm working on for Spyder and the FBI also includes the Assembly. Maybe a guest will be there who might run into me as I'm working on the case. Finley might have been afraid I'd blow my cover. I'm sure, as we're getting closer to next Thursday's party that he'll take me aside and tell me the issues if he thinks I'm going to blow the op."

"Huh."

"Or, maybe he thought some Assemblyman would have a dagger out for me."

"The Assembly doesn't know your role in taking them down."

"No. They're not supposed to, anyway. But the Assembly permeated every aspect of the political and economic power grid in America. I *think* my role is secret. Spyder and I worked under the radar as we brought them down. Indigo's death happened when they'd have no way to identify my role. And all of the records were burned when Omega torched their own headquarters. Some minion along the way..." I glanced around the empty street. I didn't even like bringing it up here in the car.

"Are you thinking of someone in particular?"

"No."

"What about that guy that came to your father's funeral."

I slid a hand down first one arm, then the next as if I was scraping off a film that had settled on my skin. "I don't know. He and Spyder had some symbiosis at the funeral. They communicated with a glance. They were teamed up to help get Mom to the car when her wheelchair mired in the mud. At that point, Spyder was fine with him. Today, Seth Toone was confused when he saw me. He didn't know Mom had died. If he was paying attention to my parents or me, he would have known."

Double whammy: My parents crowded forward. *Pay attention!*

And at the same time, I heard a *knowing* blare, "Take the keys and lock her up, my fair lady."

20

When I opened the fridge, dinner fell on the floor.

I balled my fists and growled my frustration.

"Lexi, sit." Striker said, all calm and shit. "Let me handle this."

"I've got it," I spat out.

"Do you need me to remind you, you aren't a superhero?"

"I'm very clear on my human frailty, thanks, Striker." I grabbed up the broom and dustpan to scoop the remains of my casserole.

"Not even close to my point. I was going to say that it's been a hell of a day, and I'd like to help you relax. And, Dr. Carlon said that you have to get a good night's sleep. The alarm is going to be sounding way too early for your liking. Why you accepted that crazy schedule—"

"I took the schedule that the quitting waitress already had on the books." I dumped the food into the trash and moved to the sink to get a rag and wipe up the last of it. "I love you," I said past the blast of water. "I appreciate you. You know that, right?"

"We take care of each other. The appreciation is mutual. Now, shall I call for some pizza?"

I pulled my hairband from a hook by the soap dispenser, bent back, gathered my hair up into a loose bun, then moved toward the spill.

Striker took the rag from my hand and pointed to a chair. I sat gratefully while he sopped up the mess. "I could make breakfast for dinner," I suggested. "Do you want eggs?"

"I'm fine with a bowl of cereal. I'd rather you sit." Striker finished up, tossing the cloth in the pail to go down to the washing machine. "Sometimes, you find solace in cooking. If that's the case here, then make whatever you want. If this is a chore on your to-do list, let me do it."

I caught the way he was assessing me. I knew I wasn't fooling him at all. I didn't even feel up to this much. I certainly didn't want to eat. I was just play-acting to get to the point in my day when I could fall into bed, hopefully early and by myself, so I could just lay there and cry. Let my body release this sucky day. I stood up to get myself a drink of water.

"What do you need right now, Chica?"

I swept my hands over my face. "Just being here with you is pretty darned good."

He reached out and pinched the edge of my dress between his thumb and forefinger, his mind working the problem. He was a SEAL, through and through.

Releasing the cloth, Striker reached under my arms and lifted me onto the counter, so we were eye to eye.

I rested my hands on the broad expanse of his shoulders and just felt the latent strength. These arms had the capacity to do great harm and the ability to take up great burdens. I loved Striker's shoulders. I leaned in and laid a kiss on the rounding dome of his muscle.

When I lifted up, Striker's lips met mine in a slow kiss.

Gentle and sweet, I felt my stress slide to the side. There it was, crouching on the floor, watching for another opportunity to grab my attention.

I was determined to leave the stress there, ignored.

As my body softened, Striker pressed my knees apart and stepped forward, snuggling into the space between my legs that was all his.

I flexed my feet to make my flats clatter to the ground. Wrapping my legs around Striker's waist, I crossed my ankles behind him to keep him there in the place where he belonged between my thighs. To keep him doing the things he was doing with his mouth. A swirl, and a lick, a nibble, and a dance with my tongue.

He brushed at a wisp of hair that found its way to my cheek and was tickle-itching me. And as he did, he sent a look of curiosity toward the dining room. "What I think you need is a distraction."

"Yes." I sighed out. That was exactly what I needed. A concentration of this energy and then an explosion of release. "That would be wonderful."

He drew my hands to his neck, then wrapped his arms around me. "Hold tight," his voice carried a smile.

What is he up to?

Lifting me up, he walked me to the dining room. There he held me fast with one arm while he scooped my skirt up and out of the way before he set me down on the white paper-covered table.

"It's the Nancy Drew dress that's got you heated, isn't it?"

"That's turning me on? It's you. All you." He gave a slow tug to my zipper. "I think we could have some fun in here."

"Oh?"

"Mmm." He lifted the dress over my head and cast it to the side.

Every move, sensually slow.

Striker in play mode.

"Is this what you want?" he asked as his lips found the delicate bones beneath my neck, tracing a string of kisses from one side to the other. He stopped and looked up to catch my eye.

"This is *exactly* what I want." All day, my muscles had been banded and ready for a fight, physical, intellectual—moral, even.

I had learned over our years together that Striker had a magical ability to shift my consciousness.

It was like hypnotism.

With the tone of his voice, the strokes of his hands, the world fell away.

I was sensation.

Connection.

My life's experiences had taught me that I could blow the *now* by allowing the ugly and violent world to encroach on sacred space.

I purposefully and consciously put up an etheric do not disturb sign. I would focus on nothing but Striker.

Making love with Striker had many moods.

But mostly, it was about allowing a bubble to surround us, a partition, a designation. *This is now. Here is where my focus lies. This is my body, my mind, my soul, and I share it with you.*

I released my legs from encircling him. With my hands pressing into the tabletop, I scooted farther back on the paper, wondering what Striker was concocting in that creative brain of his that kept our sex life so passionate.

He lifted his chin. "A little more."

I complied.

"A little more." Striker kicked off his boots and toed off his socks. He whipped his belt from the loops of his tactical pants and let it drop with a thunk to the carpet. Then slowly, making sure I was watching, he tugged his uniform shirt over his head.

I licked my lips.

A demigod worthy of being a sculpture. An underwear model

on a five-story billboard in Times Square. He was beautiful. And the way he looked at me made me feel beautiful, too.

He popped the top button of his pants.

Room to grow, I thought as my body warmed.

He reached across his chest, tucking his hand under his arm. The fingers of his other hand stroked at his chin. Contemplating.

He angled his head this way, then that, then walked to the dimmer switch on the wall, adjusting the light up, then down. Squinting his eyes, fussing with the brightness until I was illuminated just the way he wanted.

Moving back to my side, Striker pulled free the elastic that had been holding my make-do bun in place.

A gasp escaped my lips as the warm silkiness of the strands tickled over my shoulders and breasts.

I recognized this energy Striker was putting out.

The artistic inner space.

It was the place he went into when he was designing a new canvas. Striker preferred huge expanses where he usually painted stormy seas in slashes of violet and indigo oils, connecting some inner emotion with his brush strokes.

He swept my hair back and dropped one of my bra straps down my arm.

Then the other.

"This just needs to go." He reached over to unclasp my bra, sliding it off and tossing it to the floor. He took my hands in his. "Will you lay down for me?"

"For you?" I gripped his fingers tighter as I lay back, wondering where this was all heading. "I would do most anything."

I was rewarded with a slow sexy smile. The one that promised good things to come.

His gaze shifted to rest on the pots of finger paint, then back to me. A questioning tilt to his head.

"That would be so cold. Don't you think?"

"I have no idea. Shall I try?"

A burst of laughter bubbled up from my belly and filled the room. It was part delight, part I'm not sure about this, part anticipation.

His fingers snapped at the sides of my panties. "These are very pretty. I don't want to get any paint on them."

"Thank you," I murmured, pressing my weight into my heels to lift up.

He inched the lace over my hips, then slowly, slowly down my thighs, and untangled them from my feet.

Striker had a way of making me feel graceful. He had a natural rhythm, an elegance to him that would be lost to those who only knew him in hardened operator mode.

Well—ha!—hardened as in body of steel ready to go after evil and malice.

I was the only one who got to experience *this* kind of hardened operator mode. I reached out and traced my finger over the tip of his erection, wrapped in underwear and not happy to be constrained. "These come off too, please."

I didn't have to ask twice. He peeled off the rest of his clothes, then crawled naked up on the table with me, lifting the pot of blue and showing it to me.

I shivered with anticipation.

He dipped his finger in, his eyes scanning over my body. He started at my calf. In cursive, he traced out the word *silken*.

Twisting, he looked at my belly, quivering with this new game. There, his index finger drew *soft*.

Striker bit his upper lip, tipping his head from side to side. He lifted my hand above my head, then slid off the table, crouching low, his head resting against the flat surface. He was focused on my side that had been slashed by the serial killer. Over a hundred stitches tugged me back together. Those scars were vulnerable to me.

Striker dipped his finger into the pot. I watched in the mirror over my buffet table as he looped *voluptuous*.

That was what he saw when he looked at my side? Not damaged?

Trading for a pot of white, on my arm, from wrist to shoulder, *strength*.

Caress on the other arm.

Nibble worked its way up my neck.

I kicked at him as he traced *tickle* across the arch of my foot.

Lifted to my elbows. It was erotic as heck watching him paint *arouse* on my inner thigh.

Oh, yeah, I was aroused all right, and I was gratified to see the drip of moisture shine the head of his cock, letting me know this was doing good things for him, too.

I knew from our years together that Striker liked slow. He enjoyed the idea of using sex as an escape into physical sensations of love and joy, and he felt no reason, except when I was asking for a quickie, to hurry things.

Tonight, there was no rush. Slow was perfection.

This was so much better than a massage. Striker's fingertips swirled over my body, making me feel beautiful and treasured.

His little kisses, licks, and nips punctuated the loving words he coiled over my skin.

"I think the base is done."

When Striker started a canvas, he did just this. He began by painting words. Thoughts that he wanted to consider as he added the next layer of paints building the oils up one step at a time so that there was depth and intricacy.

The base was done. We had just begun…

I closed my eyes and let myself move to a meditative place,

experiencing the sensation of his fingertips creating serpentine lines as they stroked over my most vulnerable places.

My muscles would clench and release as he moved over my body.

Lifting, repositioning, pausing as he contemplated.

"What are you painting on me?" I whispered.

"You are Eve. The *only* woman. You are brave enough and strong enough to reach for the apple of knowledge. I'm painting you into that garden."

His fingers swirled on my hip. "In your garden, you can be all things, but mostly, you can breathe the heady perfume of the flowers. You can swing lazily from the vines. You can just experience and rest."

"Mmm."

When his fingers finally left me, Striker whispered in my ear, "I just need to wash off the paint for the other places I want to explore."

I let a lazy smile slip across my face as I listened to him climb down and move into the kitchen. I rolled languidly over so I could see his handiwork in the mirror.

Striker had indeed turned me into Eve. I looked like a woman lost amongst the flower and vines of the rainforest. It was so beautiful.

When Striker emerged, drying his hands, I patted my hand behind my back. He followed my invitation. Crawling onto the table and lining up to spoon with me—his hard-on teasing against my ass.

And that just wasn't close enough.

I tapped his hip and spun as much as the tabletop would allow me to.

Striker angled himself on his side, giving me enough room to lay back with my legs draping over his hips. I rested my head back as I reached between my legs.

Watching me pleasure myself was one of Striker's biggest turn-ons.

As I moaned and writhed, my fingers finding the right rhythm, his eyes heated with desire.

I exhaled, watching him through heavy lids.

His attention was bouncing between my fingers and the mirror. Yeah, he was totally into this.

Without changing my pace, I reached out to feel his cock, satin-smooth and throbbing with impatience. I angled him into place, and he pressed his hips to me, sliding in slowly.

Rocking his hips, filling me full, he wrapped his hand around my bent knee. His eyelids closed. His face took on the tense laxness of coital concentration.

Slicked with sweat, he was so darned sexy.

He felt so damned good.

I shut my own eyes, concentrating on the building energy. Pressing my feet firmly on the table, I banded my muscles, curled my toes, and in a burst of energy, my orgasm gripped me, took over my thoughts, my breath, the beat of my heart.

Panting, I didn't feel done. I needed a more intense angle. I reached for his hand, and as I pulled, Striker stabilized me. I found my balance on all fours, then looked over my shoulder at Striker. "Okay?" I wiggled my ass.

Striker shifted on the narrow surface.

With his fingers on my waist, he guided me to an angle. Here, we could watch in the mirror as he stroked in and out.

"This is for you," I panted. "It's your turn." If I didn't let Striker know, he'd continue to work on satisfying me, holding back on his own pleasure. But really, what I wanted was to feel the full power of Striker's desire.

Nothing held back.

And he didn't disappoint.

With his fingers curling tightly around my hips, his strokes grew deeper, more demanding. His head thrown back, he came hard.

For a long moment, I felt the sting of his fingers curling into my skin, the pulsing of his cock deep inside me. It was painfully good.

A weight lifted.

And now, peace descended.

With a gulp of air, he bent, pressing a kiss onto my back, then resting his forehead there. For a moment, we stilled while our heartbeats thrummed.

As Striker came upright on his knees, he chuckled at what he saw in the mirror. His beautiful artwork was no more. The paint had taken a wild ride as the sweat and friction turned the pigment liquid.

What a mess! And I was completely delighted.

"All right, Chica." He climbed from the table with athletic grace.

Seeing his still-hard dick, revved my motors for another go. He grinned as I licked my lips.

He scooped me into his arms. "That was round one. Now, I'm carrying you up to the shower. Round two, we're playing Mr. and Mrs. Clean."

Perfect.

21

LAST NIGHT, as I shut my eyes to go to sleep, Deep rang the front doorbell. He would have no idea that I had gone to bed as the summer sunset.

I heard Striker answer and the men's voices chatting. Deep, who was Strike Force's logistics specialist, had been preparing my cover.

While Striker would try to gather the information from Deep, I needed to hear this firsthand, for safety's sake.

Pulling on a robe and tying it tightly in place, I wound my way down the staircase. "Hey there."

"Hi Esther," he said. There were two backpacks and a grocery bag by his feet.

"What do you have there?"

"Your Esther stuff. When you ran away from your cult, this is all you could carry."

"Thank you." I walked over and looked into the rumpled grocery bag first. Leftover fast food napkins, plastic utensils, a box of crackers, a partially consumed jar of peanut butter, another of jelly. Some tins of tuna. Packets of instant soup. I could survive on this food. It looked like stuff I would have secretively tucked away from the community pantry. None of it delicious. Nothing as frivolous as a bag of chips or a sleeve of chocolate chip cookies.

In the backpacks, there were clothing basics. Clean, but a little gray and threadbare from too many washings. The style was early Goodwill. Certainly, nothing cute and nothing even remotely immodest. Most of the clothes were cotton dresses that would come down to my ankles.

"Gross," I said, making Deep laugh.

"I have a clunker for you outside. It has Ohio license plates. It's registered to The Church of High Holiness."

"Huh."

"Yeah, it's not particularly inventive by design. You stole it from your cult. You'd rather the cops not figure that out. Remember that when you're parking and if you're asked to drive anywhere. For example, you might want to park away from where you work so that if the vehicle is spotted, the police won't look inside the diner for you."

"Good thinking. If that comes up in a conversation with Destiny, that will be believable."

"I put a couple of sleeping bags and some pillows on the back seat. There's a Porta Jane for your late-night convenience. I'm suggesting that you're living out of the car. That might give Destiny an opportunity to offer you some compassion. It would be great if that was an invitation to sleep on her couch."

"That wouldn't be great," Striker muttered. "I'd rather Lexi comes home at night."

Deep exchanged a look with Striker, then moved the conversation along.

"I heard about your shiner. Way to go saving that woman." He lifted a hand to high-five me.

And while I slapped his hand, I wasn't in the mood for

congratulations or celebration. "The piece of shit car you brought me, it's dependable?"

"If you were in a high-speed chase, you'd win every time. Bullet resistant windows, run-flat tires."

"No high-speed chases." Striker crossed his arms over his chest, and he bit down on his back teeth, making his jaw bulge.

Deep exchanged a second glance with Striker, then turned back to me, fishing in his pocket. "You decide where you want these. Driver's license, birth certificate, sixty dollars in cash." He fished in his other pocket. "Cheap ass burner phone. Once you've made a call on this phone, it erases from the memory. That way, you can use it to call us or the FBI, and no one will be able to tell. The GPS is connected to Iniquus. Control will be monitoring your location. Oh!" Another dive into his back pocket. He held up an angel medallion on a chain. "This is also a GPS. In case you get separated from your phone." He glanced Striker's way, then back to me. "I can't imagine this being a dangerous assignment from what you said." He tapped his cheek where I sported my bruise. "Except when you're a random heroine. But still, one is none, and two is one, as the SEALs like to say."

After that, I'd gone up to bed. Deep and Striker hung out watching TV downstairs. The utter normalcy of it helped me drift off to sleep.

Fortunately, I went all night without remembering a single dream.

This morning, I got up and did my morning Tai Chi.

After time on my meditation cushion, I felt much more centered and capable of taking on the day.

I had decided against my routine jog or putting in any time in my basement gym. I had to assume I'd get a thorough workout at the diner today. I'd never tried being a server, so fingers crossed it would all go okay.

Today, I changed my appearance. I wasn't too worried about

presenting one way yesterday and another today. People, in general, weren't great with holding on to details of someone's appearance. The swollen cheek would be enough of a physical reminder that I was who I was.

I used my brown contact lenses. Last night I decided to dye my hair pink. Well, not all pink. I lifted up the crown of blonde and colored the layer underneath. I thought it actually looked pretty cool. I liked it. But it was temporary and would wash out in time for next Saturday's wedding pictures. "Yeah," I told the mirror, "this is something someone rebelling against her cult might do."

What did I know beyond Dr. Gupta's lecture about any of that?

One of the important points I'd taken away: No one knows what's going on in The Grove now because of secrets. Same for whatever cult I was supposed to have escaped from.

I hoped Modesty—well, Destiny—and I got along.

I hoped she would quickly learn to trust me, and I could figure out how best to get her to agree to turn State's evidence.

I'd really like to cross this off my slate before Thursday and the beginning of the wedding parties. Disappearing for three days might prove difficult.

No reason to borrow trouble.

Leaving a love note for Striker next to the coffee pot, I gathered the two backpacks and the crumpled bag of food that Deep had put together and headed to the car.

Man, he wasn't kidding; this looked like a total piece of shit.

The yellow and rust car yesterday, the diner's would-be kidnappers', would have been a major step up in luxury.

Still, when I inserted the key and turned the engine over, it hummed.

Heading to the diner, I was thinking about Spyder.

I had concluded that he wasn't in town. Yesterday morning when he called to tell me to take the FBI meeting, that call had come through the Iniquus switchboard that encrypted locations.

I sure would like to ask him some in-person questions.

Why were we trying to persuade Destiny?

The FBI didn't tell me. All I knew was that my role on this case was to make friends and find Destiny's vulnerabilities. Those weak spots would be exploited for information, not by me, but by Finley and Prescott at the FBI.

I was getting a foot in the door. That was it.

Assuming Spyder was still working to take down the Hydra, that meant Destiny had to have information on one of three entities—well, there were three groups that I knew about. Maybe Spyder turned up another.

But so far, we had focused on the Assembly for political power, Omega for military power, and Sylanos for criminal money bags.

Did this have to do with something Destiny knew about the Assembly? About a dozen men who were sent to prison after the data dump proved them to be pedophiles. Certainly, the Assemblymen might have exploited youngsters in a cult. Was she a victim? Did she know of others who were?

Omega Security… I couldn't see how Destiny could have anything to do with them. Besides, after their corruption was exposed, those that weren't scooped up for trial headed overseas. They were based out of Moldova—with no United States extradition—and took contracts mostly in East European countries and Africa.

Now Sylanos, on the other hand… That was an interesting thought. He was part of Hydra whose head we didn't cut off. He was working out of South America, where he was constantly changing his locations. It had taken me over a year just to prove he was still alive and working his crimes.

Yeah, it would be amazing if Spyder finally had a way to take down Sylanos. Though, what Sylanos would have to do with Modesty Blackburn from The Grove…

I took the long way to the diner, driving by where the apartment building where I grew up used to stand. After it burned down, city developers swooped in and made modern shop spaces with offices above.

Such a shame.

What a cultural and personal loss.

Driving in the direction that Spyder and I used to jog, I'd admit it. I did it on purpose, trying to remember anything that would help me figure out why I was experiencing this odd connection with my parents.

It was out of the blue.

And while it might have been chicken shit of me, I didn't mention this to Dr. Carlon. She didn't have information about my having advanced psychic skills. I was sure if I told her about the sensations, she'd think I was hallucinating—a big red flag for brain trauma survivors.

I wasn't a hundred percent sure I wasn't.

That was the crazy-making thing about having psychic skills. Until I had some kind of confirmation or affirmation, mostly the things that bubbled up for me just made me feel crazy.

Slowing to a stop in front of the red light, I looked up at the new construction, thinking about how I would walk this sidewalk to the library, pulling my red wagon behind me to load up with books.

In the blink of an eye, I remembered the kitchen at my old apartment. It was a day after dad's funeral. Could there be information here?

I let the memory engulf me:

. . .

Spyder pushed open the door to the apartment with his arms full of grocery bags. He ducked his head to cross under the doorframe and moved directly to the kitchen to put away the food he'd brought. "How is she?" he asked, referring to Mom.

"Conflicted." I focused back on the task of reading medicine bottles' labels, making sure the pills were counted and distributed properly in her labeled, plastic, prescription organizer so Mom's medication would be dispensed precisely each day.

I felt Spyder waiting for more information as the cupboards opened and then shut.

"She was all geared up to die, and now she doesn't feel that she can. She missed her opportunity." I snapped the lids shut on the pill dispenser. "She wants to go on and be with my dad, but then where would I be?"

The water ran at the sink, then stopped. "Is your mother asleep now?"

"Yes, I gave her a sleeping pill an hour ago—for my sake, not hers. I couldn't stand her crying anymore. I needed a break." The brown paper bags crunched as Spyder folded them to put away in the pantry. I stared out the window at the brick wall across the way.

When he came back into the main room, Spyder carried a sandwich on a plate with a sliced apple. "I don't want you to think about this food. I just want you to eat it," he said. Spyder was my godfather, but that's not what I called him—I called him my second dad. He was stern with me, and his love for me was palpable and something I'd never question. He was a man of great serenity and a man of great depth. It surprised me today that there was so much turmoil in his eyes. I braced myself because I knew that something horrible must have happened to slide him away from his Zen-like quietude.

I wiped my mouth with a paper napkin. "Just go ahead and say it."

He nodded. "The man who caused the car accident was named Memphymus Hanasal. His blood-alcohol level at the time of the accident was .24. He ended up in the emergency department for alcohol poisoning and survived."

I mechanically chewed a bite of the sandwich. It was tasteless. I was also chewing on Spyder's information; it was habanero hot, and the capsaicin-like information burned its way through my system. My eyes stung. I was panting. Sweat glossed my skin. I swallowed hard, trying to rid myself of the sensation. "So they're charging him with what? Vehicular manslaughter? Murder? DUI? I'd like to be at the arraignment if it hasn't happened yet. I want to see this guy. Look him in the eye."

Spyder wrapped my hands in his and looked down at the floor. He was very quiet. For the first time in my life, I saw tears on his lashes. He shook his head slowly back and forth. I couldn't make out what that might mean. My lips pulled down as if gravity had hooked into the corners and applied so much weight that the skin on my chin pinched.

"My dear, he has been let free."

I tried to pull my hands back, my muscles bunching as if in a physical fight. Spyder didn't let go of me. With one hand, he held me fast, and with his other, he petted down my arm. He continued until I forced my body to slacken.

"He has diplomatic credentials from Almajidni."

"There's no such place." Surely, there was. I'd just never heard of it.

Spyder sat still and waited for me to lift my chin and look him in the eye. "It is a small island country near the Gulf of Aden in the Arabian Sea. This man is the cousin of the king's first wife and is married to one of the king's daughters."

"The first wife as in she is deceased, and he remarried?"

"First wife among three. She holds a great deal of power."

"That means that Hanasal's immune? But they could waive that, couldn't they? The king could."

"He could. He has declined."

"This Hanasal guy, he's been recalled to the island? He's leaving the US?"

Spyder shook his head.

"So he's here and moving on his merry way as if nothing happened? As if he didn't kill Dad?"

Deep sadness, ocean-deep, turbulent, churning, Spyder's eyes told me how profoundly this injustice moved him. Again, I was shocked to see, for the first time, something other than intelligence and placidity shining through his coal-black eyes. "I am afraid so. I am so sorry."

I rocked back and forth in my chair, antsy for action, though what that meant, I didn't know. "Why isn't the United States putting more pressure on the king? I don't understand."

"It is a politicized world. That island has the potential to be of great importance to the United States, logistically. There will be no overt pressure."

My eyelids slid shut. When I opened them again, it was as if they were no longer flesh but metal. A steel door sliding open. Rigid and unyielding. The law was not going to stand up for Dad. But I would. This conviction absorbed into my flesh and sinew, and I felt my body hardening, finally solidifying after days of being vapor. I had exploded into a million droplets in the car crash. Translucent. Weightless. Purpose pulled me back together. My lips pursed tightly.

"Lexicon, I can see that you have decided to take matters into your own hands."

I looked at him dispassionately. He could read me like a book. So what? It didn't matter to me what he was going to say now. I had made up my mind; it only took me a nanosecond. How could I live with myself if I didn't stand up for Dad?

"You have all of the skills you need to effect revenge. To avenge your father's death." He acknowledged what I already knew. I had the power; I just needed the will. And I had that in spades. "You can track, and fight, and shoot. You have the ability to do these things, and I will not stop you. But I wish for you to give yourself a day to process. I wish for you to reflect on the phrase, 'What is yours will not pass you by.'"

Though Spyder had been friends with my parents since long before I was born, he had only been my mentor for the previous four years. Spyder had taken me under his wing when I said that I wanted to follow in his footsteps and go into the intelligence field. He taught me the things I would need to make me physically and mentally ready for the rigors of the job of staying alive against the odds. Quotes were among his favorite teaching tools—something from how he was raised in who knew what part of the world—the application of philosophical phrases to one's situation. "Beacons of wisdom," he called them.

The stare I sent him was filled with acrimony. My taste buds were painted with bitterness.

He leaned forward and kissed my forehead. I looked down at the deep darkness of his skin as he continued to hold my hand, the blue-blackness that was so beautiful to me. So exotic and interesting. I hoped the kiss meant he was going to leave. Listening to his voice was like listening to ocean waves or a singing bowl. They quieted my soul. Right now, I preferred my soul to be roused, to be fiery hot, ablaze with righteousness.

"I will come back later when your mother is awake. I will be the one to tell her about Hanasal. I can see that you would prefer to be alone so that you might better reflect on the phrase I have given you."

He was being my mentor. He was being my godfather. What I

would have preferred was that he'd put on his special operator's hat and help me get this guy.

A long brutal blast of car horns roused me from my memory, bringing me back to the here and now.

I lifted a "Sorry!" hand as I pressed the gas pedal and headed on to the diner and my first shift with Destiny.

22

THERE WAS a rhythm to this gig. It was going to take me a day or two to get it down. Already Jim and I had had a battle over the trash. No, I wasn't going out back alone, not after what happened to Barb. Sorry.

I knew I was on thin ice there, but I thought not being a little feisty and self-preserving might have come off as inaccurate for the character I was playing.

The room seemed to be filled with regulars.

I recognized most of the faces and the name-embroidered uniforms from yesterday.

Man, yesterday…so much had happened in such a short time.

When Destiny got there, I sent her a smile. "I have to thank you. I was so hungry yesterday. You could have made a stink. I appreciate you letting me get something to eat." Her brown hair was pulled back in a tight bun with a dancer's net holding the wisps in place. She had a broad closed-mouth smile that hid teeth that hadn't been straightened with braces. Not unruly, just not perfectly aligned. Her blue eyes were bloodshot and had a wariness to them. Otherwise, she was perfectly average. Forgettably attractive. These were good qualities to have if you were on the run.

"Yeah, I've been there. I know what a pinched stomach feels like. Tips aren't lavish here, but no one's stiffed me yet. You'll be okay now that you're working."

"Yeah, not bad. They might be treating me nice because I'm the new girl. But I have enough for my gas tank now."

"You have a car?"

"If you can call it that." I gave her a one-sided smile. Gathering up a pot of decaffeinated in one hand and high test in the other, I made a circuit of all the customers. This was just colleague chatter. I wanted to make sure that I didn't come off as too interested in her. Keep it light. Keep it natural. And keep it moving.

We worked side by side, and things seemed smooth. She didn't take advantage of my willingness to work, nor did Destiny act competitively, trying to get all the tips.

As my shift was coming to an end, I carried the dishes back to the staging counter. I filled a to-go container with the portions that hadn't been touched and set them aside. Eventually, I had three.

Destiny bumped her hip into mine as I scraped the scraps into the bus bin. "Don't let Jim catch you doing that. He doesn't care much about health regulations and such. But he wants us waitresses hungry and needy. If we eat the scraps, we have more money from our tips to spend on other things. Like a way out of here."

"Seriously?" I whispered. "Thank you. I'll find a way to sneak this out."

"If he catches you, you'll get fired."

"Okay." I glanced around. "But I could take them to the restroom with me and eat in the stall before I go. Then he'd never know."

She gave me a nod as Jim banged his spatula on the pickup bell. "Order's up."

"I'll cover for you. Go on and eat."

I carried the containers to the bathroom and flushed the food down the toilet, stuffing the Styrofoam boxes deep into the bathroom waste basket.

I was at the sink washing my hands when Destiny came in. "Nicole's here."

I lifted my brow.

"She's another server. The one who takes over your shift. I told her you were in the bathroom, so she's started on your customers. You're going to lose those tips, but it was just Grover, and he always leaves a dollar no matter his bill."

"A dollar's a dollar."

"Where are you staying?" she asked.

Since she didn't move to use the facilities or wash her hands, I assumed this was the reason she'd come into the bathroom.

"Me? I was traveling through, and since I just got the job, it'll be a while before I can afford someplace to stay. Right now, I'm sleeping in my car."

"I've done that. It's not very restful. You have to keep an eye open and a bat in your hand. Cold is cold, and hot is hot. And not being able to straighten your legs makes for a bad day carrying the trays around."

"Yeah." I let my face droop. "Though I will tell you, I'm kind of excited about tonight. I found an Internet coupon for a campsite on the ocean. I've never seen the ocean before. For fifteen bucks, I'm going. I've always wanted to know what it feels like to have sand between my toes. And salt water. After I take a walk, I'm going to take the longest hottest shower."

"Do you know how to swim?" Destiny asked.

"Me? No. Where I grew up, that's not something the girls were taught to do. There was a watering hole. The boys would go down there and swim in the nude. We weren't allowed anywhere near there. But someday, I'll learn."

"Still lock your doors at the campsite. Stay safe."

"Would you like to come?" I already knew she was on the schedule for the red-eye shift that I had worked today. She wouldn't be able to accept my invitation.

I was keeping Little Guy and the neighborhood kids tonight.

She shot a glance at the door, then her watch. "I don't have a car." A non-sequitur. She must have had a thought running below the conversation.

"Was there somewhere you needed to go? Can I give you a lift?"

"No." She waved her hand in the air. "Just…we seem to be in similar situations. Poor, I mean."

"Destitute for me."

"Yeah. And I thought that if we pooled resources, we might be able to get our feet under us faster."

"Not following."

"You have a car. Look, I have a place. I mean, it's a piece of crap—a single bedroom. But you're welcome to crash with me. If it works out, we can split rent, and that'll help us save faster. Just like this job is under the table, so is my apartment. It's above a detached garage. The owner of the house is an old guy who I think is kind of lonely. I get the rent for cheap, but I have to knock on his door every day and say hi."

"Why?" I leaned my hips into the sink.

"I'm guessing partly because he wants some human interaction every day and maybe for safety. You know, if he falls or has a stroke or something, I don't think there's anyone who would know. He'd just eventually die wherever he falls."

"Man."

"Right? Anyway, you interested?"

"I'm… what?"

"Do you want to split the rent? Your share would be one-twenty plus utilities. So far, that hasn't cost me much. Thirty dollars a month, your share for everything should be less than one-fifty."

"Serious?"

"I have some rules. No visitors. Absolutely no men."

"Amen to that," I said.

"Yeah. You in?"

I paused so I didn't look too anxious. "Is it far from here?"

"I walk. It's a long walk, especially after a tough day. If I helped with gas, I wouldn't mind having a ride, especially after a night shift. Walking home in the dark scares me."

"Is this a bad part of town? What happened yesterday with that waitress, Barb?" I was wearing Barb's uniform and name pin.

"No idea."

"Do you think she told the police? Made a report?" I was still worried the cops would see me on their dash or body cams and come in to get my details.

"Oh, heck no—do you think she wants her name and address anywhere public? She's on the run. Her ex went off the rails. Put her in the hospital for two weeks. I get why she quit."

"Those are the choices I made too. You?"

Destiny looked at her shoes.

"Thank you so much for inviting me to share your space—I don't sleep restfully when I have to have my mind checking for my safety. There was this one time," I lowered my voice to build intimacy, two girlfriends chatting, "I had to sleep at a train station. I put on all the clothes I owned. Partly to stay warm and partly because I was afraid of being raped. I figured there were a lot of layers to get through. And, if I looked homeless, that might be a deterrent."

"You were homeless."

"Well, yeah." I laughed. "Anyway, I put my sunglasses on

because the lights were so bright. When I woke up the next day, I discovered that someone had stolen them right off my face."

"What?"

"How creepy is that that someone came up to me while I was sleeping and slipped them off. I didn't feel anything. I felt so vulnerable after that."

"But you have your car." She lowered her voice to match mine.

"Now, I do. That story was from the first time I ran. This is the second time."

Destiny reached out to grasp my arm. "Are they looking for you?"

I was afraid that she'd pull her invite away. At the same time, I wanted her to know I was on the run. "I don't think so. Not this time." I shrugged. "Never can tell, so better I work somewhere under the table. Keep my life in cash and no contracts."

The bathroom door pushed open. "Yo, I can't handle this place by myself. So if Jim didn't give you diarrhea from his crap food, I could use some help out here."

The door swung shut.

"Enjoy the beach." Destiny reached for the door handle. "I'll get a copy of the key made, and tomorrow, if you'll meet me here after my shift, I'll show you the place."

23

———

Striker would be home soon, and I had just finished a bowl of garlicky cold tomato soup from my favorite sandwich shop just a mile from my house. Garlic and welcome home kisses weren't a great combination.

I climbed the stairs to go brush my teeth and gargle.

Sleeplessness was building up in my system. Dr. Carlon had impressed upon me how important it was for my brain health to maintain good sleep hygiene. This included a set go to bedtime and a set time to rise and shine. Luckily, the kids were all pretty good about having their fun, then falling asleep fairly early. And all of them were good at sleeping in at my house.

Though their parents would tell you a different story. Apparently, when they slept in their own beds, the kiddos liked to pop awake with the bird song.

I picked up my toothbrush and squeezed out some paste, dipping it under the flow of water.

This would be my last night in my house until I could find a nerve to press on Destiny. I needed to talk to Prescott about this. Destiny seemed like a nice girl. She certainly didn't seem like she was playing loose with the law. Was this FBI interest safe for her?

I had seen how FBI missions could go off the rails, and innocent people were caught up and made vulnerable. I didn't want to be part of putting Destiny in any kind of danger.

Now, if the FBI's interest would ultimately keep her safe, then I was all for it.

Besides the lecture that Dr. Gupta provided to help me lay a better foundation for my own background story, nothing was shared.

Not unusual.

Just unsatisfying.

Yup, I needed to make sure there was a plan in place for keeping Destiny safe. And I'd ask some pointed questions about my own safety if I were living with her.

Forewarned is forearmed.

It could wait for Monday, though. I spat out the toothpaste foam and rewetted my brush to take another pass as I scrutinized myself in the mirror. My fatigue was reflected back at me, along with the bruise that was entering into the violet and lime color spectrum.

Some theater makeup would help.

Maybe some eye drops to clear the red…

I spat out the last of the toothpaste, rinsed it with water, then opened the medicine cabinet to grab some mouthwash.

When I did, my pack of birth control fell into the sink.

I picked it up and stared at it. Every single pill in the pack was still cuddled into the little plastic blisters encased by the foil backing.

Every. Single. One.

I checked the date to see if this was for next month. But no. It wasn't. I hadn't been taking my pills.

I grabbed my phone and checked the date. I should get my period in two more days.

Okay, the chances that I got pregnant while I was playing the canvas and Striker was painting The Garden of Eden was just about zilch.

I rubbed the knuckle of my index finger between my brows, trying to self-soothe so I could think clearly. Striker had been downrange much of the last two weeks.

Had I gotten pregnant without discussing it with Striker first?

It felt calamitous to have been this absent-minded.

Okay, first things first, I told myself as I shoved my phone into my back pocket and scrambled down the stairs, grabbed my car keys, and leaped down to the sidewalk.

Reaper was just getting home, and I brushed past him with a hand up in the air that I hoped signaled, "Hey, how are you?" and "Sorry, I'm in a rush" at the same time.

I calmed my system as I started the engine, stalling to take a deep breath so that others would be safe around me when I drove —a quick trip to the pharmacy. Grab a box of PlanB and an early detection pregnancy test. Get home and pee.

There was no point in freaking out until I knew there was a reason to freak out— Wow, it was possible that I had just had a fight with three steel-toed gang bangers when I should have been protecting my child.

As I thought that, cold sweat slicked my skin.

Holy moly, what had I done?

Still no reason to freak.

Pharmacy. Home. Pee.

I could do this.

As I sat impatiently drumming my fingers on the steering wheel, waiting for the light to turn green, I decided that either way, I needed a GYN appointment. If I was pregnant, to do what-ever it was that pregnant women were supposed to do, vitamins or something.

And if I wasn't pregnant—oh please, please, please, don't let me be pregnant without talking to Striker, to begin with, and making a plan.

I meant, if I was pregnant and it was a total accident, the pill failed as it can do, Striker would be a thousand percent supportive of me,

But this wasn't a mistake.

This was me failing to live up to our agreement that I would take the pill, and we would stay baby-free for the first five years of our marriage.

Of course, at the time, we thought that our wedding was taking place last month.

It was all called off because the CIA failed me.

Yup, now that I thought about it, our wedding date was the time when I stopped taking the pill.

Self-sabotage?

I was about to find out.

"Hey there, what did you get?" I asked.

Striker set a bag of groceries on my kitchen counter, where I was mixing up a bowl of sugar cookie batter for the kids to decorate.

I'd cleaned up the art supplies after yesterday's fun.

It would be weird to watch the kids' finger painting after the whole me as a canvas sex thing.

Glancing over my shoulder, I watched as Striker pulled out a jug of milk. A poem my mom loved pressed forward, grabbing my attention. *Pay attention.*

"...tomorrow before brunch?" Striker paused.

"What?" I sent him a knitted brow. "I'm sorry, I was somewhere else and missed that. What were you saying?"

"I was asking if you have to go in to work in the morning before the neighborhood parents come over for brunch."

"Oh. No. No, I have the afternoon shift. Then I'll spend tomorrow night over at Destiny's apartment. We're going to be roommates."

"Good job. How are you explaining that you aren't sleeping there tonight?"

"I told Destiny that I wanted to see the ocean. I've never put my foot in salt water before. I'm heading to the beach to sleep in my car at a campsite. I asked her if she wanted to come, but I knew she was on the schedule for the breakfast run."

"How'd she respond to your plans? Any sign of distrust?"

"She asked me if it was a good idea to sleep in my car. Other than that, she seemed happy for me that I was going to get to cross something off my bucket list."

"I prefer it when you're sleeping in my arms rather than the floor in some low-rent apartment."

"Duty calls."

"What were you thinking about just then?"

"When?"

"When you didn't hear me talking to you."

"Oh. You know, just before Spyder called to let me know that the FBI would reach out, I was having a very long, very physically strenuous dream about rowing a boat."

"I remember."

"It reminded me of one of the poems that Mom took comfort in. It's by Kahlil Gibran. Mom and I both found richness in his poems."

"Yes…"

"This one—I think I'm remembering it because of the water theme of that dream. It's called "Fear," and part of it goes: 'It is said that before entering the sea/a river trembles with fear./She looks back at the path she has traveled,/from the peaks of the mountains,/the long winding road crossing forests and villages./And in front of her,/she sees an ocean so vast,/that to enter there seems nothing more than to disappear forever./But there is no other way./The river cannot go back./Nobody can go back./To go back is impossible in existence.'"

"As Spyder would say, 'Now apply that to your present situation.'"

I snorted and put my wrist to my mouth. "Oh my god, he would say exactly that, wouldn't he? Uhm, let's see. I told you that I felt my parents." I waggled my hand over my right shoulder.

"Still?"

"Yes. And when I think about them, memories bubble up. Most all of the things I'm remembering are from the time when my dad died, not my mom. With this being her birthday week, I would think I'd have more Mom memories. It's a bit surprising… Curious."

Striker crossed his arms over his chest and leaned into the counter, focused intently.

"Perhaps because around my dad's death, I have a lot of self-recriminations."

"But why?"

"Like, did my actions or inactions at my father's death—did I cause his death? I think that was one of the reasons I was so gung-ho to join the rescue squad and learn everything I could to protect my mom. And not make any mistakes. I lost one parent by my not having the advanced knowledge that I needed."

"Wait. You think you were part of the reason your dad died?"

"I bet every loved one has similar thoughts, even if they flit in and flit out—did I do enough? Did I do too much? Did I add to their suffering?"

"Survivor's guilt. I experienced that when missions went sideways when I was still with the Navy."

"You know, I once heard a woman speaking about being in a car accident with her husband. He died on the scene, and she emerged without a scratch or a bruise. And she could not let go of the guilt. Before the accident, she had just reached for his hand and had laced their fingers. Had she not reached for him, would both hands on the steering wheel have made a difference? Who knows? This woman was absorbed by the fact that she must have been left alive for a specific purpose. It was driving her nuts."

"Was she able to get psychological help?"

"Medical help. She donated a kidney and saved a young girl's life. Saved that child's family from grief. As soon as her kidney was gone, the survivor thought, 'Okay, good. That's why they needed me here.'"

"Okay, maybe I shouldn't even whisper this, but organ donation is a thing. Had she died in the accident, they could have harvested a lot more from her body and saved a great deal more people."

My mouth hung open.

"I know, gruesome."

"Totally. And yet, you're right. It hadn't occurred to me. Wow. I hope that doesn't occur to her either."

This was nice, hanging out in the kitchen with Striker.

But I needed to get up the courage to tell him what I'd done. Or, more precisely, what I didn't do. I hated it when I failed him.

24

———

STRIKER STRODE through the living room, opening the door to find Kate standing on the porch with Little Guy.

I had followed along behind, peeking around Striker's broad shoulders.

Little Guy was mewling and rubbing his head into the crook of Kate's neck.

"I thought I could get him to sleep before I handed him over." Her words formed an unnecessary apology. "Sorry, he's had a rough day. He just cut a new tooth."

"Aw, poor little thing." I reached for him, all snuggly and warm. "No worries at all. I love rocking babies."

Kate set the diaper bag inside the door. "If you need anything for him, you have a key. Just help yourself."

"Okay."

"And we'll be home around eleven. I'll come pick him up. I'm not yet ready to be away from him overnight, even if I know he's right next door."

"I totally get that."

Kate put her hand on Little Guy's back and looked like the last thing she wanted to do was leave.

"I'll take excellent care. I promise." I sent her a warm smile, hoping to ease her angst.

Reaper was on the porch behind her now. His eyes got warm and crinkly as he watched his wife's conflicted emotions. "Kate? Lexi has this. We can go enjoy ourselves."

Kate frowned and nodded, then turned and left with a backward wave.

I sat in my rocking chair, snuggling the baby into my chest, rhythmically patting his back. Bolero played on my sound system. I rocked with the beat, closing my eyes, letting stress just wash away.

Babies were magical.

I continued to rock long past Little Guy falling asleep.

I heard Striker come in and sit on the couch. I could feel his energy reaching out with curiosity and…stress. Yeah, well, I'd left the pregnancy test on the sink for him to see.

I opened my eyes. Striker held the plastic test in his hand. "Can we talk about this?"

Gesturing lamely toward the stick, I said, "I'm not pregnant." I needed to own up to my infraction with Striker.

"I see that." He stared down at the single pink line. "But you thought you might be?"

"I have to apologize. I didn't take the pill this month. It was unconscious. I just…don't know. I didn't see them. It didn't occur to me." So very lame.

Striker nodded slowly. "We want kids."

"Yes."

"We decided to wait five years. Give your body a chance to recoup from all the things that have happened these last couple of years."

I rolled my lips in and nodded.

"I want to be a dad when it's safe for you. And when we feel the time is right."

I nodded some more. Man, guilt was a painful mantle to wear. "I'm sorry," I whispered.

His gaze caught mine. "Are you ready to be pregnant?"

"No."

Striker waited.

"Are you?"

"I'm looking forward to being a dad. I'm looking forward to your being pregnant. But I'm not going to rush you into anything. You have to decide when you're ready. That's body, mind, and spirit. I'd prefer that it was a planned pregnancy and not a mistake."

"I'm sorry." My focus was on the floor, contrite.

"No need for sorries, Lexi. None. I just want to be on the same page with you."

"I made an appointment with the GYN. If you'd please wear a condom until I get a prescription for a no-brainer method..." I lifted my hand from Little Guy to waggle in the air. "The ring or a patch or something."

"Not a problem. I just want you safe, and," he dipped his head to the side and sent me a full-dimpled grin that righted everything about this fiasco, "I want to make sure we get to keep our sex lives in overdrive."

I affected a cheesy Parisian accent. "I want you to paint me like one of your French models."

Striker laughed.

He stood and strode the two steps to the rocking chair. He dropped a kiss onto the now sleeping Little Guy's head then gave me a long, slow kiss that told me everything was calm between us. "If it's okay with you, I'm going to hit the gym down in the basement and take a shower before the invading horde gets here."

"Enjoy." I smiled. How did I get so lucky? In a sea of white-caps and swells, he was always the miracle of calm and steady.

Little Guy made cooing noises, and his lips pulled back into a smile. "Milk dreams."

Striker looked thoroughly charmed. He dropped a kiss into my hair. "When you're ready, you're going to be an amazing mother, Chica."

"If we can ever get married."

"We don't have to be married to be parents." He held up his hand. "I know it's important to you. I think some of that importance is that the CIA made a mess of things."

"Angel says he always thought he'd be dead pretty quickly, and it would never be a problem. That thought hurts. I want him alive and well and living his life not married to me, not lying to me, not putting me in line to commit crimes that I had no idea I was committing. Not being able to explain why we put off our wedding means people are speculating. Maybe we aren't as in love as we said or as committed to each other."

"Let them. What they think doesn't count."

"Still, I'm going to admit it, I'm a little jealous of Gator and Christen. I really hope they enjoy their new lives together. It just seems like our happily ever after keeps getting snatched away from us."

25

___

THE NEXT DAY, on the way to pick up Destiny from her shift at the diner, I drove a circuit.

It was a lifetime ago that I had been in this part of town. And every time I drove down the road, memories came up strong.

This morning, I pulled over in front of Hanasal's house. This was the elite neighborhood for the uber-wealthy and not at all like the neighborhood just a few miles away where people led a life paycheck to paycheck.

A young mother came out of Hanasal's house. She had two youngish kids with her dressed for soccer practice. Fobbing her way into a Subaru, she strapped the kids into their car seats.

As she drove by, she sent me a concerned look. It seemed to me, she was noting my license plate.

Cars like the one I was driving didn't belong in this area. I wondered if she would call the police and ask them to check why I was parked there, staring at her house.

Still, I wanted to take this time to remember back to what had happened. It felt like there was something there. Something more.

Hanasal was dead. But that didn't seem to have ended things. There was obviously a loose end that needed to be tied up. Why else would my parents be—yeah, I didn't have the right word for this—haunting me?

Seven years.

It felt like panning for gold as I reached out with my sieve, trying to discover the nugget that would solve the mystery:

After Dad's death, Hanasal's house wasn't hard to find. Dad's friend, Stan, didn't mind giving me the address and the license plate number on the guy's new car from the police database.

It hadn't taken long for the diplomat to replace the car he'd totaled and move on. Hanasal didn't get a scratch on him in the accident. I only got fifty stitches scattered around my body, and Dad got dead.

I hated Hanasal.

I hated that he had whistled as he climbed into his car as if he hadn't a care in the world.

Spyder had given me the directive not to act for a full day. I wouldn't disrespect Spyder by lifting my Springfield and popping a hole in Hanasal's head, though, man, it would have been so darned easy.

I'd waited.

Determined to figure out the best time and place for my retribution, I wasn't going to add to Mom's woes by having her see me in handcuffs. Besides, I was better trained than that. Spyder took his mentorship very seriously. As did I. I meant to be the best of the best someday and protect my country.

Spyder didn't hand out vague information. He spoke very little, and the things he said all had meaning. "It is a politicized world. That island has the potential to be of great importance to the United States, logistically." What I heard him say was, *don't rock the boat by doing something overt.*

I loved my country.

I wouldn't want to do something that would cause our soldiers harm down the road.

So I had to be cunning.

Sitting outside of Hanasal's house, I had chewed on the bone Spyder had given me: "That which is yours will not pass you by." On the surface, it had to do with destiny and karma. Quickly, I could say it was Dad's time to go, and karma would bite Hanasal for me—if not in this lifetime, then in the next. But Spyder never gave me a phrase that could be deciphered that easily. There was more meat on that bone, but my head wasn't willing to be still enough for deep thoughts.

Instead, I had decided to do two things. One: gather intelligence on this guy so I could make my plans. Two: make sure he wasn't driving drunk and destroying another family. I was being proactive, and that always felt better to me than treading water in a cesspool, waiting. But Hanasal had better freaking stop that whistling. In the moment, I only had but so much control over my emotions. And he was pushing my finger a little closer to the trigger with Every. Single. Note.

The woman was back, knocking on my driver's side window. She must have circled the block.

I tapped the button and lowered the glass a few inches.

"Are you lost?" she asked. She didn't actually sound like she wanted to be helpful, just wanted me to move along.

"Do you live here?" I pointed at the house.

The woman scowled.

"I thought Mr. Hanasal lived in this house, but then I saw you come out, and you're not his wife." If she knew that name, then she'd think I was there legitimately and not call the cops on me.

"Oh, dear." Her face slipped into a frown. "Are you his friend?"

"It's been a while since I've seen Mr. Hanasal." Friend? Even to get me out of this situation, no, I would never call him a friend.

"Yes, sweetie. Mr. Hanasal died in a car accident. We bought the house from his estate. That was seven years ago."

"That long…" My eye caught on the dash clock. "Okay," I said, starting my engine again. "Thanks."

"Are you all right? You look so sad."

"Well…" Sad? No. Overwhelmed by having to relive all this? Absolutely. "It's okay. Thanks. Thanks for checking in with me." I added with a finger wave, so I seemed legit. Of course, I knew Hanasal was dead. I'd watched it happen.

She stepped back, and I drove off to collect Destiny.

Was it a coincidence that she chose that name when her case brought me to this particular part of the city? Or was this a message from the universe?

26

It was walking distance, Destiny had said.

Well, it was walking distance if you liked a good hike. Two miles wasn't bad if you were fresh from a good night's sleep. But two miles coming home from eight hours on your feet would be miserable.

Especially in this heat.

Destiny was sitting shotgun in my POS car, looking wrung out. "It's there." She pointed.

I had picked her up from her shift. Mine wasn't for another hour—just enough time to move my backpacks and jar of peanut butter into her place.

Finley and Prescott were pleased by my arrangements. The fact that I'd gotten the job and was now moving in should keep the mission heading right along. We were speeding ahead with the case, and I was told that was imperative. And more importantly to this moment, Finley had told me that they didn't think anyone was actively looking for this woman, though, yes, if she was found, she'd be in danger.

Destiny knew what was on the line. That's why I was here.

They hoped it wouldn't take more than a couple of days to figure out her Achille's heel so they could wrap her into their program.

"Why are you driving past?" she asked as I turned the corner and parked off the side of the road.

"Uhm…" I chewed on my lip, trying to come up with the right feel for this information. It needed to align me with her situation but at the same time not make her feel fearful of having me with her. "So this car comes from the place I ran away from. It was mine to drive while I was there, maybe not quite so fine for me to have driven off in."

"Stolen?"

"Borrowed," I said. "Ohio plates. No one in D.C. is going to care. But, all the same, if my plates came up on some cops computer system, I'd like to make it hard for them to track me down." Now I needed to switch things up. "What about you?"

"Me?"

"Barb is on the run from her ex. You said Jim hires women who are in danger. Who's after you?"

Her lips sealed tight. Her teeth locked.

"It's okay. You don't have to tell me. Just scale of one to ten, how dangerous is it for me to bunk with you?"

She looked at her lap for a long moment. "I don't know," she whispered.

Wow. *Not* what I expected. I'd have to run that by Prescott and Finley. If this was an imminently dangerous assignment, things needed to be reworked. I was not an operator.

Minimally, Iniquus would have me covered with Strike Force back up. They'd be running all kinds of systems and diagnostics. I wouldn't be dangling in danger's way without support.

"We'll just need to stay low profile," I said. "Get some money in the bank. Head down to Costa Rica and start a charmed life filled with coconuts and fresh fish." I pulled the keys from the ignition and opened my door.

"How was the beach yesterday?"

I closed my eyes with a smile and inhaled like I could still smell the salty air. "Perfection." I tugged my backpacks and sleeping bags from the backseat. "I haven't got much. Would you mind lending a hand?"

We walked back up the street. I waited in the drive while Destiny went and rang the guy's doorbell. "Hey there, checking in."

"All's good, chicky. You got a friend?" The homeowner's wife-beater dangled from bony shoulders. His pants were belted under a rounded belly. He was barefooted and could use a shave, a shampoo, and a haircut.

"Yeah, she's gonna hang around a bit." Destiny turned. "I'll check in tomorrow." She skipped down the three brick steps and walked around the back of the house.

A two-story garage was tucked under the trees. The stairs on the right looked untrustworthy. I climbed behind her. "I have a key for you. I'll give it to you upstairs," Destiny said over her shoulder.

"Thanks."

She unlocked the door handle and the deadbolt above, pushing the door wide.

Well…it was safer than sleeping in my car, I guessed.

It was clean.

The linoleum floor looked like it was laid in the seventies. That and the wood-paneled accent wall. The other walls were dingy neutral. Two massive, upholstered chairs looked like they'd either been left by the previous resident, or Destiny had dragged them from the curb before the garbage could pick them up.

I looked in the bedroom. She slept on a single mattress on the floor. Her clothes were folded in neat piles and lined up along the wall.

I moved to the bathroom with its avocado-colored ceramic

toilet, bath and sink, and turquoise walls.

The galley kitchen was part of the great room.

"Get yourself settled in. I'm going to take a cold shower. No air conditioning." She leaned over and turned on the box fan. "It's not terrible. The trees keep the sun off. On really hot days, I go to the library and hang out. It's two blocks past where you parked your car."

Destiny went into the bathroom with a change of clothes tucked under her arm and shut the door.

I took the opportunity to do a security assessment. I'd need to report the situation to both Strike Force and the FBI.

Pulling my phone from my back pocket, I videoed the setup's locks, doors, and windows.

Fire trap. It looked like the only exfil was the door we came in.

Destiny didn't have a fire extinguisher in the kitchen.

Peeking in her cupboards and fridge, I discovered there was little in the way of food. It looked like Destiny ate sandwiches.

She didn't even own a pot.

I stalled at the kitchen window, looking between the trees. In my mind, I was trying to position myself geographically.

When I angled myself correctly, I could see the bar where Hanasal had been drinking the night he killed my dad.

Sometimes I loved how the universe worked, putting me in the right place for the right thing. I wasn't thrilled about this. My parents were sending me a buzz. *Pay attention!*

Why was I here? What was I supposed to be remembering?

At seventeen, I thought I was bulletproof.

Since then, I have learned just how vulnerable a person can become.

Spyder knew what I was up to, and he allowed it. He let me

act as if this was my op. Though I later learned that while I was working to bring justice for my dad, Spyder had his eyes on me the whole time, or someone did. He knew my every move. Always.

I never figured out how.

Spyder would never reveal his strategy.

When I found that out, though, I was annoyed that he hadn't trusted me and the training he gave me to handle the situation myself.

Ah, the many things I would tell my teenaged self now that I knew better.

For example, I've learned the importance of having a team at your back, the buddy system. You don't swim alone.

Back then, after I found out that Hanasal couldn't be held responsible, I decided that a bad guy did bad guy things.

I had just needed to find something with enough oomph to force him home.

Prison would have been great, but off U.S. soil had been my second-best outcome:

Four days after my dad was buried, two days after I was given the news about Hanasal, I was justice bound.

It was twenty-one thirty hours military time; I was in military mode. I had dressed in nondescript clothes and tucked my hair under a skullcap; the cap pulled low over my eyebrows. Most people started their identification process with the forehead and brow. So why feed people information? In my baggy clothes, I could be male; I could be female. I'd certainly blend into almost any background in these mousey colors that looked like pale winter dirt and cement.

So far, Hanasal seemed to have no clue that I was watching him.

I had to be careful; Spyder had taught me that I had to look at things around my target. The human brain feels the sensation of eyes on them, a limbic survival holdover from our earlier caveman times when those eyes might belong to a sabretooth tiger or some other predator. If a person felt the eyes, the target would scan to find the source, which would out you quicker than quick.

Once I had identified Hanasal, I shifted to focus on the things around him. I looked at his shoes, at his tires. I tried not to even think his name. I needed to guard my covert action.

Hanasal was driving a new car. Black. Shiny. He kept his diplomatic license plates.

Screw you.

He headed into the nearest low-rent neighborhood and pulled into a bar. The same bar where Hanasal was drinking the night of the crash.

Obviously, my dad's death didn't shake him loose from his drinking habit.

Pulling to the side of the lot, Hanasal parked face-in under a light, which told me he had no counter-surveillance training. And there he waited. My car didn't fit in with the kinds of cars that parked in this lot. Mine was battered, rusty, and old. These cars were mainly middle class—except for Hanasal's trophy of prestige and success.

I had parked on the street.

With my monocular, I watched Hanasal sitting there, drumming his fingers on the steering wheel. He was waiting for someone.

I had slid from my car. Lightly shutting the door, I crossed the street, moved up the block, and circled around to stand in the shadows of a broad, winter-naked elm.

A car drove up beside Hanasal's, and Hanasal's window powered down. The motor buzzed against the backdrop of bar music. The passenger window on the new car slid open.

Hanasal reached out to receive something, amber, and white. It looked like a prescription bottle from the pharmacy.

Are you a druggie, too, Hanasal? I shot video of the exchange. Or whatever it was. I held perfectly still as the other car drove away.

Then Hanasal went into the bar.

Checking my watch, I had waited for twenty minutes, making sure Hanasal had settled inside. Until I could get hold of his key fob, getting under the car's hood or to the fuse box was going to be a problem. Crouching low, I moved toward the back tire and hammered a piece of metal that I had brought for just this reason through the tread. Air hissed as it escaped. I waited to make sure the tire was fully deflated, then did the same on the front. I laid a few more pieces on that side of the car— See? Someone left some building materials, and he pulled right in on top of them. Surely two flat tires would stop him. But just to make sure, I monkey crawled up onto the thick limbs of the tree and made myself as comfortable as I could.

My plan had been to call the police if Hanasal tried to make his way out of the parking lot on his two good tires.

"That which is yours will not slip you by." Hanasal was mine. I would not let him slip away.

That's not what Spyder meant.

But screw Spyder.

No, I don't mean that. I quickly sent out the erasure thought in case Spyder caught hold of my words in the ether. *I'm just really angry, Spyder. Lava-in-the-veins angry, and I'm about ready to erupt.* I had to slow down my rage. Slow down my blood flow and my respiration as I perched on the limb.

I found it most helpful to pretend to be a lizard in the sun when I was tasked by Spyder to do stakeout practice. Stakeouts meant long, long, long periods of nothingness. But if the mind wandered, if I fell asleep, if I lost my focus, then I might lose my prey. I had found this twilight place somewhere between meditation and alertness. I tasked my brain with noticing my surroundings, searching out that delicious fly so that I could flick my tongue and savor the rewards of lying so still. It was a place where I didn't feel my legs falling asleep from draping over the side of the branches or feel the cold wind bite at the tip of my nose.

It was a place of nothingness and expectation.

Eventually, the doors on the bar had banged open, and people trickled out and toward their cars. Hanasal wasn't one of them. I checked my watch—something I tried not to do during stakeouts, lest I be discouraged that only one or two minutes had passed. I was rewarded with the surprise of last-call o'clock.

What do you do in a bar all alone for so long?

Ah, not alone.

I slowly pulled my phone from my pocket and videotaped Hanasal stumbling across the lot with his arm draped across a woman's shoulder. He pulled out his car keys, pointed in the vague direction of the sedan, and pressed the fob. His car barked twice as his lights blinked, and he grinned a wide toothy grin. Startlingly white teeth. A Cheshire cat. The woman who was with him steered them to the car, and they climbed into the back seat.

What the heck? I was too high up to get a good angle on the backseat interior. I rounded to the back of the tree and shimmied my way back down. Lying on my stomach, I crawled on my elbows toward his car. It was the only vehicle left on this side of the lot. I slid my hand up alongside the door frame between the front and back windows and videotaped what was going on inside. When the woman spoke, I slowly lowered my arm and snaked my way back into the tree line.

The woman exited, made a phone call, walked to the street, and waited for the car that came five minutes later.

Hanasal stayed in the back of the car.

I opened the video. It was very dark in the interior, with the only illumination coming from the parking lot lights. From what I could make out, Hanasal pulled a wad of money from his breast pocket, peeled a couple of notes off, and handed them to the woman. The woman tucked the cash into her purse and then slid her dress bodice to the sides to expose her bare breasts. Hanasal licked at them greedily. He squeezed them and tweaked at her nipples. The woman grimaced and moved her hands over his to stop him from hurting her. She smiled and cocked her head to the side, then petted a hand down his chest and said something to him.

Hanasal slid his hips forward on the seat and spread his legs wide. Thank goodness the angle was bad, and I couldn't make out the image. From her position, though, I'd imagine that she had unzipped his pants and dragged out his dick.

Huh. I wonder what the king and his daughter would think of you getting your wanger sucked off by some woman—and in public, no less?

Would this video be enough to get him called back? Maybe it was traditional for men in that kingdom to have certain forms of relations outside of the marriage. I certainly couldn't hand this evidence over to the police. His being a john couldn't be prosecuted. His willy was free to get sucked in public, no problem. *Shithead.*

I had closed the video and waited. Nothing. I prowled toward his car.

Hanasal was stretched out in the back seat. With his mouth hanging open, his tongue draped loosely over his lip. He was passed out, his dick lying limply under his hand.

The alarm hadn't chirruped when the woman exited; the alarm wasn't engaged. I edged the door open. It was as cold inside the car as it was outside, but I still slid onto the seat and pulled the door almost all the way shut so the wind wouldn't rouse him from his alcohol-induced, post-orgasmic coma.

His keys lay on the floorboard. I pocketed them. With the tips of my fingers, I stroked along the breast pockets of his jacket where I had seen him put his money. There was nothing there. I continued down to check the outside of his pants' pockets, hunting for the prescription bottle. I didn't find it, either.

I had searched the car seats and along the floorboards, finally pulling the container out from under the driver's seat. The lid was separate from the bottle. Whatever had filled the bottle was now gone.

After snapping a picture of the label, I exited the car and headed home.

I remembered thinking that I was supposed to train with Spyder in just a few hours. He'd have questions. I had no new answers.

"Hey, are you okay?" Destiny asked, coming out of the shower, her hair wrapped in a towel, frayed at the edges with faded pink stripes.

I fought to pull myself back to the here and now. "Okay?"

"You're very still, staring out that window."

"Yeah." I sent her a smile. "I was just—whew!—kind of over-whelmed by a memory. There was this man. He did…really bad things. Sometimes he pops up unbidden, and I relive that time."

She gripped at the top of her dress, pulling the rounded neck-line tighter around her throat. "Bad?"

"Yeah."

"I'm sorry."

"You and me…We're going to be okay. Eventually. We're both going to right our ships and sail off into a gilded sunset."

Destiny's focus wavered off. "I hope so," she whispered.

27

———

THE NEXT DAY was very much a repeat, only it was my turn at the red-eye, and Destiny took the early bird dinner shift.

Yesterday, Prescott and Finley assured me that Destiny was safe. And I was safe to hang with her.

They should know, but compartmentalized secrets sure did wear on me. I wanted to know everything rather than dangling in the dark.

Trust.

I missed Striker already. We'd only been apart these two days, but he'd just come home from his own assignment.

We were two ships passing in the night.

It was important that when we were together that we made it special.

I needed to figure out how to uncork Destiny's information and hand this mission back to the FBI. Sleeping in my own bed with Striker would be my reward for fast action. It would be helpful if I knew what was relevant. Tomorrow, Monday, Finley had set up a meeting for us. We'd do some information exchange then.

And to that end, I had a plan. I didn't have warrants, so I

couldn't place audio in the garage apartment, but nothing stopped me from placing nanny cams. They covered the apartment except for the bathroom and would send to a feed in the cloud. We could go back and scan them later to see if Destiny had any visitors when I was away or if she led us to any top-secret stash of information.

Though, Prescott said that what they needed was all in her head.

So nothing for me to find wandering around the near-empty apartment.

I was lying on my sleeping bag with the box fan blowing air across my body, making my next tactical plans, when Destiny came in and double-locked the door behind her.

"If you had called, I would have come to get you," I said, waggling my phone.

"That's okay. I got a ride from Huahine."

"Whose that?"

"Short order cook on the weekends." She picked up a towel. "I'm going to go take a shower and wash away this fry grease."

She moved to a window and forced it open. "There's supposed to be a storm later tonight."

"That'll be a welcome relief from the humidity." I gave an exaggerated yawn. "Right now, it's sapping me of all my energy."

I closed my eyes and must have fallen asleep, waking again with the shriek of unoiled hinges as Destiny exited the bathroom.

When Destiny emerged, she was wearing a loose cotton dress like the ones that Deep had put into my backpack. It fell nearly to her ankles and had a Laura Ingalls vibe to it.

So did her hair, now in a thin French braid, hanging down her back all the way to her hips.

"Oh my goodness." Frowning down at my burner phone, I clutched the top of my shirt with my other hand as I cast my hook.

Destiny looked up and froze.

"No way," I mumbled in astonishment. I scrolled up the article that I had queued as my way to broach my own past and hopefully demonstrate a parallel with Destiny's. "Wow." I lifted my gaze to catch on hers. "Did you read the news today?"

"No. I have enough troubles of my own. No need to go borrowing any."

I canted my head. "Then how do you know?"

"What?" Her face was a blank.

"What's going on in the world? What's safe and unsafe? I mean, growing up, I wasn't really aware of anything that happened outside of our compound. It took me leaving and, you know, expanding my awareness to see all the things that I had no clue about. Things to keep me safe, things to make me think. Even laugh." I smiled and turned back to the article. "Things that make me grateful that I had the courage to separate myself from my upbringing."

That set the hook. Now I just needed to slowly reel her in.

Destiny moved over to the chair in the living area. Spinning it, she could face me where I lay. "What does the article talk about?" She pulled her feet up onto the chair and wrapped her arms around her legs, peeking at me from behind the barrier.

"Well, let's see." I scrolled back to the top. "This is out of Denver."

She leaned forward and rested her chin on top of her knees.

"It says here that they've arrested seven members of a cult-like group." I glanced up at Destiny. "Cult-like? In my experience, you're either in a cult, or you're not."

She nodded tight little bobbles without lifting her chin.

"Though people in a cult *really* hate the word. I only learned it once I'd run away." I didn't wait for her to show surprise or ask any questions. As I looked at my phone, I could feel her concentration as she laser-focused on me.

"Craziest thing—which is saying a lot for a cult—it looks like the seven are being charged with abusing a corpse and child abuse."

"The child that was abused was it some kind of sacrifice or something?"

"No. The kids—" I scrolled down to that part. "According to the sheriff who found them, there was a thirteen and a two-year-old."

"Not hurt, though?"

I shook my head. "It says they're fine. They were taken in by social services."

"Okay." She breathed out. "What happened about the dead body?"

"Let's see…Okay, here it is. They had the corpse set up in the corner of the back bedroom. It was wrapped in a sleeping bag and draped with strings of Christmas lights. And they had put glitter eyeshadow on the face, but there were no eyeballs." I glanced up from my phone. "Mummified. Do you think they did that ritualistically like, I don't know, like the Egyptians?"

Destiny stared at me wide-eyed, shaking her head.

"Maybe they just left the body outside in the desert? I read somewhere that if you bury a body in the sand and it kind of bakes under high heat, the body mummifies by having all the moisture vaporize. I can't tell you if that's true or not, something I read."

"It says mummified?" She made a stink face.

"Yeah, they think it's the cult leader who told everyone she was a god." I swiveled to look out the window and said kind of under my breath. "I wonder what will happen to the adherents."

"What did they believe in?" Destiny asked.

"Seems like from the rest of the article, that the followers were brainwashed, and their money was handed over. But who knows? Someone who's never lived communally with others and worked for the greater good always thinks it requires brainwashing." I chewed on my top lip, thinking. "There are some people who are just tired of thinking and want to hand over the responsibility to someone else. I was told that was the best way to go about life, you know? That if someone told me what to do and what not to do, then things are easier. I was led to believe that if I had too much information, I'd just be lost and anxious, not knowing the right way to go, what to think, and do." I caught Destiny's gaze, trying to read her. "I'm finding that as I live life, and get out in the world, hearing ideas, trying on different thoughts, it's kind of freeing actually. I'm making my way in the world. Making decisions that are best for me. And I'm still young. I have time to learn."

"Do you think you'll have to give that up when you get married? You know, give yourself over to your husband, honor his wishes through your obedience."

"Oh, I'm already married." I wrinkled my nose.

She dropped her feet to the floor, wrapped her arms around her stomach, and leaned forward. "Where is he?" she whispered, then sent a frantic glance toward the door.

"Don't worry. He's not coming here. My husband Zebedee's not abusive, and he's got five other wives to manage. He was doing what he was told to do by his leaders. And I left so I don't have to do that anymore. Zebedee has no idea where I am." Now I just had to remember that name. I had meant to say Zebadiah, but it had come out wrong. Call him Zeb, I told myself.

"How old were you?"

"When I got married? A teenager. It had been planned by the elders before I even met Zeb. I mean, it was a small place. We all knew each other, but the men stayed away from the women. The women were supposed to serve in silence. I only got to know Zeb, you know—talk to him, for three weeks before we had the ceremony. Yeah, I don't recommend that. Especially because he's pretty old." I wrinkled my nose to show my distaste. I was thinking about what the rules were at The Grove when I made up this tale.

"But if you're married, that's kind of it, isn't it? You're stuck until one of you dies."

"That's what they told me. But it turns out, that's not what the laws say. A man is only allowed to marry one woman at a time. Our marriage wasn't legal. So…yeah, I guess I'm not married." I laughed. "Well, there's a realization for you. And up until I said that, I thought I needed to save for a divorce. Are you married? Do you have someone in your life?"

"Me? No. Well almost. Same thing. A man was chosen for me. He was my uncle."

"Isn't that illegal?"

"The place where I grew up had its own rules. Barnabas was his name—still is." Her face had blanched. "His name is Barnabas. He's fifty-four and looks every minute of that age with his paunch belly, varicose veins, and comb-over." She gave a full-body shiver. Her face scrunched with distaste. "His teeth were yellowy-brown from tobacco chew and crooked." She gestured at her mouth. "All crowded forward into a glob. And his breath always smelled of beer. *Always*. First thing in the morning, he came into the office reeking of beer."

"Was this at a business?"

"Business… yes. You know, when you talk about things, it sounds like we might have left the same kind of environment. I was homeschooled like you were. And I was in a compound like you were. The male elders told me what I could and couldn't do. Where I could and couldn't go. What to believe. What to think. Whom to marry." She picked at her nails and chewed on a cuticle. "My biggest problem right now is that what I was taught doesn't seem to be reality." She pointed at a science book on the floor that still had its friends of the library twenty-five cents sticker on the cover. "I'm reading that, and it's crazy what I'm learning. Back in California, I was told that the saints saddled T-Rex's and rode them around like I might ride a horse."

I nodded.

"And what schooling we got was mostly what was useful to the community: reading, writing, computer data entry, math. I'm very good at math, and that's why I got to work in the office. My friends, they had to work in the fields growing our food or in the arts house."

"What did they do in the arts house?" I turned on my side resting my head on my bent elbow.

"Crafts that they'd sell online. Mostly hammocks."

"The office sounds better. Unless Barnabas was there."

"He was there a lot. But still, it was better than being out in the fields under the hot sun from dawn to dusk."

"And that's why you fled? To get away from having to marry?"

She stilled. Finally, she rotated her lips in a circle as if unsticking them from her teeth. "Why did you leave?" she asked.

"There was a fire that burned down the compound's storage warehouse. I thought it was the perfect opportunity to just disappear. Something just snapped for me that night." I pulled that story from my family's tale of how my great (to the seventh generation) aunt escaped from Williamsburg to go spy in Seattle. Something familiar. Something I would remember if it came up again. I was throwing out a lot of details that I'd need to keep straight. *Destiny was supposed to marry Barnabas. I was already married to Zeb. She's from California. I'm from Ohio. Don't mix up the details!*

"Yeah," Destiny was saying. "It was time for me to get married. I climbed out of my bedroom window and took off barefooted across the fields." Her face drooped. "I left my siblings behind."

"How many?" I peeked down to make sure my phone was still recording this. D.C. had one-party consent laws, and I definitely consented to having this information heading to the FBI.

She paused again.

I raised my eyebrows to my hairline. "A lot?"

"Don't judge."

I shook my head.

"My mom was one of twenty sister wives, and I have seventy-three brothers and sisters."

I threw my head back and laughed. It surprised the shit out of me, and by the wide-eyed look on her face, it surprised Destiny as well.

"Sorry. I was picturing you trying to save your siblings, and in my imagination, it looked a lot like a clown car."

A smile spread across her face. "Yeah. You're right. Well, there was no way to pull them out of that situation. I couldn't care for them. It took me this long to start to care for myself. They're going to have to save themselves."

I lowered my voice to a whisper. "Do you think they're looking for you?"

"Yes."

"Why? I mean, if you don't believe in their message, and you want to go, why not just let you?"

"If I had worked on the farm or in childcare or even in the craft room, I think they would have since I'm an adult." She stared at the door as if she was waiting for it to burst open and the boogieman to be on the other side. "I don't think they'd drag me back, no. Because then they'd have to watch me too closely. They had used my brothers and sisters against me. You know, like if I did something wrong, they didn't whip me. They picked up one of my younger sisters and belted them in front of me. Of course, that gave them all the control they wanted. But I figured out that if I wasn't there to see the belting, then they wouldn't do it because it served no purpose."

"So, what do you think they'd do if they found you?"

Destiny stood up and walked toward the kitchen. "Huahine set aside a to-go order that no one came to pick up. Weird because they paid for it over the phone with a credit card. He didn't want it. He eats his fill as he goes along cooking. But he knows we're trying to get our feet under us. If we're careful, there's like two-three days' worth of food in there."

"Serious?"

"Yeah, come fix up a plate, and I'll start the oven. We can just stick them in for a few minutes to brush the cold off."

I'd pushed as far as I could. But this was information. She knew something from the office that made her a target. She was in fear for her life. It was in her eyes. In her posture. In her inability to just answer my question.

If I was on the run like she was and had time to contemplate and make a plan, one thing I'd do was bring evidence out with me. A safety measure. Surely, that was what she'd done.

I hoped that after I introduced her to Finley and Prescott, she'd tell them where it was hidden.

28

MONDAY MORNING, Destiny got up before dawn. Today, she was scheduled at the diner for the four to noon shift. The breakfast rush was the most lucrative, and Destiny said she liked getting the work done and having a long afternoon to sit and read her school textbooks, learning what the rest of us had in grammar school.

My shift was the tail of the breakfast rush through the lunch crowd—seven to three. This worked out perfectly because this afternoon, I needed to meet with Prescott and Finley, and tonight I was having bridesmaid's cocktails for Christen, who'd just come in from Iraq.

I'd told Destiny that after work, I would drive around D.C. and scope out some of the tourist things to do and make a list. I wanted to see Arlington Cemetery, the Smithsonian, and the memorials. I didn't invite her to join me and had crossed my fingers that she wouldn't ask to come along. She hadn't.

Destiny picked her uniform off the plastic hook and headed into the bathroom to get dressed while I pretended to sleep.

I took advantage of the privacy to position myself cross-legged on the floor with my pillow doubled under my sits bones, my palms facing up as they rested on my knees.

In my training, both Master Wang and Spyder had taught me that the present is all there is.

But as I scanned my body, focused on my breath, and tried to descend into an altered conscience, my meditation this morning was interrupted with memories.

I knew better than to fight them away.

The goal was to not have a goal. To sit. To breathe. To allow quiet to find me.

But my busy buzzing hive of a mind did not allow for my normal meditative state. Typically, I sat, focused on my breath, and went blank. An intruding physical sensation might tug at me, an itchy nose, a strand of hair on my cheek. A feeling might bubble up—anxiety, what have you. A thought—I can't forget to call… But rarely was I offered memories, especially memories that I was being force-fed.

I decided that rather than fighting it, which was a meditative no-no, I would let it run its course. Stand back and observe. And just like that, in my mind, I was back to being seventeen:

"Spyder?" I asked after meditation one morning.

"Yes, Lexicon?"

"I've been researching the laws of Almajid."

"And what did you find?"

"They don't allow alcohol, and they don't allow homosexuality. As a matter of fact, an act of homosexuality is punishable with the death penalty." I smiled.

"And you have tapes of Hanasal hiring multiple men engaging with him sexually. Do you wish for him to be put to death for homosexual acts? Would this align with your morality?"

I dropped my head. "No, *of course,* it doesn't align with my morality. But his being put to death would align with my sense of justice."

"The means to an end are an important part of your ethics as an intelligence officer."

"They aren't my laws. Those are Almajid's laws."

"But by handing this particular information over to their king, it would be you who is assigning him to death for this specific reason. Does that align with your sense of ethics? Yes or no?"

"No." I was ashamed. But I was also left without much to work with. "You knew I was taping his recreational activities with the prostitutes in the bar, and some of them happen to be men. Hey, how the heck can you do that? How is it you're following me?"

"That is not what this lesson is about."

"Okay, then answer this. Why is it that you're just watching? Why aren't you helping me?"

"Have you needed my help?"

"I don't know… Maybe?"

"When you need my assistance, you will ask for it. In the meantime, 'That which is yours will not pass you by.'" He smiled gently at me, his eyes warm with fatherly love. "Are you going out again tonight?"

"Yes, sir."

"The videos of heads bobbing in the back seat are not a fruitful direction." He stood and left.

Clanging in the kitchen dragged me back to the present, here in the crapola garage apartment. Yeah, meditation wasn't going to happen today. I'd try again tomorrow.

I wandered into the kitchen to see what Destiny was up to. I needed to build my bond with her.

Destiny had come home with a stockpot yesterday with no explanation.

She double folded washcloths and had lifted the pot from the stove, carrying it to the sink. I peeked over the rim. It looked Destiny was boiling socks and underwear. Clever.

She tripped over a loose flap of the linoleum, the pot tipped, sloshing the hot water on me.

I shrieked and jumped back.

In reality, the water was overly hot but nowhere near boiling, I discovered. Destiny must have brought the water to a boil and let things cool while getting ready for her day.

But the reality part of my brain was a step behind the survival part of my brain.

My flinch reaction assumed the water was scalding and would burn me. I'd whipped my shirt over my head and threw it toward the sink.

I stood there in my bra and jeans.

Destiny put the pot on the counter and grabbed a towel in one fluid move. "Are you burned? I am so sorry!" Her face turned red as her eyes brimmed with tears.

"I'm fine, Destiny," I said. "It's fine. I was just startled and frightened, that's all."

She patted over my arm with the washcloths, drying me off. Her focus was on my chest and abdomen, where fine scar lines created lace patterns over my skin.

The modus operandi of serial killer Wilson was to hold a chloroform-sodden rag over the victim's nose and mouth, tie her up, sliced her skin with a razor, then Wilson woke her by pouring vinegar or salt on her wounds.

On my wounds.

The plastic surgeon had spent hours in the OR gluing me back together.

Now, Destiny's finger traced down the scar that ran from ribs to hip, a hundred and fifty stitches, the scar that Striker had painted over with the word "voluptuous," covering where Wilson had tried to skin me alive the second time he found me.

I let her look. Process. Conclude.

Tugging the washcloth from her hand, I held it over my chest. "I'm fine. I wasn't hurt. I just…" I exhaled loudly. "I've had a rough past, and it makes me jumpy."

Destiny panted some unpronounced emotion.

"It's a habit now that I'm trying to unlearn because that was a ridiculous thing for me to do just now. The water was hot but not burning. I found that my abusers wanted me to experience pain. If I tried to be brave or stoic, the punishment got worse. If the moment they touched me, I screamed in pain and sobbed for relief, the abuse was less. They just wanted the power of the reaction. Now I react—overreact—as a habit."

As I said that, I wondered how much of that was true. All these memories around my dad's death and the sensation of my parents hovering and warning me to pay attention…

Was that all just my brain pulling a con job, trying to give me a manufactured story to explain away my angst?

29

Night and day from my undercover job, I was now fluffed, buffed, and dressed in a cute little black dress.

I walked onto the patio with a view of the Potomac, where I was meeting up with Christen and the other bridesmaids. I thought about Steve Finley. He was, for the most part, a desk jockey at the FBI. It's not where he wanted to be. He had always enjoyed working undercover.

More power to him, I thought ruefully.

He had been working a case where, I guessed he'd been undercover too long, his handlers weren't paying attention…something.

It had all gotten out of hand.

He fell in love with his asset. Like "Let's get married and live happily ever after," in love with her. And it had messed up his perceptions and endangered too many people along with the mission.

I liked Destiny. If I was really who I said I was, we would be friends. But I had to learn from Finley's horror show of an outcome. My relationship with her—from my end—was professional and not at all personal.

I checked my watch. I couldn't be out too late. If I was back at the apartment by ten—ten-thirty, that might be reasonable. Any later, and Destiny might grow anxious.

Though, maybe she'd be asleep and not notice. She had asked to switch our schedules so she could have my red eye since I'd be out late.

Fine by me.

Still, the sooner I built trust, the sooner I'd be home in Striker's bed.

Incentive to get out of here early.

"Hey!" Auralia called with her arm raised.

Gator's sisters, Auralia and Genevieve, sat at the round table with Lula and Christen. Someone had brought Christen a headband with a four-inch bridal veil that she was wearing in her pixie haircut like a good sport.

Colorful drinks sweated in glasses. Platters of ooey-gooey hors d'oeuvres had been picked at. Everything was so normal. The smiles so wide.

This is about Gator and Christen, *not* about you, I reminded myself.

While Lula and Christen were besties from childhood, they'd each gone their own way. Christen into the Army. Lula to law school—and into her covert job at the CIA, where she was one of the color code. Johnna White.

The problem was, that was top secret.

I shouldn't know.

Unless and until Lula was the one who told me that information. I had to act as if that information didn't exist in my brain.

Lula was not responsible for my issues getting a divorce from Angel.

I wasn't going to let that beast rear its head here.

This was about fun. Friendship. And last-minute details for the wedding.

And I would play nice.

"Yay! You're here!" Genevieve was up from her seat, giving me a massive hug. Followed by Auralia.

The waiter showed up. "What can I get you to drink?"

"Perrier and lemon, please."

"What, you're not drinking?" Auralia asked.

"I have work later tonight. And I'm driving. Besides, my stress fell off the minute I walked into this place. Hey, Christen. Welcome home."

She raised her glass of champagne. "I've been looking forward to this for so long. Glad to finally be here."

30

———

As FUN as it had been to hang out at the bar, it made it that much harder to pull on my "Esther" outfit of jeans, a T-shirt, and beat-up tennis shoes.

My back was sore—my shoulders. My feet throbbed.

I could say for sure that being a server wasn't my happy place. I was exhausted and yet felt like I hadn't had exercise in days.

Bed would feel excellent, even if it was an air mattress, a couple of crappy pillows, and a sleeping bag. Right now, I'd be fine curled up on the back seat of my car.

All I needed was some darkness and some quiet.

I'd left my shift this afternoon at the diner and met up with Prescott and Finley. They debriefed me. Checked to see how I was handling the situation. Reviewed the tapes and videos and pronounced things to be on track.

Fast track, I hoped.

I needed to come up with excuses for being away Thursday night for the Davidson's reception. Then, of course, Friday, everyone in the bridal party would be hanging out at my house. And Saturday I'd be gone all day for the wedding.

Fake an illness?

Tell Destiny I was going on another bucket list adventure?

I already had off Friday and Saturday, so that might work. I could say I was going to Hershey, Pennsylvania, to see how kisses were made or something.

Next time I talked to Finley I'd see if he had a better game plan.

Climbing the rickety wooden stairs to the upstairs door on the side of the garage, I noticed the bedroom light was on.

As I reached my key toward for deadbolt, heebie-jeebies lit my nerves.

I stilled.

A long, slow inhale quieted my mind as I expanded my senses, trying to understand the threat.

I hadn't seen anything on my way up the street, my car was parked around the corner, and no other vehicles seemed to be in this area.

Just this morning, I'd talked to Destiny about heightened reflexive actions, but this was heebie-jeebies, and they had *never* been wrong before.

Resting my ear against the door, I held my breath to listen.

Nothing.

I turned to put my back to the wall. With one hand shielding my eyes from the overhead light, I searched. Too late, my night vision had been corrupted. Around me, the night sky was moonless.

Pulling the door toward me and slowly turning the knob, so there would be no squeak or rasp, the door gave.

Unlocked.

Unusual.

My heart thrummed.

Now, I exhaled. Reprocessing, I released the knob slowly so that it made no sound.

Stepping back, Striker flashed into my awareness. After I

jumped into the fight in the parking lot, I'd have to be very careful here.

Calling in backup was the right thing to do, even if it felt a little like overkill.

I sidled soundlessly down the steps to the ground. Hugging the shadows, I wound my way around the garage.

No dogs barked in the neighborhood.

The guy who owned the house was elderly and hard of hearing. He usually fell asleep in his recliner in front of the TV, and then around ten, he'd make his way to his bed.

When I drove past to go park a moment ago, the blue light of the television had been flashing in his curtainless picture window. By the time I parked and hiked back, the front room was dark.

All of that was normal.

So far, the only abnormal thing going on in the tiny apartment above the garage was the lights on, and the locks weren't engaged.

To be honest, the few days that I had "lived" here weren't enough to get a baseline for behavior.

But Destiny was fairly paranoid and systematic.

I had seen the bedroom and bathroom lights on as I walked through the yard earlier. And here was the window in our main room with the lights ablaze.

Destiny had hung sheets as curtains, and usually, the thin flat surface meant I could see shadows moving around if someone were walking inside.

I thought about our schedule for tomorrow. Destiny had the red-eye breakfast shift. She would normally have gone to bed around eight with a sleep mask over her eyes to protect her from the sunset's last gasp, sending the rays straight into the western-facing window.

Why were lights on in the bedroom now that it was ten?

I sent a text to Iniquus Control. **Closest available. Stage in yard at the garage.**

'Closest available' was a designation of extreme need. If I were wrong, I'd do my mea culpas later.

By typing 'closest available,' the monitors in Iniquus overwatch would figure out where I was on their master board and find a force operator in my area not actively engaged with a different mission and deploy them to my situation.

It was the seven-alarm blaze of calls. No one wanted to drop everything for a nothing burger.

Blowing my cover by having some operator showing up would be bad.

I didn't know what else to do. My heebie-jeebies meter was pinging brightly, but other than that… I had nothing.

If Destiny was in trouble, she needed help.

Closest six-minute ETA. En Route Ridge and K9 Zeus, Cerberus Tactical K9. Advise.

Ridge was a retired Delta Force Operator. And Zeus… Well, Zeus was a highly trained tactical K9. Zeus and I had a special bond. He was the K9 that helped me escape my kidnappers.

Having this duo at my back would be excellent.

Outside perimeter, pretend to be walking the dog to blend. Weapons ready, I texted.

I rounded back to the side. Clinging to the edges of the steps up next to the handrail, I used my shadow walking skills to climb back to the door.

I didn't like the light shining on me.

"I said lift higher." It was a male voice raised loud enough that I could make out the words.

I didn't hear a response. Was he talking to Destiny?

Destiny insisted on no visitors at the apartment and absolutely no men.

This could be the owner doing some maintenance. But at ten o'clock? That was improbable.

Besides the folks at the diner, did she even know any men in the area? I never met that guy she'd said was a short-order cook. They seemed friendly from our conversation. Maybe it was him, and he was helping Destiny with some issue?

That would explain the locks…

Licking my fingers, I reached up to turn the lightbulb, listening to my spittle hiss as it evaporated from my fingertips.

I pressed my back against the wall where I wouldn't be seen immediately if the male voice popped the door open to investigate.

Shadow walking in the black of night would be easier if I weren't wearing a bright white T-shirt.

A long minute passed, and I decided to edge the door open. Maybe I could hear what was happening inside and determine if I could call Ridge and tell him it was a false alarm. He was still about three minutes out.

I put my ear to the crack.

"Stop. Is she breathing? Did you check?"

Ice slid down my spine.

"How do I do that?"

"Put her in the bathtub and spray her with cold water. See if that brings her around."

Drugs? Alcohol?

This all seemed wrong.

But if there was a chance that Destiny wasn't breathing, she needed an immediate intervention to save her life.

I pressed the door open just a smidge and looked in.

With the roar of an engine, and headlights bouncing along the road, I could see the Iniquus Hummer pulling up on the street in front of the bar just on the other side of the copse of trees.

I pulled out my phone: **Garage apartment. Second floor.**

Intruders. Two male voices. Possible life-threatening medical emergency. Move in.

From my vantage point, I saw the back of a man. Destiny's bare feet were tucked under his arm as he disappeared into the bathroom.

In my mind's eye, Ridge had gotten his new information, and he was climbing from the cab, gathering the medical bags and defibrillator, releasing Zeus from the kennel in the back.

Iniquus wouldn't mess around with this, they'd send an ambulance, and they'd call our client to find out whom they should send in as support—the police or would the FBI go themselves?

Inside the door, five gallon-sized jugs of muriatic acid had been lined up. I had seen them inside of the garage the other day. It was the kind of acid that one used to clean the driveway.

Why would anyone have brought these jugs upstairs?

"Just turn on the cold shower. If she's not dead, she's gonna scream her head off when we douse her."

A man moved into the living room, and I froze.

"You left the damned door open." He stalked over.

"I didn't. The wind must have blown it."

The guy leaned out. "You think someone came up here and saw what was going on?"

"Like who?"

"The roommate?"

I froze where I was. Push come to shove, I could leap over the side, drop, and roll.

"Stop being a chicken shit. Check and see if she's dead and let's get this over with. I wanta collect the money and…"

I was shadow walking. But shadow walking has its limitations, and I just pressed up against a major one. Shadow walking doesn't hide my shadow. If he looked down…

With the door swung open wide and the interior lights beaming outward, a man stepped out past me.

He looked down the steps and saw nothing.

He leaned over the rail to the ground, and there was nothing.

Get here, Ridge!

How many times had I sent out that kind of psychic call for action to an Iniquus team member?

It never worked on humans. But Zeus and I communicated in the ether all the time. This time when I sent out my thought waves, Zeus barked his frustration, furious that he couldn't do just that.

When the man turned to go back in, he focused on the platform outside the door where my shadow stretched.

The guy reached out and grabbed me by my shirt, turning me and thrusting me into the apartment.

The thought that was foremost in my mind was, *don't let him hit you in the head.*

A ridiculous concern since he was reaching under his shirt in his back waistband.

A gun?

He now stood between me and the only other exit in this fire hazard of an illegal apartment. With a snarl, he slammed the door shut.

Reaching to the side table, I picked up a drinking glass, half-filled with water, and I threw it with all my might at his head. It bounced off and clattered to the floor, leaving a bleeding welt near his temple.

He staggered a foot out to the side to try to regain his balance.

At that moment, I crouched then leaped into the air in a hitch kick, raising a knee to distract him from my true strike.

His hands fumbled wildly behind him for his weapon as my other leg kicked up under his chin. His head snapped back, catching his spine on the metal coat hook.

He crumpled to the ground.

I stepped forward, stomping on his crotch with vicious heel

strikes. If he came to, I didn't want him to be able to stand. He lay right in front of the door where Ridge and Zeus needed to enter.

I reached for the guy's pants to turn him and get to his weapon when his buddy emerged from the bathroom. "What the—" Instead of finishing the sentence, he roared.

This guy was a monster. His bald head dissolved into a tree trunk of a neck. Tattoos covered most of his visible skin. He wore a black T-shirt with the sleeves ripped off and jeans. His biker boots had studs that could do immense damage.

Intimidating as hell.

Holy cow, but he was big.

Protect your head was the marginally helpful phrase circulating through my mind, taking up strategic space. I worked to cast it off. To focus. Concentrate. Plan my moves and execute them.

He dragged a knife from the sheath on his hip.

All right, here we go. My brain shifted gears pressing the fear to the side, moving me to the chess board. It was all about thinking. Strategy. Interpreting his upcoming moves so they could be thwarted or used to my advantage.

This was what I trained to do since I was five years old and started my daily private lessons with Master Wang.

Stepping back, I snatched off my t-shirt, hoping that such a bizarre choice would buy me a moment of goon brain stutter.

Loose T-shirts were a liability, I had found. They gave the bad guy something to grip and hold me with. And a T-shirt was its own kind of weapon. I whipped it out, stinging the guy across the eyes. It was enough that I could safely take two steps forward, wrapping the cloth around his wrist gaining some control of his knife-hand.

With a quick twist and tug to lock his arm out, I tried to break his elbow by dragging his arm down as I raised my knee.

No go.

He was a behemoth.

But with a second try at jamming his elbow into my knee strike, the knife spiraled through the air. With my peripheral vision, I tried to keep track of where it landed. It needed to be in my hand, not his.

I flicked the t-shirt again and again at his face.

Irritation, possibly some loss of immediate vision, I was merely trying to keep him away until Zeus could get a bite in.

This last swipe, he grabbed the hem of the shirt.

With his size, and the close confines of the room, honestly, all I could do was try to keep him off mental equilibrium.

Pulling on the T-shirt, I spun into him, lifted my foot, and grazed the edge of my tennis shoe down his shin, an excruciating strike that lights up the nerves up and down the leg. Right leg, his dominant leg, based on the side he carried his knife.

Slamming my heel into his toes, I fisted my hand, dropping it over the back of my shoulder, so my elbow strike hit him under the chin.

I needed to get his jawbone out of the way.

My next strike was a punch to the throat.

Chugging air past his collapsing windpipe, the ogre snatched the T-shirt from my grasp and wrapped it around my throat, pulling me up against his chest. This time, there would be no headbutts and broken noses. Not only would that be a strike to my head, but the man was just too tall. He wasn't in my striking range.

I could hear Zeus outside frantically barking.

Ridge's shoulder was hitting against the door.

The ogre lifted me off my feet.

The worst thing I could do is try to wrestle with the cloth.

I reached over my head, trying to press my thumbs into his sockets to dislodge his eyeballs. Or maybe just inflict enough pain that he'd give me a little breathing room.

Not working…try…something else.

Reaching behind me, I undid his belt, whipping it from his loops. I flipped the prong up and jabbed it back at his face. I felt it slide into his flesh. It elicited a grunt, and that's all.

Ridge had the door open, but the guy had passed out in front of it. Ridge was having trouble getting through.

I lifted my legs. Pressing my tennis shoes into the goon's thighs, I tried to lift up higher to release the pressure. My vision was getting blurry. My eyes bulged. My tongue extended from my mouth, trying to make room for more air to get into my lungs.

As I lifted up, I slammed my elbow first left then right toward his temples.

Then, like an avenging angel, a fur rocket vaulted into the room.

Zeus brought his jaw down on the ogre's bicep, dangling his weight while he shook his majestic head.

I was tossed aside as the ogre screamed.

When I hit the ground, I rolled to the knife, afraid that if it should somehow end up in the guy's hand that he'd hurt Zeus.

I grabbed the unconscious guy's hand and crawled backward, scooting on my butt as I dragged him far enough into the room that Ridge could make his way in, gun in hand.

"Call off your dog!" The ogre bellowed.

"On your knees." Ridge's voice was ice.

I slid further back on my butt until I made it all the way to the kitchen, where I opened the fridge and stuck my head inside, looking for a blast of cool air to right my systems.

31

Destiny was dead.

Dead.

Dead.

A deep moan escaped from the bowels of my being.

I hadn't left the galley kitchen, hadn't crawled up from the floor. I sat there with my legs extended in front of me. Zeus laid across my lap, his focus intent on the comings and goings in the room. En guard.

The two men had been cuffed by the FBI guys in their tactical gear and hauled away for interrogation.

The medical examiner had come and gone with the body.

Ridge stood out of the way, vigilant.

Prescott and Finley moved into the kitchen and sat on the floor with me.

"I'm sorry, Lynx," Prescott said. "You handled yourself beautifully. But that should never have happened. We thought we were monitoring The Grove effectively. I can't imagine this originated with them. We would have picked up some chatter."

"There are other players, though, that you couldn't manage?" I asked.

"We didn't think they'd become aware of Modesty's living arrangements," Finley said. "And if they did…well, Modesty had done a good job for someone with little knowledge of how the world works at keeping herself under the radar."

"Was the muriatic acid already up here?" Ridge asked.

"Not when I left for the diner earlier this morning."

Finley and Prescott looked at each other. "Well, it's strong enough that it might make her unidentifiable. Destroy her fingerprints."

"If they had DNA, they'd still be able to figure out what she looked like. There's an artist in Seattle that can make a fairly realistic mask out of Destiny's genomic material, enough that a picture on the news and someone would recognize her. Of course, mostly Destiny only knows—knew people from the diner and The Grove."

"What are you saying about the artist?" Prescott asked.

"Can I tell you about that later?" I asked. My stomach was queasy and talking made it worse. I was so glad that all I saw of Destiny was her feet as the goon carried her into the bathroom. I had no idea how they killed her and had no desire to be caught up on the case.

As far as I was concerned, I was done.

Though Spyder was involved…

Prescott reached out and patted my leg. "This will keep. Let Ridge take you home. Try to get some rest."

As he said that, Zeus climbed from my lap.

Finley stretched out a hand to help me up.

"Do you need to go by the hospital?" Prescott asked.

"Yeah, just to be sure. Strangulation, even as lightly and for as short a time as it happened to me, can have bad outcomes. I should probably check-in and make sure I'm not going to swell up and die in my sleep."

32

"HEY, SPYDER," I said when I found him sitting in my living room. Somehow, I wasn't at all surprised.

Ridge and Zeus had escorted me away from Suburban Hospital with my clean bill of health. Ridge let Zeus sit on the floorboard in the front with me in the SUV.

Zeus rested his head in my lap, and I got to pet his soft fur. He was balm to my heart.

I had bent forward and kissed Zeus between his velvety ears. "Thank you for saving me from the bad guy," I whispered as Ridge pulled up in front of my house.

Dawn would break soon.

Striker met me at the door with a hug and a kiss. I could tell he was trying to keep things light. He wasn't going to ride me.

Good choice.

"I am sorry that things unfolded the way in which they did." Spyder was sitting in the rocking chair. The length of his legs made it look like the chair had been made for a child.

"It wasn't the way I thought things would go, that's for sure." I moved toward him to offer a kiss of welcome.

Hopefully, now I'd get a clearer picture of what kind of mess I'd been playing in.

After Striker took his place on the sofa, I toed off my shoes and curled up against his chest. "Now that Modesty is unable to provide information, do you have another route to whatever it was that you were trying to figure out?"

Man, that sounded cold. Modesty was a young woman who hadn't even met her prime or her potential. She'd been brave enough to try to save herself. I didn't want her to be forgotten or considered a statistic. But too, there was some personal relief from thinking about her in the abstract. I'd have to reevaluate those thoughts later. Was that a safe and sane way to handle this? Compassionate? Yeah, much to meditate on.

"Modesty, or Destiny as she reinvented herself, tried to remove herself from a situation far more concerning than being raised within the confines of The Grove. As we know, treachery happens when seeking wealth."

"Yes, sir."

"As it happens, this case has some ties to your social activities this week. You will be attending Christen Davidson's wedding."

I pushed to sitting.

"The Hydra includes Sylanos, who owns many ships from the times when he engaged in software pirating. And some Assembly men, since the data dump that sent many into hiding and others into prison, have sought a new relationship with Sylanos to engage in a new way to rob Uncle Sam's pockets."

"Christen's dad, William Davidson?" I curled back into Striker, who held me close.

"While William Davidson walks a fine line between the criminal and the innocent, it is his son who displays the black heart."

"Karl," Striker said.

"Exactly." Spyder laced his fingers, steepling his index fingers, and pressing them into his chin.

"So Karl is into energy monies, especially around fossil fuels and natural gasses," I said, thinking back to the debacle where Gator and Christen had met last July. "including helium."

"Exactly."

"And this goes together with The Grove and Modesty Blackburn?" I asked.

"Indeed. Allow me to explain. A little history first. In the 1970s, well before you were born, there was a petroleum crisis. It was quite disruptive to America. There were long gas lines, and drivers were only allowed to fill up their cars on certain days."

"I studied that." I nodded.

"As a response to our dependence on foreign oil, the U.S. government thought that it would be wise to mandate the use of biofuels, those made from soy and corn oils, for example."

My brows pulled together with concentration.

"The science of creating biofuels has a place in understanding the current crimes. Vegetable oils and oils taken from restaurants cooking vats—for example, from your beloved Burger Go! restaurant." Spyder sent me a wide smile. "All of these oils are high in triglycerides. To make them useable in vehicles, one mixes the vegetable oils with an alcohol such as methanol as the beginning of the transformative process. This is very expensive to perform."

"Okay."

"And as you well know, our planet is facing an emerging catastrophic state due to the levels of carbon monoxide in the air, among other issues."

"Yes."

"To try to combat this, and here is the crux of the issue, Congress decided to subsidize the biofuel market by creating billions of dollars in incentives."

I scowled. I could see how Karl Davidson would both be knowledgeable about such subsidies and have the Assembly help manipulate things behind the scenes. But The Grove and Modesty?

"B100 is the name of the fuel stage where the vegetable oil has been treated with some form of alcohol. A step in the process of being able to use the fuel in our vehicles. Those who produce B100 are compensated by the government."

Striker and I nodded.

"In order to claim subsidy money, every gallon of B100 that is produced is provided with a specific number so that it might be tracked. Big oil producers, such as the Davidsons, are required to buy biofuel. They are supposed to mix the B100 with diesel to make B99."

"I'm following. Sort of. The Grove? They're in California near Hollywood."

"Patience, Lexicon. One must take all of the steps on the path to proceed without mishap."

"Yes, sir." I shifted against Striker, and he rubbed his hand up and down my arm, which helped me calm my impatience.

"A gallon of B99 creates a dollar in tax credit, which is paid directly from the IRS. Skipping to our friends in California. Barnabas Blackburn was welcomed back to The Grove and offered the first of his wives when he came up with the scheme of producing B99. Even with the enormous governmental incentives, he was barely breaking even."

"I'd imagine shipping costs were eating into his bottom line. He'd have to ship the oil from the mid-west, right?"

"Precisely. One would have to do that to be legitimate."

"Ah."

"From what information I was able to glean, Karl Davidson approached Blackburn with a deal that included Sylanos."

"Selling your soul to the devil," I muttered under my breath.

"If one believes that such an entity exists." Another broad smile. "Barnabas Blackburn, who was Modesty Blackburn's uncle, agreed to work with the Hydra. And it was quite lucrative for him and those who lived at The Grove. He brought in millions, which meant that many eyes followed him and became curious. This is especially so as The Grove is protected from taxes and other requirements as The Grove claims to be a religious order."

At the mention of Modesty, I needed a moment. Holding up a "please pause" finger, I asked, "Can I get anyone anything in the kitchen? I need a cup of tea. My throat."

Both men shook their heads.

I had called Striker from the SUV on the way home from being cleared at the hospital. Ridge and I updated him about the status of the mission, the apprehensions. It seemed like Striker had decided not to be a mother hen. He said nothing to my throat comment.

I was glad to have a long moment while the microwave heated the water. But having dunked in a teabag, it was time to hear the reason behind Modesty's murder.

"Are you ready?" Spyder asked.

I curled back into my place under Striker's arm, pressed up against his chest, my tea mug balanced on my knee. "Yes, sir. Excuse me for interrupting."

"Not at all, my dear. I was about to talk with you about the Three-card Monte."

Striker nodded. "In that grifter's card game, the dealer wants you to follow the ace and point it out. But it's shuffled in with two kings. Through sleight of hand work, the ace is shifted, and the dupe loses his money. Back in my early Navy days, I had a friend who made a lot of money that way. Ended up in the brig."

"Darn."

"What is this 'darn,' Lexicon?" Spyder raised his brows in question.

"I was at the CIA looking over some information for them last week. I used the metaphor of Monty Hall's three doors game to explain to them what I saw happening at the crime scene."

"A car and two goats?"

"Yes, sir."

"This is very similar. They are built on each other."

"Yes, but your metaphor is much more elegant."

Spyder offered me a slight bow of the head. "Here is how they played their game. Barnabas purchases some B99 oil silently financed by Karl Davidson. It is mislabeled as 'cooking oil'"

"Cooking oil is B100, not yet mixed with alcohol," I said.

"Correct. This oil is shipped straight down the Mississippi. Cheaper than overland. It was loaded onto a Sylanos ship. This ship goes to Central America, where it is off-loaded, driven across the breadth of the land, then reloaded onto a second ship. The second ship takes the product up to The Grove in California."

"Barnabas takes the mislabeled cooking oil and says tada! B99?"

"Yes. And each gallon provides a dollar of government subsidies."

"Paid straight from the IRS," Striker added. "That's quite the scam."

"Indeed, quite the scam if it circulated only once in this way. However, they need not purchase another supply of B99 to mislabel as B100. Once they have started this circuit, there is no reason to stop. The same product just continues to move in a circular pattern."

"Why go through all of that trouble?" I asked. "With the unloading the ship and driving it across. There's the Panama Canal."

"Yes, shipping is Sylanos's specialty. Corrupt shipping more precisely. Paperwork is the reason. Of course, with this seeming volume of production, the EPA and the IRS are stakeholders in preventing fraud. By shipping the oil in this manner, there would be legitimate documentation that masked the falsified records. Faked invoices and production records looked correct when layered with the port and customs paperwork."

"Ah," I said. "I can see how Karl would use his Assembly contacts with all of their law enforcement and judicial members playing their games to keep things running smoothly."

"Indeed."

"How did Modesty fit into this picture?" Striker asked.

"Modesty was offered to Barnabas Blackburn as his newest bride. She was seventeen at the time. She escaped and went to the FBI for a walk-up appointment. She had run away barefooted and in a nightdress in the middle of the night. Quite the brave young woman. Because of her appearance at the FBI walk-up and her fancifully strange story about B100 and B99—"

"Which few people would have heard of," I threw in. "I know I've never heard of it anyway."

Spyder nodded his agreement. "They discounted her tale. Word, though, did reach me. I found her here. One presumes she came to Washington D.C. thinking this would be the place to find safety. From the FBI intake interview back in California, I learned she believed that if Barnabas was arrested, she'd be safe. She felt like she knew too much, and they would chase her down. Along the way, she stopped trusting authorities. The FBI and I determined that you would be a means for her to grow in trust and that we could work with her."

"I didn't save her."

Striker tightened his arm around me.

"Saving her was not your role. I am very pleased that you emerged from such a crime scene whole and seemingly healthy?"

"Yes, sir. The doctor says I'm fine."

"Well then, we can move forward with our next mystery. Striker says that your parents have shown up hovering over your shoulder as ghosts. Shall we discuss this?"

33

———

Striker excused himself and went upstairs.

"You frown," Spyder said.

"Not having Modesty's information is a loss to stopping the corruption. But I'll persevere. We will."

"No, Lexicon. Any other action on your part would expose too much. It can't be risked." He offered me a gracious nod. "Thank you for what you've done."

"You're welcome. Though, I feel like I failed."

"This is the beast of our work. We see things and pass them on, and we almost never know what comes of it. It is a difficulty that many professions don't have. An architect can walk into their completed building. A movie producer can watch their final product on the big screen. We must be contented to know that we did our part, but we are merely components of a whole."

"Isn't that a metaphor for human existence?"

"In many ways, it is," he acknowledged. "Now, tell me how you are."

"I am living the human condition—we suffer, then we die."

Spyder threw his head back and laughed. "True. May your

suffering be a mere inconvenience. May your death be in the distant future."

I picked up my mug and held it aloft as a toast. "And to you."

"Now, to your parents."

"Mom's birthday was last week. It seemed that the day before…a couple of days before, my parents arrived with some kind of warning for me."

"I see."

"It's possible this has to do with the area of town where I lived and worked with Destin—Modesty. I passed the site of Dad's crash. I was staying in a garage apartment just on the other side of the road from the bar where I used to watch Hanasal."

"Tell me one of these memories." He flicked a finger at me. "Lie down comfortably. Close your eyes. And tell me what memory bubbles up for you."

"Yes, sir." I arranged myself as instructed. I let myself go back in time and relived the memory:

Sixteen days since my father's burial, fourteen days into my mission, Spyder and I went on our typical six-mile morning run. I thought that Spyder had upped our normal pace considerably. Maybe it just felt that way on three hours' rest. Sleep hadn't come to me.

Panting and holding the stitch in my side, we went inside to meditate in front of the altar in my living room. It was adorned with orchids from Dad's funeral. Mom had added a bowl of salt to represent our tears and a lemon to represent how bitter life could taste. I sank into my practiced place of peace, but it was short-lived. Eventually, Spyder dinged the bell, bringing me back to my earlier state of angst.

We unfolded from our lotus positions and pushed our kneeling pillows under the altar.

"I was surprised by your stamina this morning after such a long night out."

I went to the counter, poured a glass of green juice for Mom, and put her pills into a small dish. I raised a brow at Spyder as I walked without a word from the kitchen to Mom's room to wake her just long enough for her to take the pills, then go back to sleep.

I walked back into the living room and sat on the couch as Spyder slid his phone into his pocket. There was no censure waiting for me. There never was. According to Spyder, there is no such thing as a mistake. Everything—the bad and the ugly as well as the beautiful—had a place of teaching in our lives. Once we learned a lesson, that didn't mean anything except that one's soul was now free to learn another lesson. A cycle of pain and joy. Both had importance. I hadn't yet internalized this philosophy. I guessed it would come with maturity. Still, I waited to hear just how much Spyder knew about my activities last night.

"Show me what you found in the backseat."

Ah, he knew everything. I was out-surveilled. He had been watching me, and I never knew. Obviously, I had more to learn. If I had no clue Spyder was trailing me, then others with his experience could put me in their crosshairs when I was a real intelligence officer working for the government. I chastised myself for not considering the possibility that I, too, would be followed.

I showed him the picture. White label; his name, the name of the antibiotics. Child-proof cap. If I was the woman who gave this guy a blow job, I'd want the antibiotics, too. I didn't blame her at all for taking them. Spyder examined the photo and video and handed my phone back to me.

"What else?"

I reached into my pocket and pulled out Hanasal's key ring. It had a fob, a car key, and what I assumed was a house key.

"Hanasal experienced some grief this morning when he came

to. He had to have the dealership tow his car to their lot for repairs. He had to take a cab to his house to get his spare set of keys. A locksmith came to open his door. And then he had to return to get his car. Well done."

I lifted my chin. Well done? Wait. How would he know this? Spyder was running with me this morning. "Someone just called it in?"

"My partner took over the watch when forces split, and you drove away."

"Two people were watching me? You and who else?"

Spyder chose not to answer me. "What are your plans?"

"To make sure this guy never kills an innocent civilian again."

He nodded. And waited.

"I don't know what that means. I'm gathering information and waiting for my anger to calm. There's another beacon of wisdom I need to follow: 'Revenge is a dish served best cold.'"

Spyder said nothing.

"I'll go out every night until I have a better handle on things. I'll videotape if I see something that I think might be helpful. I'll keep his car from functioning if he's drunk."

And that's exactly what I did. Night after night. Night after night. Days started to head into weeks. I was exhausted.

And Spyder said nothing more to me.

Mom did, though.

She noticed I wasn't getting enough rest. It made her worry. Her worry made the pain worse.

It was as if I had invited Hanasal into our living room to hurt us some more.

I was getting tired of my watch duty. Nothing new was happening. The pattern was fairly well set.

One night, I sat in the tree looking down at Hanasal's newest car. This was the third one. Spyder said that Hanasal was threatening to sue the dealership because the cars didn't work. This had been going on too long. Certainly, I would be caught on some video feed if I kept this up. To get his newest fob, I had to walk by Hanasal on his way into the bar and sleight-of-hand it from his jacket pocket. I didn't want my face anywhere near his, no matter how good my disguise was.

XYJ, the license from the person who continued to meet him in the parking lot, showed up again. And again, the windows went down, and a prescription bottle changed hands. Hanasal walked into the bar. I gave him time to settle, then started wiring his car with a remote kill switch and a GPS. I figured it would be a heck of a lot more fun to let him drive down the road a bit, kill his engine when it was safe for other drivers that I do that, wait for the tow truck, and flip it back on. I snapped the panel back in place. That's when I looked over at the pill bottle tucked between the seats.

I used my t-shirt to take the vial with me. I could sit in my car around the block, and my phone would alert me if Hanasal's car moved. I looked at the vial. It was the same antibiotics as before, just a different date on the label. I twitched my mouth to the side and checked on the date. Had I lost a day from my lack of sleep? No. This label was definitely for tomorrow. I snapped a picture of the label.

I pulled on a pair of nitrile gloves, unscrewed the bottle top, and looked at the pills. I checked the label again. I knew this antibiotic from dolling out Mom's medications. It should be a bright yellow solid pill. This was a blue and white capsule. This wasn't the drug from the label. I folded a piece of paper and emptied the vial into the crease. One by one, I lifted and examined each pill. Why not? I had hours to kill. There were forty-two pills in all—three times a day for fourteen days. On the twenty-sixth pill, something was different. When I rolled it between my fingers, it didn't feel like granules that shifted as they were pressed. This felt solid.

Slowly, I pulled the capsule apart—no medicine granules. Instead, a piece of paper was rolled tightly and shoved inside. I reached into my glove compartment and pulled out a tool kit. I picked up my pointed tweezers and ever so carefully pulled out the contents, spread the slip of paper—smaller than a Chinese fortune —on my lap, and read what it said. There was an Internet website address and a time. I took a photo and then worked to put it back exactly as I had found it. I inspected the rest of the pills. One other had information, too; this one said Dusty Roads. I swallowed hard, took the picture, put everything back in the vial, gave the vial a shake, and replaced it exactly as I had found it in Hanasal's car.

At the library on the other side of town, the day after the pill bottle date, I looked up the web address and found a forum for "hipsters who like ferrets." I scrolled through the messages until I found one posted by Dusty Roads. It looked like a recipe, half in English and half in gibberish, and at the end, it said, "Lastly, add the .onion" and stir.

.Onion meant this was a deep web address.

Last night, Hanasal had received another vial, and I replicated the task and had found another website and another code name. Its posting would go up tomorrow. I waited and got that information as well before I approached Spyder.

"Spyder, I need your help."

"And how is it that I might assist you, Lexicon?"

I went through my pictures and my actions. Spyder nodded with the utmost of attention and seriousness. "I don't think I should search the dark web from the library computer. I don't want to let anyone know that I have this information—they might erase what's happening. I thought perhaps you might take this to your office at Iniquus and use an encrypted computer."

Spyder leaned forward and kissed me on the forehead, then left.

That night found me behind yet another tree. There was another handoff, and I wasn't sure what to do about it. I had just decided to slip forward and grab hold of the vial when my phone buzzed against my hip. Spyder. I swiped the screen and sniffed so he'd know I was there.

"Take cover," Spyder said.

Cover? Cover. Cover meant weapons would be out. Conceal would mean make sure I wasn't getting caught. *Weapons and cover usually meant guns*, I processed. I ran behind the brick wall and plastered my eyes against a crack so I could see what was going on. My phone buzzed again.

"Good girl."

"You can see me, Spyder?" My eyes traveled around. I saw nothing and no one that I didn't expect to see.

"I want you to watch for Hanasal and let me know the second he comes out the door."

"Yes, sir."

I couldn't see the door from where I was crouched. I duck-walked to the edge of the wall and held out my phone, so I could use the camera to see what was happening at the entrance. After a while, my hand got tired, and my arm sagged ineffectually. I perched my wrist on my knee and waited. And waited. *Oh, dear god in heaven, seriously*? I waited. *Finally,* Hanasal came staggering out with his arm around the shoulder of some guy. I buzzed Spyder.

"Cover," Spyder said, then hung up.

Within seconds the parking lot was filled with FBI SWAT. They were fearsome to behold in their black armor and balaclavas. Hanasal freaked. With his mind mixing alcohol and adrenaline in vast quantities, he took off at speed I would never have attributed to a man of his bulk. He dashed away from the SWAT unit, out into the street where a shriek of tires and a loud thud was quickly followed by screams as the driver leaped from her car to hover over Hanasal.

Sirens soon followed from around the corner, where I guessed the SWAT unit had staged an ambulance—a precaution they took when they thought their arrestee would fight. Certainly, they wouldn't have foreseen him running in front of some woman's car.

I stayed behind my wall. A good operator didn't risk being seen. But I could see. I saw the local PD come and administer a field sobriety test. I saw the woman's wrists being cuffed behind her back and saw the police officer helping her into the back of his police cruiser. I saw the ambulance pull a white sheet over Hanasal, slide his body into the back of the rescue squad, and leave without lights. I pumped my fist in the air victoriously. It wasn't my kill. It wasn't even my intention. But Hanasal was dead. Just desserts. Killed by a drunk driver—now *that* was karma biting him back. I wanted to feel triumphant. But my little victory dance felt like a farce. I slunk back to my apartment, feeling oddly defeated.

Sliding my key into the lock, I pushed the door open to find Spyder waiting for me in my living room. "An eventful night, Lexicon."

"Yes, it was. Why was the FBI on scene?"

"The Darkweb addresses turned out to be a plethora of information about illegal arms trade with Al-Qaeda operators. Hanasal was involved in terrorist activity. We wished we could have him under arrest for interrogation. But destiny cannot be thwarted. You helped that along."

I nodded. I thought I'd feel more fulfilled than I did. Lighter. I thought if Hanasal had died, that some kind of burden would be off my shoulders. But I felt just as bad this morning as I did yesterday morning—as I did every morning since Dad was killed.

· · ·

"My dear, keeping your eyes closed. I wish to ask you if I may use hypnotism."

"Why is that, Spyder?"

"I have latched onto your phrases, 'I wanted to feel triumphant. But my little victory dance felt like a farce. I slunk back to my apartment, feeling oddly defeated.' There is something rich there. Some piece of information that your mind knows but is hiding from you. I wish to explore it, if I may."

34

HYPNOTISM WAS a technique that Spyder and I had used frequently. As he moved his chair over to the couch where I lay, I followed his instructions into a trance.

"Find the place and time that will give you the most information," Spyder instructed.

I was back at the funeral. Back in the mud. Spyder carried my mother. I held the umbrella. Her wheelchair was lifted from the mud and was being carried just behind me. I described the scene to Spyder.

"And what did I do?"

"You put my mom in the back seat. There was a pillow there, and she clutched it to her stomach. It took a moment to get her to be aware enough that she released the pillow for you to put on her safety belt."

"Continue."

"A hand reached toward me, 'May I have the keys? I'll put the chair in the trunk.'"

"Do you recognize the voice?"

Did I recognize the voice…?

"Go back in time and listen to the voice asking for the keys again."

I nodded.

"Do you recognize the voice?"

"I do."

"Who is it?"

I shook my head.

"Move to a time where you can see the person who has that voice. Tell me when you're there."

"There."

"Where are you?"

"CIA headquarters with Striker. We're leaving a meeting."

"When is this?"

"Thursday as Striker and I were leaving Langley."

"Who was it?"

"Seth Toone."

"The name of the man who carried your mother's wheelchair was Seth Toone. He worked closely with your father at the CIA. And since your father's job was clandestine, he was the only representative for the CIA at the funeral."

"Ah."

"Which doesn't resolve the question."

"No."

"Go back to a time and place that will give you the most information. Tell me when you're there."

"There."

"Where are you?"

"I'm at my father's crash."

"What do you see?"

"Hanasal is getting out of the passenger's side of his car. He's stumbling toward the tree line. Places his hand on the trunk. Is vomiting."

"What do you need to see, but your brain is afraid to show you?"

"Hanasal gets out of the passenger side… I'm in a fog, thick enough to slice. I couldn't see anything."

"Bring in a device. What could dispel the fog?"

"A sun gun."

"Use it."

"I'm picturing myself with a water squirter beaming out rays of sun, burning through the mist. A man got out of the car's driver's side. He shook himself off. Looked at me where I was crawling from the window onto the road. He turns and walks away."

"Zoom in on the man's face. Do you recognize him?"

"Yes, it's the guy Seth from the CIA."

There was a long pause.

"I was with Seth Toone the night of your father's death. We were on a mission. He was not there."

"Then my brain must be conflating the two images."

"Not necessarily. No. Not necessarily at all. This is taking an unexpected turn, Lexicon. Let us close this session so we might speak. You are deep in a meditative state. As you rise back to the surface of consciousness, you will bring all of your memories with you. Stress is removed from these pictures. They are in the past, and they now serve as vehicles of information. That is all they are, pieces of information. There is no reason for old wounds to open, old pain to be revisited. You step up from ten to nine, eight, seven, anxiety and pain are left behind as you climb back to the here and now. Six, five, four. You are starting to feel your body in present time and space—your feet on the arm of your sofa, your sits bones on the cushion, your back flat against the fabric. Three. You have weight and take up space. You are back in the room. Two. Your eyes are fluttering. You take in a deep breath, still comfortable, still just receiving facts that do not attach to emotion. One. You are fully present, solid in your body."

I blinked at Spyder, giving myself a moment.

Spyder sat patiently to my side, no pressure, no rush.

In Spyder's philosophy, we are given bodies. Our bodies are alive to learn lessons. We are destined to repeat our lessons until we learn our lesson, which does not bring us anything but new lessons. Circular.

There is no better 'here' than here, no greener pasture, no reason to fight our destiny, and by destiny, he means the lessons we're sent to learn.

In fighting them, we just add struggle to our lessons list.

So for Spyder, there was no rush or pressure that was connected to his actions or inactions. And certainly not in the process of meditation, which is how Spyder frames hypnosis.

Spyder believes in non-effort. But for him, it is the non-effort of an elite athlete.

Studies have shown that when an athlete gets attached to an outcome, their performance declines.

Working with elite athletes both from the sports world and the special operators' world, the scientists have found that one must train to hit one's peak, that's body and mind. In mind training, visualization, meditation, or hypnosis, the goal is always to perform one's best.

Striker, for example, was trained that after the team had planned an attack on the tabletop, they tried it out in the shooter house. They would practice and tweak, practice and tweak until their very cells remembered, without thought, the exact moves that they need to make.

The exact angle of the gun.

There was a truism in the SEAL world that no plan survives first contact.

But that doesn't lessen the imperative of having a plan, practicing, coming up with contingency plans.

Once this was developed, the team would meditate on the action. They meticulously moved through each step in the exact way they wished it to be performed.

That was the action and performance, not outcome.

There was no, "and then I got the gold medal of freedom" at the end.

There was no, "and then I killed the bad guy, and the world became a place of peace."

No.

If a shot was to be taken to down a bad guy, there was no "get." There was no "win." There was simply the physical action of positioning the gun, finding the mark, pulling the trigger, hitting the mark.

That was what hypnotism was supposed to be for me.

Information. Preparation. Separation from a need to have a certain outcome.

Of course, my desired outcome was to know why my parents were hanging over my shoulder (information), warning me (for my preparation). It was the separation that I found so hard.

It was a push me pull you.

Spyder wanted me to rid myself of the distractions. Yet, my psychic mentor, Miriam Laugherty, taught me how to allow those very experiences—again, for information and then remove the distraction.

That was often easier said than done.

Especially with the newest *knowing,* "London Bridge is falling down," setting off my alarm systems.

35

"MY DEAR, I wish you to bring me your box with your mother's journals."

My mom's journals, filled with sketches and doodles, miniature paintings and poetry, her thoughts. I couldn't imagine what Spyder wanted with these.

Setting the box in front of him, Spyder reverently lifted one journal after another. Opening the front page, he glanced, then gently placed it on the floor.

Finally, he found what he was looking for and handed it to me.

"You will excuse me for a moment." Spyder stood and walked through my dining room, my kitchen, and outdoors to the garden. I supposed this was all bringing up difficult emotions and memories for Spyder as well. My parents and Spyder loved each other with a deep kinship.

I looked down at the book in my hand.

It was a journal that I hadn't seen before. I thought I'd read them all over and over throughout the last few years since mom had died.

I opened it, and a flurry of yellow papers fell out.

The first was an obituary. A young woman who looked a bit like me. She was killed in a car accident. She'd been seventeen when she died. "Molly Toone. Beloved daughter of Gloria and Vincent Toone. Mourned by her family, including her uncle Seth Toone…"

The next article was about the police and ambulance being called to Molly Toone's funeral. It said that the father, Vincent Toone, had severely beaten Douglas Rueben—Dad! My eye scanned the article.

It said that my mother was driving the car that killed Molly.

My nerves buzzed.

There was something there. Back, back, back in my memory. My dad had been covered in bruises, his arm in a sling…

There was a copy of my father's obituary.

And now the last slip of paper. The one that felt like acid on my fingers. The one I didn't want to read.

"I was aiming for your daughter. You should feel what I do."

It's funny how the brain stutters. How it creates magic tricks.

"The years of evil" was how I internally referred to the time between when I got my first stalker note from Travis Wilson up until the time when I found out my dead husband wasn't really dead but had just chosen a life doing black ops for our government. And during those years, I had the support of friends and later Iniquus colleagues, and especially Striker and my team.

But the support and help I needed were from Spyder.

I had lamented the fact that he was off-grid, and I had no way to contact him, no way to send up a distress sign.

Or so I thought.

But he had given me a bat signal.

We had been at a Chinese restaurant where Spyder liked the idea of the fortune cookies. He used them as teaching tools.

I had a different mentor, Mrs. Drinkwater—a terrible name.

She was an English woman who actually drank tea—lots of it. And there was nothing she liked better than to have me around for high tea and chatter. A pagan, Mrs. Drinkwater, was trying to learn to read tea leaves. She was rarely accurate. She was better with tarot cards. But the thing that I liked best was her bag of tumbled semiprecious gemstones.

They were an act of trust.

After tea, she would pull out the bag, and centering myself, I meditatively reached in and let three stones land in my palm. I pulled them out, and Mrs. Drinkwater would pronounce their meaning—compassion, strength, gratitude. Those were the words that I should carry with me for the day.

The interesting thing about those stones—and the similar way that Mrs. Drinkwater pulled her tarot cards, not for a foretelling but more as a compass—let me hold different words in my consciousness, seeking to incorporate those aspects into my day.

When I carried a stone that represented gratitude, when I could finger it in my pocket and be reminded, then my day filled with gratitude.

Spyder's use of sayings and quotes was similar, I guessed.

At the Chinese restaurant, we'd ask for our fortune cookies while we waited for our meal to be prepared. We worked on the assumption that this would be a message that the Universe conspired to provide us with.

We'd snap open the cookie and drag out the information— rather than prognostication. And we'd see what meaning we could find, what instruction I could use in how I comported myself that day.

I remember it vividly. Spyder had slipped my paper from my fingers and read the Confucius quote: *Virtue is not left to stand alone. He who practices it will have neighbors.*

He looked me in the eye for a long moment. "My job pulls me

to a different location. I am not abandoning you. You are my priority."

My heart had gripped. I didn't want him to go to a "different location." I wanted him there with me. At least until I got my feet underneath me after Mom died.

He passed me the fortune. "There are no insulated events in this world, Lexicon. Everything transpires as it should. This fortune, for example, is well-timed. Very suitable, wouldn't you say?"

I frowned at him.

His eyes smiled back in his fatherly way. "Lexicon, this will serve as our code. When there are no other options, and you send me a message with these words, I will dismiss all other obligations and return to your side." He paused. "I trust you will use the code wisely."

I put it in my pocket and immediately forgot all about it.

Through the fire, the stalker, the kidnapping, the healing, the craziness…

Then at precisely the right time on exactly the right day, I was having lunch with a work acquaintance Leanne. I opened the fortune cookie, smoothing it out on the table. *Virtue is not left to stand alone. He who practices it will have neighbors.* And like the good witch waking Dorothy from her spell-sleep, I woke up. I remembered.

Leanne knew how to contact Spyder—of course, she did. Why hadn't I considered that avenue before?

Spyder had actually come into town the night before to bring me along as he fought the Hydra.

Yeah, the serendipity of it all seemed magical.

So I had experienced this weird brain magic before—if I was inclined to paint this as esoteric.

I had been through these boxes hundreds of times.

Read every word on every page.

And yet, here was a journal I had never seen before, and when I opened it, this is what fell into my lap.

The confusing part was, why now?

Surely, it had to do with my sensing my parents' concern.

"Row faster, Lexi!"

If only I knew where I could find a safe shore.

I SAT THERE TRYING to remember. I was glad that Spyder was outside, giving me this space to adjust to the newly discovered information.

I was very young at the time, maybe four years old?

I was in the car with Dad. We were coming back from a picnic at one of my parent's friends' houses. Mom drove there with me. But I had pitched a fit. I wanted to drive home with Dad. I remembered thinking I might be able to convince him to buy me an ice cream cone.

I remember the sound of brakes squealing—the sensation of being thrown forward. Of Dad yelling at me to sit very still, he'd be back.

Spyder walked in and sat down. "Are you ready?"

I nodded.

"Your mother was driving home from a party at Seth Toone's home. It was his birthday. He celebrated it with his identical twin brother—"

"Vincent."

"Precisely. Seth's niece had run to the store for more sodas for the party. Her name was Molly, and she was seventeen."

My lips went numb.

"As your mother drove, she passed out at the wheel. Her car veered into the oncoming lane, hitting Molly's car in a head-on collision. Molly died on the scene. Your mother was rushed to the hospital. She was diagnosed with brain cancer."

I nodded.

"Your father went to the funeral. He was…filled with grief. When Vincent saw your father, he lost control and beat him severely. Your father did nothing to protect or defend himself, and he was hospitalized. You might remember this time. You went to live with Snow Bird and Master Wang. You worked with them in their dry cleaners across the street. It was at this time that Master Wang began to teach you martial arts."

My frown was so deep it felt weighted like it could pull me over.

"As your mother was in the hospital and they were trying to offer her a diagnosis and a path forward, the Wangs told your father that he would best take care of his wife and the back and forth to the hospital, and they would keep you until your mother was home from the hospital. You were having a great time at their home. So that's what your dad did. It was an enormous help. This gave your father time to focus solely on your mom, and it gave him time to physically heal from the beating."

"You were there?"

"I was."

"And you allowed it?"

"If your father had wanted to stop the fight, it would have been very easy for him to do. As good a fighter as you are, Lexicon, your father was one of the best I have ever seen. He *allowed* Vincent Toone to beat him."

"Why?"

"The man was filled with rage over the death of his child. Your father thought that he needed to hurt your dad to dissipate some of his own hurt. The grief he experienced with the loss of Molly was immense."

"You said you were with Seth Toone the night of Dad's accident."

"I was."

"Vincent Toone figures out where we'd be. He gets a diplomat who won't be held accountable for vehicular homicide. He had Hanasal drink heavily, so he couldn't remember, then he drove into our car. He was protected by the airbag. He must have unbelted Hanasal, done something to make it look like he had been driving and flung? But Hanasal got out of the car to puke. That I remember clearly. And Vincent, he just walked away." I reached for the note I'd found in Mom's journal. "Vincent Toone wanted Mom to suffer, so he was trying to kill me but killed Dad." The words barely squeaked up my throat. My voice was helium.

When Spyder canted his head at my last sentence, I held up the note to my mother, and Spyder read it over.

"Did you know about this?" I asked.

"This your mother kept from me," Spyder said, rubbing his fingers over the blue ink.

"He needs to be held accountable." *Obviously.* But how could I prove this? It wasn't like I could go into a court of law and say, "I was hypnotized to remember. Oh! And my folks are ghosts hanging out behind my shoulder, and they were trying to catch my attention so I could remember for some reason."

"Perhaps with time," Spyder responded to me, saying Vincent needed accountability. "Not right now. It is a seed that I *do not* wish to plant in your mind."

Vengeance was that seed.

So many times in my adult life, I have seen revenge and hate be the impetuous for terrible outcomes.

I had to be on guard myself against those thoughts. I'd tried those lessons with Hanasal.

He died.

I was not healed.

Had I not learned anything?

37

CHRISTEN and Gator walked into the ballroom at the Davidson's private social club. An enormous turn of the 20th-century mansion just outside of DC proper in Maryland. Twenty-foot ceilings, walnut-lined corridors, period-stained-glass windows made for an elegant setting.

Kira, London Davidson's college roommate, had made the arrangements, and she had done a lovely job.

She had devised a World War II vibe with vintage war posters, WWII model airplanes, and the catering staff dressed as GIs at a USO dance. A swing band, now getting up from their instruments to take a break, had been set up on the dais. A nationally competitive jitterbug duo had shown off their routine.

There was a lovely buffet with period dishes, Waldorf salads, and salmon in aspic.

Everyone seemed to be having a good time. And so far, I'd just stayed huddled with my friends at our designated wedding party table—safe.

All of Strike Force was here; Randy and Axel came solo. Deep and his wife Grace, Blaze and his girlfriend Faith, Jack and his fiancée Suz, Reaper and Kate, Striker and I rounded things out. Gator would have his teammates stand with him as his groom's men. Lula and I would stand with Christen's soon-to-be sisters-in-law Genevieve and Auralia on the bride's side.

Gator's biological brothers weren't due until tomorrow morning, getting here in time for the rehearsal.

"Where are your mom and sisters, Gator?" I asked, looking around. Their name cards weren't on our table, and I wondered where London would have seated them since they were strangers to everyone else.

Gator looked down at his phone, texting.

A moment later, a scowl crossed his face.

"What is it?" Christen asked.

Gator swiped his tongue across his teeth. And pressed the dial symbol. "Where'd you get that address?" he asked without a hello. After a long pause, while he listened, he said, "Sit tight. I'm comin' to pick you up and bring you to the correct location. I won't be long. Promise."

Christen laid her hand on Gator's forearm as he swiped the screen closed and dropped his phone back in his tux pocket. "Did they get lost?"

"London gave them the wrong address. They're on the other side of the city."

Christen's gaze scanned the room, stopping on London, who was dressed like a 1940s Hollywood starlet in her vintage Dior evening gown. Christen glared so hard that people who encircled Christen's stepmother all turned as they felt the thought daggers flying toward London. "I'm coming with you."

"Christen," Lula said. "This party is for you and Gator. Why don't I go get Mrs. Rochambeau?"

"Because," Christen said, still glaring, "this party has zero to do with Gator and me. This is schmoozy Assembly crap. It's so my dad can say during negotiations, 'You came to my daughter's wedding celebration. We're like family. Let's line up our interests.'" She turned her attention back to Lula. "It's only about business. And I can imagine London, never having met Gator's family, assuming that because they live in the Louisiana Bayou that they would come and act like hicks."

"Christen," Gator started, but whatever he was going to say fell off.

I thought Christen was probably right on that account. London probably gave the Rochambeaus the wrong address, so they'd come in late when no one would notice when the toasts were made, and they wouldn't need to be identified and welcomed to the family.

So ugly.

"I'm coming with you." Christen slid her hand down Gator's arm, lacing their fingers together. "And we're going to eat while we're out instead of this food. Then we're going to take the longest, slowest way back. And when London asks where her honored couple is, Lula, you can tell them the truth, we went to get Gator's family."

"Sorry." Lula frowned. "That's pretty crappy behavior."

"We'll be back," Gator said.

"Maybe," Christen added, and they walked away.

"Awkward." Lula scratched at the side of her head.

"Hey, White!"

Both Lula and Axel turned and looked for the person that had called out. I watched a man slap another on the back of a guy, then they shook hands.

Axel—Dr. Axel White Ph.D.—I understood why he turned.

Up until this point, I'd had to pretend that I didn't know that Lula LaRoe was also Johnna White, CIA. What just occurred to me, though, was that she was also the woman walking up the hallway toward the elevator bank at Langley. She was the tiny woman in the white pantsuit and the tall red heels walking next to John Black.

It *was* her. I knew it in my bones.

As the rest of our group peeled off to get drinks or mingle, I snagged Lula's arm. From her expression, she knew she'd messed up.

"Good to see you again."

"Yeah, it was fun getting to know you at the dinner." Lula smiled.

"I obviously just put the puzzle pieces together. As you well know, I was on the team that helped pull Gator and Christen out of the ocean when Christen's brother Karl threw her overboard, trying to kill her. I was on the team that offered support to get *you* off the island when you were stuck there when homicidal psycho Karl was trying to kill Christen's dad last summer."

"Christen's dad doesn't believe that his son wanted him dead."

"Delusional in his old age." I shrugged. "Doesn't matter. Karl's hiding out in Saudi Arabia, well away from here. I guess what matters to me right now is that you warned John Black that I was there in the hallway when we were at Langley."

She said nothing.

"You know why I needed to speak with him."

She rolled her lips in.

"It's a problem that needs fixing."

Nothing.

"Can you get a message to my husband?"

Nothing.

"Or to John Grey?"

Lula scanned the room to make sure no one was overhearing these names. She exhaled. I could see her mind racing at full gallop.

Her eyes came back and fixed on mine, but I was pulled away from the conversation.

Holy moly!

There was Vincent Toone in the flesh. He'd aged terribly. But, yes, it was him. And I knew for certain because I could feel the agitation of my parents just over my shoulder.

My sixth-sense systems were going off all at once.

Heebie-jeebies sparked my electrical grid. It was my run! Run now! Run fast! Sensation. I scanned the room for Striker as my jaw dropped to pull in more air.

London Bridge is falling down! Circulated the *knowing.* Whatever had been flowing through my system these last few days was now *over*flowing.

Warning. Warning.

But I couldn't see a single thing that was wrong with this picture.

I spun when the double doors opened.

A man walked in dressed as plastic army soldiers kitted out in a WWII uniform. He was green from head to foot, including one of those green face hoods used in the movies as green screens. The door shut behind him. Moving to the top of the room, he found a place on the dais.

His arms spread wide to gain everyone's attention.

Everyone turned with polite welcome clapping.

The guy on the mic called out, "Ladies and Gentlemen, an homage to our brave soldiers from the greatest generation."

As the MC made a gestural flourish, the double doors opened. Two of the green soldiers stood on either side, holding the doors wide.

A green soldier with a professional movie camera backed into the room.

Pay attention! My parents pressed on me. To what?! I felt like screaming out.

My eyes landed on Vincent, opening his phone with the typical Z pattern. And as I stood there all by myself, watching him, I felt a great push from behind me, forcing me to stumble forward in Vincent's direction, though no one was anywhere near me.

The phone! The phone!

Fine, I said in my head, *the phone.*

The music blared, *This is the Army, Mr. Jones.*

Through the doors came parallel lines of men dressed up as toy soldiers. Where the children's toy had green puddles below the legs to hold the plastic toys upright, these men sailed in on green hoverboards.

The partygoers moved to the edges of the room to make space for this new entertainment.

I turned back to watch Vincent Toone slide his phone into his pocket. He looked expectant and nervous. His eyes scanned the room and stuck when they found mine.

He audibly gasped.

My gaze shifted as I did a quick search for Striker. He was over near London. London was sporting a plastic "what the heck?" look. I wasn't sure if it was because Striker was reaming her a new one or if the entertainment took her by surprise.

I sent a barbed look at the back of Striker's head and glared.

He turned. Smacking Blaze across the chest, they headed my way.

Vincent grabbed my arm and tugged. "Are you Alexis Rueben? You are, aren't you?" he asked. "Your dad was a friend of my brother. My brother won't have anything to do with me anymore. He doesn't *know,* but he knows, you know?"

I shook my head and looked back to see Striker's progress was impeded by Army men.

"I didn't intend to kill him," Vincent said so quietly that his words were almost lost in the music.

The phone! The phone! Pay attention!

"I don't know what I meant to do. I mean, it's one thing when you're high as shit. Angry as shit. Just fucking pissed at the world. I heard your mom had brain cancer." His grip tightened on my arm as he pulled me away from the green men.

"She's dead," I said it exactly as I had to his brother Seth at the CIA.

"Hell of a thing." He rubbed his hand over the back of his neck.

I took advantage of the move to reach out and do a sleight of hand trick, removing his phone from his pocket, sliding it into my bodice.

"I didn't know she was sick. All right? I'm sorry, all right? I was messed up. It's all messed up. I didn't mean it, okay?"

Things were getting weird. Where was Striker? My whole system was in flames.

"But now my nuts are in a vice, you know? They're screwed down so tight, I can't make a move. You see?"

"I…"

"Yeah. You pull something like that. And Karma bites you. Hanasal died, you know? In a car accident. Just desserts. For him. Not me. But when they figured it out. And man, Hanasal had some friends in some very high places. I mean. Wow. Right? Yeah. Nuts. Nuts in a vice." He was dragging me back to the wall.

I wasn't sure if I should be fighting him. Maybe he was just trying to get us out of the way of the entertainers.

I tried to keep my face neutral. It wasn't easy. This was the man who *murdered* my dad.

The green army men made a circle in the center of the room. They lifted their guns to their shoulders. The MC announced, "And the enemy is defeated!"

"Get out. Get out now. This is your chance!" Vincent spat as he turned and grabbed my shoulder. He opened a door that was hidden as part of the wall. He thrust me through.

"Consider yourselves conquered by the invading army," the MC called as the door slammed in my face.

Through the wall, I could hear muffled clapping.

I tried the handle, but it was locked. I looked around me. This seemed to be a staging room of some kind.

I didn't see another way out.

The clapping turned to screams.

Striker was in there!

38

______

A STRAFE OF GUNFIRE SOUNDED.

I flung myself to the ground as pieces of the plaster wall rained down on my back.

Screams erupted from the reception hall.

Looking up at the holes left behind as quiet descended anew, I noticed that they traced along the top of the wall.

Cover fire.

It was meant to send a message, to gain compliance, to shock the shit out of the people in the room. It wasn't meant to kill.

I crawled to the door and tried the handle a second time. Locked.

My team was inside.

What was happening?

I scrambled toward an open door at the other end of this space. Dressing room. Not much here of use. A sink, a makeup table and mirror, an empty costume rack with metal hangers. Some janitorial equipment. My purse was back at the table in my clutch where I had been standing when I confronted Lula— Johnna White.

Patting at my bodice, Vincent's phone was gone.

Crawling on all fours, I scrambled back to where it had fallen out during my dive to safety.

Then back again to the dressing room. From what I could tell, this was behind the dais, so I should be relatively safe from flying bullets.

With my back against the cinderblock wall, I drew the Z that I had seen Vincent draw moments ago. Boom, the phone's security allowed me in. What was he texting when I got the psychic message of my own?

Vincent: **Karl, everything's in place. We're a go. They're coming through the doors now.**

Karl Davidson?

Karl: **He he he. I'm watching on my computer. We have a good feed. It's worth getting up at the crack of dawn. Enjoy the show. I'd say break a leg, but what I really mean is break some necks.**

Karl. He was in Saudi Arabia, where, indeed, it would be the early hours of the morning.

Holy hell. I was pretty clear on who was in that room, Omega Security. After all, William and Karl Davidson had sat on their board prior to the info dump that Spyder had set off a year and a half ago, driving their organization out of the country.

Not to say everyone left.

Management had changed locations.

I used every trick in my book to calm my nerves to stay focused and rational. Work the problem. Stay out of the emotional cascade that would drown me in inability. My team needed me.

What this text told me was that Karl was making another run at a billion-dollar inheritance.

Last summer, Karl the psychopath had drugged his sister and thrown her over the rails of the Davidson's yacht, trying to kill her.

He had headed right for his father's private island with a vial of poison in his pocket destined for his dad's evening cocktail.

Instead, Christen, with Gator's help, survived. She showed up in time to scoop her dad up in her helicopter and get a shot off, aiming for her psychopathic brother. The bullet pierced Karl's leg, and he was now an amputee with a lot of rage.

Of course, Karl would show up in some manner and try to destroy her wedding.

Thank goodness for London's pettiness. It kept Christen and Gator safe. *If* they'd stay away.

A lot had gone on for the Davidsons last year. William had faced a possible natural death with a tumor scare. London had given birth to a fourth son/fifth heir. And …

London. Oh no.

Karl needed London dead. Was that what was happening here? I tried to think that through. If William and London were killed, there might be an inquiry that might hold up the distribution of the inheritance, *but* if many were dead in a criminal event…

After London gave birth to their son Archie, William Davidson had significantly adjusted his will. While he said he didn't believe Karl was trying to kill him, a seed of truth must have been planted.

Christen insisted she wanted nothing to do with the Davidson wealth.

Gator told me that while she was still stationed in the forward operating base in Iraq, she'd had a lawyer draw up papers saying that if anything came her way, she would immediately liquidate the assets and distribute them to charity. She would take no control and have nothing to do with the Davidson wealth.

It was after she presented those papers to her father that the will changed.

Gator told me that William Davidson had sent the new will to

Christen, showing her that she was no longer listed as a recipient. Christen's role in the last will would have given her control of her share and that of all of her siblings under the age of thirty. She was supposed to balance Karl's hot-headed ideas until such time the younger siblings were full adults.

We had all surmised that this would keep Christen safe from a murderous brother.

But what it did was move the crosshairs from Christen to London.

Man!

Okay.

I was here on this side of the wall. They were there on the other.

I had been "saved" by the man who had tried to kill me and who had taken my beloved father.

My brain was working on overdrive, searching for anything that would help me puzzle out a way through.

This was a lot. There was a lot going on.

And I didn't have time to mull.

I had time for action.

What action could I take in this odd space with no exit…well…?

Shit.

I pushed against emotions that wanted to burst through the barriers of logic.

Stop freaking out and think. Your team needs you.

Outside, Christen and Gator. They wouldn't be back for, say, an hour. Would they realize something was wrong? Or would they just walk through the doors and be caught up in this horror?

Inside, there were men with skills, Strike Force. Kira's date, Ty Newcomb, Delta Force Operator. But they weren't strapped with weapons: eight men and the seven women they loved.

A gun was a gun was a gun.

And while there were indeed superheroes in that room, they were not superhuman.

A bullet could stop them cold.

39

———

THAT ROOM WAS full of people I love. My team. My heart, Striker.

I went back to the door, hoping it would give, if even an inch, so that I might see what was happening. Or even if there was a wide enough crack at the bottom so I could shove Vincent's phone underneath to video like I had when I was surveilling Hanasal.

The answer was an emphatic "no" to both.

Though, from this angle, I could now see a square vent in a strange placement on the wall. Two foot by two foot, it must have been nestled between studs. The metal covering was ornate, I guessed, so that it would blend into the opulence of the ballroom.

I crouched to the height of someone sitting in a chair to look through.

Ah, I knew what this was for.

With no wings on the stage. This space must be where performers prepped and exited to climb the three steps up to the dais. Someone sitting in a chair and monitoring could see the stage and tell folks back here when it was their turn to go on.

Taking a knee, I could observe in a limited way. I needed

information so I could "work the problem," as Striker would say. Slow and steady saves her team. *Be smart, Lexi. Do it right.*

"Where is Christen Davidson?" The MC asked. The fabric stretched across his face obfuscating his features.

My brain pinged back to the CIA, where I had learned about the artist's use of DNA to create a likeness. There would be nothing to go on once these men left. Their gloved hands would leave no prints, their costume would allow for no accidentally left behind genetic material.

They would get away with this.

"Where is Christen Davidson?" He raised his voice.

Kira timidly raised her hand.

Ty's face hardened. I had known Ty Newcomb for a while now. But he had just met Kira last week. From the looks of things, the love bug had bitten him hard. Where most people wouldn't see the subtle shift in his demeanor, I lived amongst men who were or had been special forces operators. Ty was expanding his systems like a bull pawing at the ground, ready to lunge.

Calm. Wait. I sent him soothing vibes, knowing they wouldn't reach him.

"Christen isn't here. She went to pick up her mother-in-law and-and-and-and her sisters-in-law. They aren't here."

There was a stillness amongst the green Army. This was blowing a hole in their plans.

"Who are you?" MC snarled.

"Me? I'm Kira."

Steady, Ty.

"And what is your role here?"

"I'm… I'm a guest."

"You're Christen's friend?"

"I met her the other day. She's not here," Kira said.

"All right. I'm going to call out names. When you hear your name, you will come forward and form a line."

"Lexi Sobado."

I was second up. That was information.

Omega had a score to settle with me. And it had nothing to do with Spyder's data dump. Omega had come after me two years ago, and in the fight, several of their operators had been killed.

The guy twitched his gun at Kira.

"No, she's not here either." Kira had seen the guy push me out the door. Of that, I was reasonably sure. Would she tell? Would they hunt me? I held my breath. There was nowhere for me to go. All I could possibly do here was to shadow walk and stay invisible.

"She left. I… I think she left with Christen and Gator…I don't know." Kira stared down at her shoes. Her weight shifted around. I thought she might just faint.

Ty reached out his hand and tugged her back to him. Pressed her into a seat. Pushed her head down between her knees.

Good job, Ty.

A shuffling and gasps pulled my attention to the left. I couldn't see for the people standing to that side of the grate.

A muffled, "She's having a heart attack," spread person to person and rounded the room.

"Is there a doctor in the room?" a man asked.

Striker held up his hands to show they were free of weapons. He strode toward her. Ty followed. And Kira bounced up from her seat, obviously not willing to leave Ty's side.

Lula edged to the right of my grate. She tapped twice.

I tapped twice in return.

The army men pushed everyone else to the other side of the room. They were allowing Ty and Striker to help the woman. Was this encouraging?

The MC started in again.

"William and London Davidson." This time he didn't need hands to go up. He pointed directly at the couple. They were escorted to the dais, where they were made to kneel in front of their guests.

I turned back to the woman on the ground.

I remembered from Dad's car crash how that felt to press and push and pray under my breath.

"Now everyone is to get out their phones and hold them over your heads. If you don't produce a phone, you will be escorted to the corner, and you will be strip-searched. Your clothes will be confiscated."

The phones came out.

The army men with black sharpies went person to person, writing on their phones. Manipulating them briefly. Dropping them into a bag.

It wasn't until they were taking Lula's phone that I heard what they were doing. They wrote her name and the passcode. If it was a biometric code like irises or fingerprints, they were made to change to a swipe code. The batteries were removed.

As the army man moved past, I could see Striker and Ty again.

Kira was using her skirt to blow air the woman's way.

I knew from the look on their faces that they knew they had failed and hadn't given up quite yet.

Others tried to get down and relieve Ty, who was doing CPR, but they were pushed away by the gunmen.

Ty was a machine. He kept going until Lula went over and stopped him. "She's gone. Let's move her to the side." She pointed at the table to the right of my grate.

Lula was trying to amass friendlies together. Maybe she had a plan.

Lula and Kira stood on either side of the woman, tucking their hands under her back.

Ty took her feet. Striker had the deceased woman under the arms.

While Lula directed Striker over to the place she had been standing just to the left of my grate, I was worried that she would call attention to me. But she stood with her back to the wall, covering.

"Lexi," she said under her breath as she squatted to adjust the dead woman. "Man, I sure am hoping that you're crouched there trying to figure this out. "

"Here."

"Can you get out?" She arranged the woman's clothing in a respectful way.

"No."

"Phone?"

"Yes," I said as an exhale. "It's one of theirs. I'm afraid to use it lest they're monitored."

"Agreed. Weapons?"

"No."

"Plan?"

"No."

She crossed the woman's arms over her chest. Pressed her eyelids down. Ty took a cloth from one of the tables and was covering it over the woman.

"Any ideas?" Ty asked.

"Not yet," I said.

What we needed here was magic. I ran through my skill sets, shadow walking, sleight of hand, fighting…really, the only applicable skill I had was puzzling.

I was in limbo, neither part of the crime nor away from it.

Trapped.

They had finished collecting the cell phones. It looked like everyone anteed one up. No one was in the strip search corner.

"Line up when I call your name," the MC instructed.

Assemblymen, one at a time, moved forward.

I was trained by the best of the best to become an intelligence officer. Not an operator. I had little in the way of applied tactical maneuvers to protect those I loved.

I reached into my bag of knowledge. After my team came in from a mission, they went through the hot washes, explaining what they did and why they did it. Looking for holes. Looking for ways that they could better react the next time.

Eight men, seven women in our group. Christen and Gator were safe.

A gun was a gun was a gun.

I had no idea how to help. I looked over my shoulder. *Mom and Dad, if you're there, I could use some inspiration.*

40

Striker, Ty, Kira, and Lula sat on the ground with their backs to the wall with the dead woman in front of them.

I thought that was a pretty good idea. I remembered studying how some native tribes would make platforms up in the trees, away from wild animals, that served as burial sites. When other indigenous peoples passed through the area, they were careful not to disturb the sacred space. Therefore, when trappers moved through the area, they often slept under those trees, knowing that the area's indigenous people wouldn't go to that spot.

By placing the body there, my team had formed a barricade that, by human nature, wouldn't be crossed or disturbed.

I hoped so anyway.

I had to find a way out of here.

Before I could tell Striker where I was going, the MC walked up on stage and stood behind the Davidsons. "There seems to be some hesitancy. Some reluctance to do as you are being told. Let me set the record straight here. You are not in charge." He dragged a .22 caliber pocket pistol from his green uniform jacket. And without a moment's hesitation, he aimed it at the back of London's head and pulled the trigger.

BANG!

"Right? No monkey business. Just so you see the conse-quences." He pressed his foot into London's back, and she dropped from the dais to the floor.

The back of her hair was matted with blood.

Holy moly!

William Davidson passed out and was ignored.

People were vomiting and crying—the room filled with moans.

Axel and Randy came forward, looked the man in the eye, and wiggled a finger. I supposed to ask permission to move London to what was becoming a make-do morgue.

The MC gave them a nod.

Axel turned to the women in our party who were seated at the table where I'd left my purse. My phone was in there.

Helpful?

It didn't matter. None of the women scooped it up. It was left there next to my plate of untouched hors d'oeuvres.

They stood and moved over to London, reaching under her as Randy instructed.

On Randy's count, they all lifted and walked toward us.

Kira was curled into Ty, clinging and shaking.

When they got to us and were laying London out, Axel whispered, "It was a .22. She's still alive. We need to get her out of here ASAP. Hopefully, she can hang on until this is over."

"You think they're going to let anyone live?" Ty spoke without moving his lips. His voice carried as wide as the circle of operators and no further.

No one mentioned to the newcomers that I was there behind the grate.

Good. The fewer who knew, the less chance I'd be caught.

Vincent knew where I was. Will he rat me out to the MC?

I didn't see him anymore. It was possible that Vincent had done his duty and had left.

Still a worry.

The other men, Reaper, Jack, Deep, and Blaze, were slowly, slowly making their way in this direction. Every time an Assemblyman's name was called, and eyes looked around to find that person, they took a sidestep.

At this rate, it would take them a while.

The Assemblymen were brought to a computer one after the other.

One after the other, they sat down and tapped, sweating and gasping.

I assumed that they were entering passcodes into the systems and moving money.

Lots of money to someone's offshore account, I guessed.

Striker pulled Ty and Axel in front of him. "Chica,"

"Here"

"Can you get out?"

"No. I'm not sure what to do."

"Absolutely nothing. If you can't get out, you need to lay low and not call attention to yourself. It'll up the stakes. Make them twitchy on the triggers. We need weapons. All of our guns are in the vehicles. Anything you can find us."

"I'll see what I can come up with. So far, I've decided not to make a bomb with cleaning supplies."

"Yeah," he said. "Good call."

"If I find something, I need a way to give it to you. Can you get the grate off?" I asked.

Lula pushed in behind the men, crouching beside Striker. "Stand up," she told him. She pulled a clip from her hair. Her tiny frame was hidden behind Striker's bulk. "It's held with screws. I can get them out. We need weapons. Figure it out."

Shit.

I searched over every inch of the outer room and saw no way to get through.

This seemed like a bad fire design, just like Destiny's apartment had been when there was no way out past the goons besides that side door with the rotting steps.

The walls in the dressing room were cinderblock except behind the sink. I assumed they'd used drywall there to facilitate access to the water pipes.

Knocking at the drywall, it sounded hollow. Well, hollow enough that I was tempted to see what was on the other side.

Digging through the dressing table drawers, I located a pair of scissors. With the open blade, I scored down the paper, pressing hard to cut through the gypsum.

Powdery white sulfate material sprinkled down on me. It looked so solid, but this wasn't hard to do. I cut to the side of the outlet, knowing that I'd have a two-foot space between studs to crawl through. That was if this led anywhere at all. I could just be heading into a concrete wall, another group of domestic terrorists, or a dead end.

Climbing onto the sink, I lifted a leg and started through the hole into what looked like a meeting room. I spent a moment jumping up and down and scraping my feet on the rug to rid myself of any dust lest I leave a trail.

Shadow walking, I moved into the hall toward the kitchen. At least I knew there would be ultra-sharp knives in there. The staff was sitting on the ground with their backs to the walls. Green Army men kept them under gunpoint.

Two of them.

Two… No. Armed with only scissors, I couldn't fight them. If they got a shot off, even with their suppressors, it would call attention.

I took a moment to observe. Yeah, these guys were high-tech. One touched his breast bone where I was sure he was pressing a comms button. He spoke, then stilled to listen. He must have earbuds in underneath his outfit. If I had that outfit on, I could sneak into the room… to what end? How would that help anything?

Okay, nix that.

I had to get to the cars.

With another breath in, adjusting to make sure I was obfuscating my presence with my shadow walking technique, I made my way to an exit. I observed the door. If I went out, could I get back in? If I went out, would it signal anyone? So far, I hadn't seen any security cameras. But that meant little. In spaces like this private club, the cameras were often eliminated so that private conversations would stay private. Often, too, they had security cameras, but they were hidden to make their clients feel more at ease that they were in a safe space and crimes were not anticipated.

I thought if there were to be security, it would be on the exterior, and it would focus on exits. The door wasn't a good idea. I backtracked. Every second meant that the terrorists were getting closer to completing their tasks and would move on with next steps.

Every second might be London's last breath.

The MC had been cold about shooting London. Would they care about the lives of the others in the room?

I found a service staircase and followed it up. Here, in another hall, I made my way to the side of the mansion opposite the parking lot. Outside, there was a slope down to a pond that was just visible in the dusk.

This was my exit, I decided.

41

———

IN THE UPSTAIRS OFFICE SPACE, I dragged the curtains from the windows. Floor to ceiling silk, this was precisely what I needed. Tying four of them together end to end and pulling knots every so many feet, I quickly constructed a rope system that I could use to climb from the third-story window.

I was so glad that I had chosen to be comfortable tonight in a black satin jumpsuit and flats.

Using rubber bands from the desk drawer, I secured my hair out of my way.

Filling my cheeks with air, I let it go in a rush. *I can do this.*

Sure I could. This was a walk in the park, I told myself as I went butt-first out the window, testing how my shoes would do against the smooth siding.

Not good.

I pulled them off and stuck the shoes in my bra, letting my breasts hold them in place.

This wasn't my first rodeo on the side of a tall building. This was only three stories. Heck, I had climbed up a fire chute thirteen stories high when I tried to take out the Hydra. And look at

Christen, when she met Gator, she leaped into his heart when she did a parkour dive off the side of a two-story building.

It's doable.

I'm doing it.

As my feet found the solidity of hard-packed dirt and grass, I left the make-do rope in place. Those knots would help me climb back with the things that I gathered. It's one thing to climb a rope hand over hand. It's entirely different to climb encumbered that way.

I am not a SEAL.

That didn't mean that I wouldn't try to shapeshift into one.

Quickly replacing my shoes, I laid down, crossing my arms over my chest as I rolled down the hill, below the horizon, and out of view if anyone was watching out of a first-story window. I raced toward the tree line. There, I stopped to assess.

At the front gate, four army men on hover scooters stood sentry.

On the wall, I saw others crouched, observing the street, but not the grounds.

It was good that I went out the window on the other side of the building, or surely they would have seen and taken action.

Needing to be sure that they weren't monitoring the parking lot, I waited for a full five minutes to make sure my next moves would go undetected.

Yes, it was time that I didn't have. But getting caught now would serve no one.

Feeling reassured and glad for the descending night, I made my way to the Iniquus vehicles.

Per protocol, they were parked at the back of the lot facing outward.

I snaked my way up to the first one, reaching under the bumper, feeling for the code panel. This was a security measure placed on every Iniquus vehicle. Besides the normal bullet resistance and run-flat tires, Command didn't want to have the operator stuck on a scene if somehow the keys went missing.

The locks were set up like a gun safe. I laid my fingers in each of the grooves then pressed in the combination: pinky, ring finger, and thumb. When I did, the system recognized an emergency was in play. The lights disengaged, the alarm—any beeps or chirrups all disabled—the back unlatched.

Control would be notified and be listening for instructions over the intercom.

I popped the rear hatch, lifting it halfway.

"Control," I whispered, knowing that the computers would augment my voice. "May Day. May Day. May Day. Lynx from Strike Force. We are involved in a hostage situation."

"Control. Copy."

"We are eight men, seven women with an Iniquus connection. Gator is not on-site. He's with his fiancée Christen. Contact them immediately and tell them not to come in the gates. Urgent. Do not let them return."

"Good Copy. Wilco."

"There are by my count a hundred and twenty other guests. I have counted over thirty criminals. Eight that I've found on perimeter. They are dressed as green army men."

"Repeat last."

"They are dressed in Halloween costumes as green army men."

"Copy."

"Rifles with silencers. One woman has died of what seems to be a heart attack. One woman is in a life-threatening medical state with a bullet to the back of her head. One man was unconscious from an undetermined reason. Our people were unharmed last I saw them."

I crossed my fingers to give that thought extra good juju. Then sent up a silent prayer to my parents. *Please help them. Those are the people I love. Please.* Though what they could do in the ether was beyond me.

What did I know? Maybe they were the reason that Vincent had a Come to Jesus moment, saw what Hell might look like, and shoved me through that door in a bid to earn an eternal reprieve.

I'd like to believe that.

"I'm gathering equipment and taking it back to my team. Over."

"We have you up on satellite. We have operator teams deployed."

Iniquus sent its operators out in Humvees or other large tactical vehicles. One reason was that they were always on call for a fellow operator in trouble. That's how Ridge and Zeus had made it to me so quickly when Destiny was murdered.

The second reason was that the vehicles were all equipped to handle the emergencies they were called to.

I went from vehicle to vehicle with my duffel. I filled it with sidearms with silencers, ammunition, bullet-resistant vests, smoke cylinders, flashbang, the breachers bag with explosives for entry no matter what the material was that kept our operators on the wrong side of their destination. And comms.

I dropped the magnetic audio units into my ear canals and put the camera glasses on my face.

"Testing. Testing. Lynx to Control."

"Lynx, we have audiovisual. We are standing by."

All those rifles.

All those Omega operators.

Would this keep my team safe? Or would it make them target practice?

Altogether this ruck weighed more than I could ever hope to carry. But my fear-adrenaline made me Atlas.

I hefted the pack onto my back and retraced my way to the window.

There, I had to acknowledge my limitations. I wasn't climbing three stories with this pack pulling me backward.

After a moment's thought, I secured the bag to my rope, climbed, shimmied through the window, then dragged the pack up the side.

Slowly. Slowly so as not to bang or scrape and call attention to my actions, I pulled and heaved. I pressed the worry thoughts, the danger scenarios from my mind.

Adrenaline had its purposes, but I had found over time that adrenaline can be a bitch. It certainly wasn't always my friend. The biggest fears were that I would freeze, that it would destroy my fine motor capacity, or that I would be unable to think strategically.

My team was counting on me. I couldn't let them down.

I couldn't.

42

———

STANDING on a chair in the meeting room with the drywall square on the ground, I lowered equipment into the sink on the other side of the wall.

Getting back into the dressing room wasn't a walk in the park.

As I tried to heft myself up, the wall crumbled in my hands and made way too much noise.

Stacking four chairs, I was able to scramble up high enough that I could thrust a leg through the hole.

My brain was pinging with all the ways everything could go to hell.

London Bridge is falling down, falling down.

"Got it, already. I'm doing my best." I grumbled under my breath, suddenly very afraid that my weight plus the weight of the equipment might just make the sink fall off the wall.

A new challenge, I tried to reframe the situation.

Spreading my legs out wide to anchor me, with the wall digging into my hips, I leaned through the opening, silently moving the equipment over to the dressing table before I made my reentry.

It all took time.

And time was a precious commodity.

Gathering the things into the pack again, I dragged it to the vent. There I took a moment to assess. It seemed that the long line of Assemblymen digitally handing over their wealth was still in progress.

"Here," I exhaled.

Striker rubbed his hands over his face.

"I have a duffel," I explained what I had gathered. "And a sketch of where I saw tangos and hostages."

"Good. Chica, here's the plan. The men will stand. The women will step through the vent. Lynx, it's on you to get them out. And if you can't get them out, you will get them to the safest possible place."

At first, I didn't like that plan. I wanted to crawl through the vent and help in the room. But as my initial knee-jerk reaction slid to the side, I could see the benefit of this strategy.

If the men were worried about their loves, their focus would be divided. The women would get in the way of their operating.

"Reaper has to come through, too," I insisted. "I need his help, and he can't be in the room with flashbang—his head."

"Agreed." Striker stood. "Ready when you are."

Lula came through first.

One by one, the others followed: Kira, Grace, Suz, Faith, Kate. Finally, as requested, Reaper dove through. The only dad on our team, yeah, there were a bunch of reasons it had to be Reaper if I could only get one of the team free.

We moved on silent feet to the dressing room. Reaper was staring at the hole. "Good job," he said. "I'll go first."

Again, I worried about the staying power of that sink. If it crashed to the ground, the noise would be huge. It would expose us. I snagged Reaper's arm and showed him the problem. "Okay, you go first then," he said. He placed a knee on the dressing table and extended his other leg to rest his foot on the shelving. "Stand on my thigh, not the sink."

And so we did. In a train of long skirts and sequins, helping each other, keeping as quiet as possible, we struggled from one room to the next.

The next step seemed much more dangerous.

I was the only one with shadow walking skills. We would be exposed in the hallway.

Peeking, running, stopping, and hiding. Eventually, we made it to the stairs and up.

Reaper looked out the three-story window and assessed my rope with a whistle. He checked his watch. "Striker gave our exfil a fifteen-minute window."

"You planned this before I got there. You all must think I have mad skills. I wasn't at all sure I could come through."

"But you did in spades. Our plan is on track. We need to get everyone down and into the trees. You're wearing glasses. Iniquus is monitoring?"

"Yup. The cavalry is on its way."

"Moving," Reaper said. "Ladies, here's the deal. This rope is plenty strong for one person, not two at a time. That means I can't walk you down. You can do this. And you *will* do this. So tuck your skirts up out of your way. Get your high heels off and suck it up. The fear you feel here is the fear of you heading to safety. There's no gun at your head with a finger on the trigger. Better already. A little more bravery, and we'll clear this last hurdle."

Nice pep talk, but looking at Kira's face...I wasn't so sure this was going to work.

It was time for next steps.

Reaper wanted it to be him who moved out, and yeah, he was a SEAL, but, honestly, this was my bailiwick, and he knew it.

There had only been nine guns in the vehicles I had found and shoved into the equipment duffle.

Lula had one. Reaper had the other.

"I'm taking Lula with me."

"Why's that?" Reaper asked.

We were lying on our stomachs in the wooded area.

"Because you need to be here protecting our group. And Lula is the only one of us who, outside of the immediate crime scene, can legally shoot anyone."

"She's a lawyer," Faith said, baffled.

I glanced Faith's way, then turned my head back to speak with Reaper.

Reaper scratched his thumb into his chin, processing.

"Lexi's right. We can do this recon. And let the badges know what they're walking in to."

I tapped my ear to let Reaper know I was listening to my comms. "Control tells me that FBI signed contracts with Iniquus. We're clear to work the scene. FBI is scrambling, no DCPD, they don't want the chatter out over the radio waves." I held my finger in the air to indicate information was still coming into my comms. "Iniquus is sending their ambulances. The heli's in the air."

"Christen?" Lula asked.

I tapped my ear again and shook my head.

"Cerberus Alpha and Bravo are moving through the woods across the road. They're ordering that any shots be life or death. They'd appreciate the intel."

"Intel it is." Lula tucked her gun in the back of her tuxedo pants and left the jacket with a shivering Kira.

"I just went through this in Tanzania. I… this is a lot." Kira wrapped the jacket around her shoulders with a thank you smile.

Lula and I set off for the wall to count heads and give GPS positions.

Things hadn't changed much from the time I first observed their exterior security. The low lights along the wall up-lit the guards and kept us safer in the dark.

Suddenly, the sound of an explosion concussed through the night.

"Flashbang," Lula said in a crouch as she ran toward the wall. "Strike Force is attacking."

God, Striker.

My heart was hammering.

The men on the wall lifted their rifles and searched for a reason to shoot. As they turned, I saw it. "Heat vision!" I hissed for Lula and Control's information.

Lula and I dove for the ground, rolling onto our backs to keep the enemy in line of sight.

Lula aimed her pistol between her knees, getting the closest guard in her sights. There were two that could see us.

Reaper had the second gun. I had nothing. How good of a shot was Lula? Could she get them both?

The left guard called out something indistinguishable.

Both men leveled their rifles at us.

Lula took the shot.

The left guard threw his arms in the air, then tumbled off the wall.

The other man turned his head, following his co-conspirator.

Over the wall came Voodoo, magical Malinois hero-dog extraordinaire.

I'd recognize that leap anywhere.

With open mouth and wagging tail, Voodoo gracefully pivoted, snatched up the rifle arm of the green army man, and continued his flight.

Boom!

Voodoo had the guy on the ground.

The terrorist screamed high-pitched horror screams. I scrambled to their side, grabbing up his rifle. I had zero control over Voodoo. And Ryder, his handler, was on the other side of the fifteen-foot wall.

This man's screams weren't the only ones.

Cerberus Tactical K9 Team had indeed arrived.

"Good boy," I whispered as Voodoo sank his teeth in deeper.

EPILOGUE

Today was exquisite.

We stood under the broad limbs of an ancient oak.

Wooden white chairs circled around.

I stood in a simple green sundress beside Lula and Gator's sisters.

Striker was across from me. Our eyes held.

This was a moment of utter peace. It was as if the Heavens had conspired that after the flashbang smoke blew away in the wind, we would be left with this amazing day with undisturbed blue sky, perfect temperatures, and butterflies dancing across the field of wildflowers.

Christen and Gator were blind to everything. Holding each other's hands and without the prompt of the clergywoman, they recited their vows.

"Christen, would you do me the honor of loving me for the whole day?" He held her hand to his lips. As he spoke, the words whispered over her skin.

"I will make that vow to you. I will, for today, have and hold you."

"For better, for worse?"

"Absolutely."

"For richer, for poorer?"

"Why yes, Jean-Marie Rochambeau, I would do that."

"In sickness or in health?"

"I will, indeed, love and honor you for the whole of today. And what's more? Just so you know, I plan on making that vow to you every single day for the rest of my life."

These were the exact vows that Gator and Christen offered each other after their first escape from Karl's villainy.

Gator leaned low to drop a kiss on her nose.

Then scooped her into his brawny arms to bring her tiny frame up to kiss her lips.

There was cheering and joy. And relief.

William Davidson sat alone in the front row, looking shell-shocked. His wife, London, was alive but in a drug-induced coma. No one knew yet what London's outcome would be. Karl? I could guess his outcome. He'd probably escape any culpability and continue searching out wealth through terror. And I had no idea what had happened to Vincent Toone, though I was assured the authorities were searching for him with charges of domestic terror hanging over his head. I needed to make sure, now that I had the note that he had tried to kill me and that he had admitted to me at the party, that Vincent was charged with murdering my dad.

I set all of that aside. No ugly thoughts should mar today.

Kira, I saw, would not let go of Ty's hand. All of the women were a little clingy right now. We had so much less experience with that kind of military-style action.

For the special operators, it was another day at the office.

We moved to the gazebo, where there was cake and champagne.

A step stool stood in front of the entry arch.

Holding Gator's hand, Christen climbed up. "Who amongst

our little clan will be the next bride?" she asked as she turned her back to us.

The women clustered behind her, as tradition dictated.

Christen's bouquet flew in a riotous colored jumble of flowers and ribbon streamers—a celebration of love and hope, gliding through the air.

And when it approached, the women around me all lowered their hands, leaving the harbinger for me.

The group clapped as I held the bouquet in front of me. My eyes caught on Striker's as he sent me one hell of a sexy grin.

I wanted to marry that man with every fiber of my being.

If only these flowers were the good juju I needed.

But the truth was until the CIA set me free, this bouquet was just magical, *wishful* thinking.

The End

Please follow along as the men and women in the World of Iniquus live, love, and fight for a better tomorrow.

The next book in the Lynx Series is:
MARRIAGE LYNX – Look for it in 2023.

The next book in the Iniquus World is:
Danger Zone, Delta Force Echo

Readers, I hope you enjoyed this book. If you had fun reading Hyper Lynx, I'd appreciate it if you'd help others enjoy it too.

Recommend it: Just a few words to your friends, your book groups, and your social networks would be wonderful.

Review it: Please tell your fellow readers what you liked about my book by reviewing Hyper Lynx. If you do write a review, please send me a note at hello@FionaQuinnBooks.com so I can thank you with a personal e-mail. Or stop by my website www.FionaQuinnBooks.com to keep up with my news and chat through my contact form.

Please turn the page for a list of
INIQUUS WORLD BOOKS
in chronological order

THE WORLD of INIQUUS

Chronological Order

Ubicumque, Quoties. Quidquid

Weakest Lynx (Lynx Series)

Missing Lynx (Lynx Series)

Chain Lynx (Lynx Series)

Cuff Lynx (Lynx Series)

WASP (Uncommon Enemies)

In Too DEEP (Strike Force)

Relic (Uncommon Enemies)

Mine (Kate Hamilton Mystery)

Jack Be Quick (Strike Force)

Deadlock (Uncommon Enemies)

Instigator (Strike Force)

Yours (Kate Hamilton Mystery)

Gulf Lynx (Lynx Series)

Open Secret (FBI Joint Task Force)

Thorn (Uncommon Enemies)
Ours (Kate Hamilton Mysteries)
Cold Red (FBI Joint Task Force)
Even Odds (FBI Joint Task Force)
Survival Instinct - (Cerberus Tactical K9)
Protective Instinct - (Cerberus Tactical K9)
Defender's Instinct - (Cerberus Tactical K9)
Danger Signs - (Delta Force Echo)
Hyper Lynx - (Lynx Series)
Danger Zone - (Delta Force Echo)
Danger Close - (Delta Force Echo)
Fear the REAPER – (Strike Force)
Cerberus Tactical K9 Team Bravo

Coming soon, more great stories from the ex-special forces security team members who live, work, and love in a tightly knit family.

FOR MORE INFORMATION VISIT
WWW.FIONAQUINNBOOKS.COM

ACKNOWLEDGMENTS

My great appreciation ~

To my editor, Kathleen Payne

To my cover artist, Melody Simmons

To my publicist, Margaret Daly

To my Australian specialist Elisa Hordon

To my Beta Force, who are always honest and kind at the same time: C. Villani, M. Carlon, E. Hordon

To my Street Force, who support me and my writing with such enthusiasm and kindness.

To the real-world K9 professionals who serve and protect us.

To all the wonderful professionals whom I called on to get the details right —

Dr. K. Connor for her consistent K9 inspiration both through her stories and her amazing photographs.

Virginia K9 search and rescue teams for their work in our community, their dedication, and professionalism. Every time I search and train with you, I'm inspired.

Please note: This is a work of fiction, and while I always try my best to get all the details correct, there are times when it serves the story to go slightly to the left or right of perfection.

Please understand that any mistakes or discrepancies are my authorial decision making alone and sit squarely on my shoulders.

Thank you to my family.

I send my love to my husband, along with my great appreciation. T, a life with you is one of my very best decisions. Thank you for giving me a solid foundation on which to grow.

And of course, thank *YOU* for reading my stories. I'm smiling joyfully as I type this. I so appreciate you!

ABOUT THE AUTHOR

Fiona Quinn is a six-time USA Today bestselling author, a Kindle Scout winner, and an Amazon All-Star.

Quinn writes action-adventure in her Iniquus World of books, including Lynx, Strike Force, Uncommon Enemies, Kate Hamilton Mysteries, FBI Joint Task Force, Cerberus Tactical K9, and Delta Force Echo series.

She writes urban fantasy as Fiona Angelica Quinn for her Elemental Witches Series.

And, just for fun, she writes the Badge Bunny Booze Mystery Collection with her dear friend, Tina Glasneck.

Quinn is rooted in the Old Dominion, where she lives with her husband. There, she pops chocolates, devours books, and taps continuously on her laptop.

Visit www.FionaQuinnBooks.com

COPYRIGHT